SCOTCH MIST

Recent Titles by Elizabeth Darrell from Severn House

BEYOND ALL FRONTIERS
SCARLET SHADOWS
FORGET THE GLORY
THE RICE DRAGON
SHADOWS OVER THE SUN

UNSUNG HEROES
FLIGHT TO ANYWHERE

The Max Rydal Mysteries

RUSSIAN ROULETTE
CHINESE PUZZLE
CZECH MATE
DUTCH COURAGE
FRENCH LEAVE
INDIAN SUMMER
SCOTCH MIST

SCOTCH MIST

Elizabeth Darrell

This first world edition published 2011
in Great Britain and in the USA by
SEVERN HOUSE PUBLISHERS LTD of
9–15 High Street, Sutton, Surrey, England, SM1 1DF.
Trade paperback edition first published
in Great Britain and the USA 2012 by
SEVERN HOUSE PUBLISHERS LTD

British Library Cataloguing in Publication Data

Darrell, Elizabeth.
Scotch mist. – (A Max Rydal military mystery)
1. Rydal, Max (Fictitious character)–Fiction. 2. Great
Britain. Army. Corps of Royal Military Police–Fiction.
3. Military bases, British–Germany–Fiction.
4. Soldiers–Scotland–Fiction. 5. Detective and mystery
stories.
I. Title II. Series
823.9'14-dc22

ISBN-13: 978-0-7278-8069-7 (cased)
ISBN-13: 978-1-84751-370-0 (trade paper)

Typeset by Palimpsest Book Production Ltd.,
Falkirk, Stirlingshire, Scotland.
Printed and bound in Great Britain by
MPG Books Ltd., Bodmin, Cornwall.

ONE

'Bloody bagpipes! Sounds like a squad of randy tomcats on a hot night,' growled Sergeant Major Tom Black.

'But it's such a *stirring* sound,' protested Connie Bush. 'Pipers traditionally lead troops into battle to inspire them. One even played on the beach on D-Day.'

Tom shook his head. 'Wrong! The ploy is to assault the eardrums of the enemy so they'll turn and flee from earshot.'

Several members of 26 Section, Special Investigation Branch, Royal Military Police had come from their headquarters to watch the band of the Ist Battalion, the Drumdorran Fusiliers march through the huge base in Germany that was to be their new home. The troops who had all been bussed in earlier in the day were forming up on the parade ground to be officially welcomed by the Deputy Garrison Commander, and the band had decided to officially announce their arrival.

These musicians 'playing the regiment in' walked with a swagger that had their kilts swinging and the buttons on their black tunics glinting in the November sunshine. The wind moved the fur of their tall headgear and caused the long plaids hanging from their shoulders to swing with their kilts. Add long socks with a dirk tucked in and white gaiters, and these men did look very impressive, as Heather Johnson remarked with admiration.

'They'll look the same as the rest of us when they put on combats,' replied Tom, irritated by this female reaction to north of the border bravura. 'And once this tartan army mixes with our squaddies, George Maddox and his uniformed boys'll have their hands full. The run up to Christmas will create havoc in the bars and discos in town. Then it'll be Hogmanay, and these skirted wonders'll run amok amid wailing bagpipes, morning, noon and most of the bloody night. They have it wrong about the skirl of the pipes. The word is *scourge*.'

'You'll have to grow used to it, sir,' said Phil Piercey, stirring it. 'I heard they have a solo piper on each accommodation block to play reveille.'

Tom smiled sourly at the sergeant who frequently got under his skin despite his skill at detection. '*You'll* have to grow used to it, you mean. As I live outside the base it won't be *my* ears that are assaulted each morning.'

'I think they'll liven up the festive season in several ways,' Heather insisted. 'So, they'll almost certainly raise hell in town and pester the *Fräuleins* . . .'

'Who won't understand a word they say,' interspersed Piercey.

'. . . but there'll be Scottish dancing in the Sergeants' Mess, and first footing at New Year,' she finished, glaring at Piercey, her least favourite colleague.

'Arms held aloft, and a lot of pointy-toe capering around swords on the floor?' Tom asked with disgust. 'I'll keep well clear of the Mess if they start that.'

The two women exchanged looks that spoke volumes, before Connie said, 'I wonder how the Boss will react to our new troops.'

'He's pretty liberated about music,' Piercey said with a grin. 'Likes pan pipes, balalaikas, mandolins and Paraguayan harps. Bet he'll go over the top for bagpipes.'

Tom had had enough. Max Rydal, Officer Commanding 26 Section was presently flying back from the UK where he had given evidence in a civil trial, so Tom had been in command for the past three days. 'OK, back to work. I want both cases wound up before the end of the week, so get your reports written and finalize those interviews still outstanding.'

Once inside the small headquarters on the perimeter of the base, Tom headed for his office to read through all the evidence on a tricky case concerning a hitherto well-balanced soldier who had gone off the rails and attacked with a broken bottle his best friend, because he had stolen his fiancée. The woman was also a soldier, which exacerbated the loss and humiliation because he had to see her and her new love, day in and day out. It was not an uncommon situation on a large base where young, fit and extrovert men and women worked, lived and played together.

The aggressor would be given a custodial sentence which would remove him from the vicinity of the lovers, and he would be posted elsewhere afterwards, but Tom deplored this setback to the career of a promising soldier. Women, he thought, could cause havoc among normally controlled men.

He scowled at his computer screen. The Scottish incomers were sure to stir passions further. Even Connie and Heather, who normally had their emotions well under control, had gone gaga over the prospect of these brawny Scots dancing in the Mess.

Once he arrived at the house he rented several miles from the base, Tom's mood lightened. After a simple meal he would be driving Nora and their daughters back there for the evening's celebration they had been looking forward to for days, and the Drumdorrans would not yet be free to attend.

The fifth day of November meant fireworks, a bonfire, penny for the guy, Gluhwein, mugs of soup, burgers and paper cones of chips. Oh yes, the children of personnel on a British military base in Germany wanted all that despite being far away from the Parliament building the long-ago Guy Fawkes had tried to blow up. So, on that cold, clear night a large crowd assembled at the Sports Ground to watch a pyrotechnic display and the lighting of a huge bonfire. No 'Guy' was placed atop the carefully constructed pile. Experience had told the organizers that many of the smaller children grew deeply upset over the sight of it being engulfed in flames. This was mostly due to their regarding as lovable toys the 'Guys' they had made for the competition held the previous day. Burning one was more than they could take.

Fortunately, all three Blackies, as Tom dubbed his girls, were old enough to distance pretence from reality and saw those effigies they had made as works of art rather than cuddly playthings. Gina had won a prize for her avant garde entry, and clutched it somewhat ostentatiously as the family occupied tip-up seats in the stand that evening. Her sisters were unfazed. Maggie, coming up to fourteen, had her German boyfriend beside her and Beth, the youngest, was only concerned that the puppy they were to adopt a few days before Christmas would not be scared by the exploding fireworks. She expressed her fears to her father.

Tom smiled reassuringly. 'They'll be keeping an eye on her down at the kennels. Don't forget her mother's a police dog trained to remain calm in noisy situations, so her pups are sure to inherit some of her courage, sweetheart.'

Beth nodded happily. 'Of course! Strudel will be the bravest of them all.'

Not with that ridiculous name, thought Tom as a concerted OOOH! resounded when six rapidly fired rockets filled the sky with gold and silver showers. He felt Nora shiver beside him, so he put his arm along her shoulders.

'Are you OK, love?'

She pressed closer to him. 'I should've worn that heavy coat I bought for midwinter. It's colder than I expected.'

Unzipping his padded jacket Tom slung it around her shoulders. He was additionally protective since Nora had revealed a pregnancy that was unplanned and initially daunting. They had now come to terms with the prospect of a fourth child, with all that having a baby after a gap of almost ten years would mean, but they had not yet gone public with the news. They planned to tell their daughters soon because morning sickness was becoming evident, and children were now so knowledgeable they would certainly cotton on to the truth before long.

The oohs and aahs increased in volume as the fireworks programme reached a glittering climax with multi-explosions of colour behind a row of gigantic spinning Catherine wheels. At the same time, over to the right, four soldiers were applying firebrands to the base of the bonfire so that it would burn evenly. Happily, there was no wind to send smoke over the spectators, as often happened.

With attention now focussed on the glow springing up all around the towering cone, everyone began to move towards the warmth that would soon radiate from it. Children in thick anoraks, woolly scarves and gloves jumped up and down with excitement as flames began to shoot higher and higher, illuminating their eager expressions and sparkling eyes.

Along the fast emptying tiers of seats lay a scattering of empty polystyrene beakers, screws of greasy paper and torn chocolate wrappers. Refuse bins were very evident, but despite annual reprimands there were still those who seemed unable to drop litter anywhere but at their feet. It meant a team of squaddies would have to spend a morning clearing it, which annoyed Tom each year.

Gina tugged his arm as he surveyed this irritant. 'Come on, Dad, let's move or we'll never get near enough to the bonfire to toast ourselves.'

He frowned at her. 'We're not getting that close, my girl. It's dangerous.'

'I know,' she groaned. 'Sergeant Maddox and his men'll be there to keep everyone back.' With a scowl she wagged her 'Guy' at him. 'Policemen *always* spoil the fun.'

Tom did not rise to this familiar complaint from his children. Having a father in the Military Police tended to hamper their acceptance by some of their schoolfellows, particularly those whose own fathers had fallen foul of the Redcaps. Nora had imbued Maggie, Gina and Beth with her own tolerant attitude towards the undeniable mistrust of the army's police force, but the girls still suffered spiteful rejection by their more aggressive peers.

Gina was right in one sense. Sergeant George Maddox, commander of the RMP uniformed section on the base had his men stationed around the stadium to keep people well clear of the area where the fireworks had been set off. There were always those idiots who thought it clever to defy common sense and risk injury.

Beth took her father's hand consolingly after Gina's outburst. Although she joined her sisters to gang up on him over strongly felt issues, she still defended him against individual attacks. He would admit to no one, not even Nora, that he loved it. Big, tough detective going soft!

They were about fifty yards from those gathered as close to the bonfire as restrictions allowed when there was a deafening explosion. The heart burst from it, sending blazing shards of wood and red-hot chunks of fuel-soaked material flying in every direction; an incandescent fountain greater than any of the fireworks.

There was a hung moment before the evening was filled with the sound of screams and cries of pain. Tom's heartbeat accelerated as he witnessed men stamping on burning scarves and stuffed toys, women madly slapping at their singeing hair, children clinging to parents and shrieking with pain or fright.

Turning to Nora, he said tersely, 'Get them home fast,' then ran to where the patrolling Redcaps were marshalling unhurt spectators clear of the site. There was initial panic and chaos, with police, first aid personnel and all able-bodied men present trying to control the situation.

As Tom ran along the tier he was in he saw a burning chunk of wood had landed just ahead of him. He kicked it along that row, then down the steps to the concrete path running in front of the stadium. It could do no harm there. The night was suddenly full of the smell of burning which, together with the lingering smoky halo produced by the fireworks, suggested the halls of Hades.

As Tom raced across the running track he saw that the stand-by fire crew were well on the job of dousing the area nearest to the casualties. These were being helped by men trained to remain calm and deal with the aftermath of explosions. One had escaped them, however; a child with wet cheeks and wild eyes running amok and too shocked to scream. Tom veered to catch her up in his arms and clutch her tightly as she kicked and struggled.

Experienced in calming fightened children, Tom murmured reassurances in her ear while gently stroking her hair as he continued to run towards the centre of the action. He must hand the child to a parent, a responsible woman able to comfort her, or to one of the two medical orderlies who had been on duty throughout in order to deal with any minor burns or falls. They had not been prepared for this.

Hearing the bell of an approaching fire engine, and knowing that medical backup would have been summoned, Tom's principal concern was to discover what had been placed in the bonfire, and by whom. In the present world situation terrorist bombs were being exploded in any chosen area. Security was tight, but a large number of civilians was employed daily on the base. They had all been closely vetted, but one could never be certain. Only recently, six British soldiers had been turned on and shot dead by Afghans they had been training as allies.

A young, ginger-haired man in a purple anorak ran towards

Tom and reached for the child. 'Thank God! She ran off while we were seeing to our boy,' he explained breathlessly. 'He's been hurt. What the bloody hell was in that mound of stuff? I'll have their bleeding guts for what they've done.'

'So will I, chum,' Tom said grittily. 'Bank on it.'

Gradually, the minor casualties were patched up and sent on their way, or were transported to the Medical Centre for treatment. One lad with serious burns, and a woman who had been hit in the chest with a shard of timber, were rushed to the hospital in town as emergencies. The various small fires that had sprung up were being doused; all stragglers had departed.

At that stage Tom discovered that three of his SIB team had been present and helped with the injured. They now joined him and their uniformed colleagues surveying the damage. The stadium spotlights had been switched on, making the scene look even more disturbing. The grass was dotted with charred scarves, woolly hats and other possessions burned beyond saving, and with patches of vomit and faeces where children had lost control in their fear.

What remained of the bonfire still smouldered so there was no chance yet of discovering the cause of the explosion. Tom's expression matched that of George Maddox as they stood together surveying the results of what should have been a happy evening.

'You'll have a load of parents after your blood in the morning, George.'

'Don't I know it.' He wagged his head unhappily. 'I had guys patrolling here from sixteen hundred, and a full force was present by the time the fireworks began. Whoever put explosive material in that pile must have done it overnight.'

'The place has been off limits for two days, and locked during those nights. I can't see how someone carrying dangerous material wouldn't have been spotted inserting it,' Tom reasoned.

Phil Piercey came up to them just then. 'Must have been a joint operation. Several lads thought it would make this year's do more representative of the real thing; make a statement to the PM that unless he improves our lives all round a second attempt to blow up Parliament would succeed.'

Cutting in before Tom could blast Piercey with words, Connie said, 'I agree it was probably the work of more than one. To produce such a result there must have been live ammo in the bonfire, which suggests an accomplice working in the Armoury. Possibly another in the workforce constructing it to stand watch while it was inserted.'

Heather Johnson gave Piercey a derisory glance. 'If anyone was making a statement you can bet they didn't intend it to be such a massive one. I'd guess the culprits are appalled right now.'

'They'll be more than appalled when I catch up with them,' vowed Tom. 'Make no mistake, what happened tonight wasn't the result of a joke gone wrong. No trained soldier could so badly underestimate the power of explosive material.'

Connie looked troubled. 'What are you suggesting, sir?'

'That we've just witnessed a deliberate threat to human life.'

At the riverside inn favoured by Max Rydal he was enjoying a quiet dinner with Clare Goodey, the Medical Officer at the base. They lived in adjoining apartments on the outskirts of town and had become friends during the four months following Clare's arrival as replacement for the previous doctor. Their separate professional lives frequently crossed paths, and they also had personal interests in common, one being that they were both losers in affairs of the heart. Clare had just gone through an aggressive divorce, and Max had recently discovered that the woman he hoped to marry was irrevocably in love with his own father.

They were not, however, commiserating as the lovelorn are wont to do. Max had that afternoon returned from the UK where he had given evidence in the trial of four bikers who had mugged a young officer before chaining him up in a disused barn and riding off. Max had traced him four days later, seriously ill and too exhausted from freeing himself to crawl to the main road for help. He was telling Clare how the accused had spun so many wild tales the Defence had thrown in the towel, advising them to plead guilty.

'A Legal Aid guy, no doubt,' commented Clare, stripping the meat from her barbecued ribs with strong teeth. 'And did they?'

Max nodded. 'With snarls and growls, against a background of loud protests from the public gallery. Half the biking fraternity were present. Unfortunately, their united hatred of the military will strengthen, and the four accused will see their punishment as a badge of macho toughness. Street cred, if you like.'

Clare grinned with greasy lips. 'You're one of the biking fraternity now. Aiming for street cred?'

He grinned back, at ease with this woman. 'Wait until you see me in sexy leathers with a helmet revealing just my steely eyes. You'll be scared to death.'

'You think?' she jeered. 'You've forgotten that I used to race my dad around the track when he was training. See me geared up and The Stig wouldn't even compete.'

Max poured more wine for them both, feeling relaxed and appreciative of Herr Blomfeld's wisdom in dividing his expansive restaurant into small units upholstered in *Volk* style which allowed for more intimate meals. It suited his personality. Max disliked large noisy groups when dining. In warm weather he was quite happy to eat in the beer garden amid locals who celebrated with song and much merriment. That seemed appropriate in a large garden strung with coloured lights, where the river flowed past beyond the lawns and lovers drifted by in boats, but when winter came it seemed to him more appropriate to cosy-up in low-lit snugs. His late love had teased him by claiming his inclination was to hibernate in winter.

He determinedly switched his thoughts to more upbeat ones of the Harley Davidson motorcycle he had splashed out on when it became clear that he would not be buying a house for himself and a new wife. Ever since his student days he had longed to emulate Steve McQueen's dash for freedom in *The Great Escape*, but an early marriage that had ended with his wife's death in a road accident had dampened the urge to be reckless. This humiliating end to his second serious love affair had revived it, so he was now regularly and robustly enjoying cross-country scrambling with a local club.

Taking up Clare's last comment, Max said, 'The way you drove here along the autobahn suggested you were planning to resume circuit racing.'

Her blue eyes sparkled with amusement. 'You ain't seen nothin' yet. Come out with me one weekend and I'll show you *real* speed.'

'No, thanks.'

'Chicken?'

'No, ma'am, I just don't intend to give the *Polizei* the huge pleasure of nicking a British military policeman for breaking their law.'

Herr Blomfeld arrived at their table to ask if they wished for another carafe of wine, but Clare's mobile rang so he deferentially retired again. His disapproval of diners who chatted on their designer telephones during a meal did not extend to this pair he knew well. A doctor and a detective had to be on call wherever they were. The German merely deplored so many meals half eaten due to emergencies.

As Max watched Clare's expression he guessed they would have to leave, then his own mobile rang and he knew why. Swiftly settling their bill they went out to Clare's car, she concerned with the casualties waiting in her surgery and Max sharing Tom's anger over what had occurred. It had clearly not been a prank. There had been past occasions when squaddies had secretly inserted a firework or two in the bonfire, or a few empty aerosol cans for a laugh, but what Tom had described sounded far more serious. Too serious for George Maddox's team. SIB would have to shoulder the burden of bringing the perpetrator to book.

The base was home to battalions of the West Wiltshire Regiment and the Royal Cumberland Rifles, as well as to small specialized units of Royal Engineers, Royal Signals, the Intelligence Corps, the Army Air Corps and several others. In addition, a battalion of a unique Scottish regiment was due to march in today. That would add to the difficulty SIB would have to overcome. As a collector of old black and white war films, Max often thought of the cinematic phrase 'a cast of thousands' whenever a case was not clear cut.

On reaching their apartments they parted, for Clare to collect her medical bag and replace her spangled top for a plain T-shirt. Max exchanged his smart jacket and tailored slacks for wool trousers and a padded waterproof anorak, before making a large flask of coffee. It promised to be a long, chilly night.

When he left his apartment Clare's car was no longer beside his own. He hoped she would not be caught speeding in her anxiety to reach the base. She was a very competent doctor who was still fighting strong resistance to a female MO. Had she been middle-aged and motherly the troops would have more easily confessed their problems to her, but she was in her late twenties, blonde and easy on the eye. The natural instinct in young, red-blooded males was to peacock before someone like Clare, not to appear in any way less than fully virile.

Max drove thoughtfully, knowing haste was not necessary in his own case. Tom, with Piercey, Connie and Heather, was already on the spot and had actually witnessed the explosion. In addition, Maddox's men had patrolled the area prior to the arrival of spectators, and they would have details of all the activity by those preparing the fireworks display.

Even as he reviewed all that, Max wondered how someone had managed to bypass police scrutiny to sabotage the bonfire with such explosive material. Maddox must be a very unhappy man right now. However, until they could establish what that material had been, no blame could reasonably be laid.

At the main gate the barrier was down, and Max was obliged to produce identification despite being well known to the guard.

'Top security in force, sir. There's been an incident. The base is sealed until further notice.'

Privately congratulating Tom on his swift action, Max was nevertheless disturbed by the possibility that there had been some kind of enemy attack here. Had this important base been penetrated by a terrorist? Every six months troops were deployed to Afghanistan from here, but the next changeover would not take place until March next year. An attack on soldiers returning from the war zone would surely be more realistic than one on families and children enjoying fireworks. All the same, Tom had been quick to mount a red alert.

The stadium was still floodlit when Max arrived there. One look was enough to show him why Tom had reacted as he had, and Max swiftly joined those grouped near the smoking remains of the bonfire.

Noting their grim expressions, he asked, 'How many casualties?'

Tom moved away from the others to speak more privately. Max followed him. 'Corporal Crabbe over there has a list of who was treated on the spot – too many kiddies. Corporal

Meacher went to the Medical Centre with half a dozen who received burns, and George sent Corporal Stubble in the ambulance with two needing emergency treatment; a boy with serious burns and a woman hit by a metal-tipped spar. He called in five minutes ago to report that the woman has been put on the danger list.'

'Name?'

'McTavish. Wife of one of the musicians who came in earlier today. Seems she has friends in the West Wilts and has been staying with them for a week until the band arrived here from its tour of the US.'

'Has her man been contacted?'

'He's at the hospital.'

'Good. How could this have happened?'

Tom indicated George Maddox, who appeared to be giving the remainder of his section a hard time. 'He's taking it very personally, but it was just a Guy Fawkes celebration, not a royal visit requiring tight security. Nobody could have foreseen what would happen.'

'Except the guy who planned it.' Max glanced over to where his own team members were questioning a group of men shifting about belligerently in their resentment. 'They the guys who built the bonfire?'

'No, they actually set it alight. We haven't yet established if they also helped to construct it. There's some aggro because one of their mates suffered nasty burns to his arm; they resent being treated as suspects. I guess they're as shocked as the rest of us.'

Having noticed that Max had arrived, Connie Bush walked across to greet him. An attractive young woman who was a keep fit addict, her cheeks were rosier than ever from the late night chill.

'Hallo, sir. How did the trial go?'

'As we all hoped. Get anything useful from those lads?'

She gave a quick glance over her shoulder. 'Apart from a load of abuse, just the info that they had had nothing to do with building the bonfire except for this afternoon. They brought the accelerant and gave a hand with arranging the final layer. They spent more time fabricating the flambeaux they used to set it alight.

'OK, let them go. We'll check them out again in the morning.' As Connie walked away, Max turned back to Tom. 'Who was OC this event?'

'The Garrison QMS. He's gone to the Medical Centre to liaise with Captain Goodey. She'll have her hands full for the rest of the night.'

Max walked for a few minutes surveying the debris littering a wide area around the bonfire site, and asked quietly, 'What's your reading of what happened, Tom? You were right to put the base on high alert, but do you really believe we were under attack?'

'No, but we have to consider it a possibility until we can safely rule it out, don't we?'

Max grunted agreement, his brain busy considering other explanations while Tom continued.

'I tried to notify the Garrison Commander, but he's at a NATO conference. His deputy, Major Crawford, is with his wife at the hospital. It was their son who was badly injured. He gave authority on his mobile for me to raise the security level.'

'Have you managed to contact Captain Knott of Logistics, to get some of his personnel here to take a look?'

'Again, I attempted to. No response on his landline, and his mobile was switched to voicemail. Can't do anything without his go ahead.'

'So we seal this place off and post guards until we get it in the morning. Take a short break, Tom, while I go to the Medical Centre and ask Jack Strachey for the names of all his people who've been working here on the firework framework and the bonfire over the past two days. Then we'll round 'em up, drag 'em out of bed, if necessary, and get some kind of info to work on tonight even if it only allows us to eliminate them as suspects.' He began walking towards where he had left his car. 'We have to get cracking on this. If the McTavish woman dies we'll have a manslaughter case on our hands.'

TWO

Quartermaster Sergeant Jack Strachey was shaped like a box on legs; a short, broad body on very long limbs. He was tough. He had seen it all. He had been in the Army for twenty years. Tonight he was stalking up and down like an angry bull. Children had been hurt and he saw red.

Max knew the man was not helping the situation in the small ward where patients not ill enough to send to the hospital in town often stayed overnight. Right now Clare and several orderlies were using it to apply salve to burns and dressings to wounds inflicted by flying debris. Several small children were lying on the beds being comforted by a parent. Max guessed they had been given a sedative to facilitate upcoming treatment. He thought about having a quick word with Clare, then abandoned the idea. She was fully on the job right now. Tomorrow would be soon enough to get from her any clues about what might have caused the injuries.

'Nothing you can do here, Mr Strachey,' ruled Max, nodding towards the waiting room. 'Let's talk.'

'But . . . these kids . . .' he said aggressively.

'Are better off in the hands of the medics. Our job is to find who was responsible for what happened.'

'I'll kill 'em, I swear,' he growled, pushing through to the waiting room. 'With my bare hands.'

Personally concerned over the number who had suffered some kind of harm, quite apart from others who had been treated on the spot and then sent home, Max allowed for Strachey's reaction. It was natural enough for the man to feel responsible, especially as he had been present to witness the distress and panic. Closing the door leading to the ward, Max told him to sit down.

'I'm too worked up for that,' he replied, fists clenching.

'Sit down!' Max repeated with more emphasis. 'I want info

from you and I want it calmly and concisely, not thrown at me as you prowl around in self-indulgent recrimination.'

The QMS glared at Max, then exhaled in a slow release of anger before lowering himself onto one of the metal-framed chairs. 'I've sometimes had dickheads put empty aerosol cans in, but this was something very different. Legit explosive, and enough to blow that bloody pile apart. None of my lads would do that. I know them, sir. And they know me, which is more to the point. They know I'd skin 'em alive if they did something like this . . . or allowed anyone else to do it.'

Max sat facing him. 'Well, someone *did* do it, and I need to know how.'

'You and me both.' His fists clenched again on his knees. 'I should've checked every hour.'

'You could have checked every five minutes, Q, and still not have prevented what happened. Until Logistics have inspected the remains and come up with an opinion on what caused the explosion, and the Fire Officer gives his conclusions on where in that pile it was sited, all we can do is to question the men you detailed to set up everything for the display and assess when a moment of opportunity for the perpetrator occurred.'

'Must've been at night.'

'The place was locked. Sergeant Maddox has his men looking for signs of a break-in. Difficult, if he was carrying a box of ammo. Easier during the day when cartons of fireworks were in evidence and no checks made. I want from you the names of every man who worked at the Sports Ground over the last two days.'

'There were two women.'

Suspecting a hint of sexism from this long-term soldier's comment, Max said deliberately, 'We can rule them out. No woman would consider making a point by endangering families and children.'

'No more would my lads,' came the immediate fiery disclaimer.

'So you say. Once they're in the clear we can concentrate on finding the knave in the pack. Now, who was overseeing the job?'

'Corporal Lines, sir. Well, he designed the fireworks.' Seeing

Max's optical query, he elaborated. 'For something like that – a public display – there has to be a co-ordinated programme so's there's a good mix of colours and shapes, carefully spaced bangs, and a grand finale that creates a pattern or design on frames. It's not like putting a match to the odd squib in your back garden for your kids.'

Never having had the opportunity to do that, Max continued with his questioning. 'So Corporal Lines would have concentrated on setting up the firework display? No time to see what was going on around the bonfire.'

'Corporal Naish was in charge of that. He's done it other years and knows just how to erect it so it's the right shape and won't topple when it starts to burn.'

'Then I'll start with him.' He nodded at the closed ward door. 'Not in there being treated, is he?'

'No, sir. Took his kiddy home right away. His wife's about to have another one. He didn't want her worrying after hearing the explosion. He's probably back at the Sports Ground now.'

'No, we've sealed it off.'

'How about I round him up and send him to your headquarters?' Knowing the man badly needed to do something, Max agreed. 'You can round up as many of the others as you can trace and send them along, too.'

Before driving to the opposite side of the base, Max called Tom's mobile. 'Where are you?'

'Still at the Sports Ground. We've found some metal fragments, but visibility isn't good. The main search will have to wait until morning.'

'Strachey's rounding up possible witnesses. I asked for as many as he can track down. In his present mood I don't imagine many will escape him. Are Connie, Heather and Phil Piercey still with you?'

'About to leave.'

'I'd like them all at Headquarters for interviewing. And, unless you've something important ongoing, you too.'

'On way.'

Corporal Naish had been drinking. His breath was beery and his dark eyes were slightly glazed. Although Max guessed the imbibing had begun after the man had gone home with his child to reassure his wife, he asked if Naish made a habit of drinking on the job.

'No, sir, *never*,' was his vehement reply. 'I've a boy nearly two and another due next week. Can't afford to get into any trouble. I had a can just now, that's all. To counteract shock.'

More than one can, in Max's estimation. 'How long have you been in the Army?'

'Five years, sir.'

'And an exploding bonfire shocks you so much you need alcohol to help you get over it? However did you earn your stripes?'

Silence from the chunky man on the other side of the desk. He was now looking very much on edge.

'According to Mr Strachey you're an expert on bonfires. So you would have overseen every stage of construction, known exactly what material was used to create the stable cone shape which wouldn't collapse when it began to burn. Is that right?'

'Yessir.'

'How long did it take to build?'

'Well . . . most of two days.' Seeing Max's raised eyebrows, he hurriedly continued. 'Stuff was being brought in that I couldn't use. Happens every time. Crafty way to rid themselves of rubbish. Think I'll just chuck it on the pile. Doesn't work that way. You have to . . .'

'So you vetted everything that was delivered to the Sports Ground?'

Realizing where this was leading, Naish hesitated.

'Yes, or no, Corporal?'

'There wasn't nothing dangerous put in while I was watching, sir.'

'Were there times when you weren't watching?'

'Normal visits to the bog, sir, but the lads took a breather at those times, and at NAAFI breaks, so work stopped.'

'So anything could have been inserted into the pile during one of those times.'

'No, sir. The fireworks squad was on site then. We arranged staggered mealtimes with them.'

'And arranged for someone to keep an eye on the bonfire?'

Naish swallowed nervously. 'Not in so many words, sir.'

'You don't need many words, Corporal, the one will do,' snapped Max. 'And the word is no!'

Shoulders sagging, the NCO abandoned excuses. 'Oh God! I swear I had no idea what would happen when it was ignited. How could I guess someone would do that? It's not like I was building a stack of volatile ammo. It was just a bonfire. For the kids. I didn't see any need to guard it every minute.'

Knowing the justice of that, Max changed tack. 'Did you have the same team throughout?'

'Yessir, except Rifleman Carter pulled out this afternoon. He cut his hand on a nail left in a plank and had to have it stitched.'

'Nobody replaced him?'

'No, sir. We was almost finished.'

'How about the four who made the flambeaux late this afternoon? According to them they gave a hand with the final layer.'

Naish's broad face turned red. 'Mr Strachey sent them along with the accelerant. That's their field of knowledge, sir. I don't have anything to do with what makes it burn.'

'So what did they do that makes you feel guilty now?'

Still flushed, he said awkwardly, 'It was just a laugh, sir.'

'What was?'

After some hesitation, he answered. 'The four of them had made a sort of straw image of their Platoon Commander. Seems he gives them a bad time,' he added with a feeble attempt at a laugh.

'Go on,' invited Max in steely manner.

Where he had been flushed, Naish now grew pale and stayed silent until he could no longer withstand Max's unblinking stare. 'We . . . we fixed it on the side. It looked like a decoration. Nothing like . . . there weren't no harm in it, sir. Just a bundle of straw.'

'Which could have contained explosive material.' Even as he said it Max recalled that Tom had told him the explosion had come before the bonfire was fully alight. 'So what else did you allow to be attached to your perfect cone "just for a laugh"?'

'Nothing, sir, I swear. I see now I shouldn't have done it.'

'No, you shouldn't have.' Max let some seconds pass before he added. 'You're an irresponsible idiot, Corporal Naish.'

'Yes sir.' He took a deep breath and offered an irrefutable defence. 'I'm really gutted about what happened, but if I'd had any notion someone had tampered with it I wouldn't have taken my own boy there tonight, would I?'

It was almost two a.m. when Tom crept upstairs to collect a couple of blankets before settling on the sofa for what remained of the night. Sleep was a long time coming. They were treating the incident as a vicious act by an unbalanced soldier with a need to make a statement, but suppose there really was an active terrorist with access to the base who would strike at every opportunity. How would they ever flush him out? Was his own family safe here?

He awoke unrested and worried, had to compete for a shower, then shaved to the accompaniment of two different pop groups vying for volume supremacy. His normal routine was to rise early enough to claim the bathroom, before descending to the quiet haven of the kitchen. This morning he had been caught up in the daily procession of females in varying stages of undress going from bedrooms to bathroom while nattering non-stop. Before long there would be infant wails added to the chorus. It did not bear thinking about when he had so much on his mind.

Worse was to come. Sitting in a row at the breakfast bar, with bowls of cereal topped with sliced banana, his daughters wanted an account of last night's drama which they could relate to their classmates with face-saving one-upmanship. They had been very disgruntled over having been sent home so peremptorily when other children had been there for the full experience. They needed inside information to compensate for that.

'You'd like to have been burned and cut, would you?' Tom demanded across the table.

Gina said boldly, 'It was only minor stuff. We know all about it from our friends who've texted. They're all well enough to get to school today.'

'Some children won't be going. Gavin Crawford, for one.

He's in hospital with serious damage to his head and face. His hair caught alight. He's very badly burned.' There was concentrated cereal eating until Tom added, 'It seems likely that something unsuitable was mistakenly included in the mass of material supplied from various stores on the base. Until we conduct a full search of the area today we won't know what that was, and who was responsible. As soon as we know, I'll tell you.'

'John Cassidy says it was put there by a suicide bomber,' said Gina, still resentful over missing the excitement.

'A *suicide* bomber who wasn't killed when it went off?' put in Nora. 'John Cassidy will have to think more intelligently than that if he's going to be a thriller writer.'

'He's changed his mind, Mum. He's going to be a film cameraman.'

'A much better idea.' Nora left her seat abruptly, and could then be heard vomiting in the adjacent cloakroom.

After a while, Beth asked, 'Is Mum all right? She keeps being sick.'

'This is the third morning running,' put in Maggie.

'Perhaps she should see Captain Goodey, Dad,' said Beth.

'Yes, she was in a real state last night,' added Gina. 'It's not like her. She's usually so sensible when there's any kind of problem.'

Maggie pushed aside her cereal bowl and reached for the toast. 'It's probably something she's eating for breakfast.'

'No, it isn't. I'm pregnant.' Nora had appeared at the kitchen door, and she crossed to stand behind Tom to put a hand on his shoulder. 'We don't know which yet, but next year you'll have a brother or sister.'

There was a stunned silence. Maggie dropped the toast as if it was red hot; Gina returned her full spoon to her bowl. Both girls stared in disbelief which gradually changed to deep embarrassment, then to undisguised disgust.

'How lovely!' cried Beth. 'A puppy *and* a baby.'

As Tom drove to the base Beth's words depressed him further. She viewed a new sibling with the same pleasure she accorded the adopted puppy. If only a baby brought as little disruption to routine as a young dog. His initial dismay at the prospect returned. How would Nora cope with it all? Maggie was into her teens; Gina was fast approaching them. Could they be relied on to give more help in the home when they so obviously felt alienated by the evidence that he and Nora still 'did it'. Even while *they* slept in rooms just across the corridor! He foresaw a prickly time ahead unless Nora managed to talk them round, which he somehow doubted after this morning's reaction to the news.

The girls were each two years apart, so the elder pair had been too young to think beyond the fact that there was a new baby in their mother's tummy. They were now old enough to know how the babies got there. Beth's caring temperament allowed her to isolate the joy of a brother or sister who would become the youngest in her place. The naturalist of the family she took procreation in her stride, with no thought of grunting and sighing in the bedroom next to hers.

After they had left to catch the school bus – Maggie and Gina without kissing their parents, and Beth thinking up names for the baby – Tom had accused Nora of breaking the news at a very inappropriate moment. They had been on the brink of a row when Nora had to rush to the cloakroom again, which made Tom feel he was behaving like a selfish brute. In typical male fashion he departed for work in the certain belief that she would prefer to be alone. After all, pregnancy was a woman's thing, and he had to find whoever had put lives at risk last night.

When he reached Headquarters he found the entire team already assembled, and Max there in his office making a phone call. Eager to get started, Tom brought up to date those who had not been present at the Guy Fawkes event, then he posted on the board the names of everyone who had been involved in building the bonfire and who had supplied material from various regimental stores.

'Those with a cross beside them were interviewed last night and appeared clean. They can be questioned again if anything comes up to cast doubt on their statements. I want the rest of these people interviewed today, and I want lists of what was sent out from each QM Stores, how it was transported and what actually arrived at the Sports Ground. I want details of who took tea breaks and when, who left the stadium and why, and I want to know their attitude towards what they had been detailed to do. Who was resentful because it prevented fulfilling another plan for the evening; who might have a grudge against the person they felt *should* have been given the job? Make a note of anyone who seems politically motivated or who's anti-establishment. Find out who these people mix with in town; if they visit any pro-Nazi clubs or organizations.'

'Bit drastic, isn't it?' complained Piercey. 'This wasn't a bomb under the Garrison Commander's car; it didn't blow up the Ops Planning Headquarters. Surely it was simply crass stupidity at a bonfire party.'

'You think I'm overreacting?' Tom commented coldly. 'Ask Pipe Major McTavish, whose wife is fighting for her life in the hospital, if he thinks we should regard what happened as crass stupidity. This is a military base, the British have enemies, our troops are presently operating in countries hiding terrorists aiming to demoralize us. What occurred last night wasn't a jolly jape, Piercey, it was a serious attempt to do just that. Do I make myself clear?'

Piercey seemed unabashed, as usual. 'Yes, sir, I simply thought . . .'

'Well, *don't*,' he snapped, then began posting another list of names on the board. 'These people were involved in setting up the firework display. Again, those with crosses against them were interviewed last night. I spoke to Corporal Lines, who was not only OC fireworks he was responsible for the whole show. He was pretty well gutted because his wife had been hit by a chunk of burning wood, which set fire to the nylon scarf around her hair. She panicked and someone put out the flames by holding a blanket tightly over her head and patting it hard. She fainted.' His mouth tightened. 'It's not funny, Piercey.'

The Sergeant schooled his expression. 'No, sir.'

'I want someone to have another session with Corporal Lines, and I suggest Connie or Heather – detectives with more understanding and wit than some of their male colleagues.' He was more than usually irritated by the maverick sergeant today following the upset at breakfast. 'I intend to visit the supplier of the fireworks. Lines gave me the invoice listing everything he ordered, but he admitted that he hadn't personally checked the items in the boxes, only the labels stating the contents.' He tapped the board. 'Get assurances from these people that the boxes they opened did contain what they should have.'

Heather Johnson looked up from her notebook. 'Private Brooks told me last night that he believed somebody lodged a rogue rocket in the bonfire unaware that it would react so violently, and his mate, Fiddler, told me rockets are well known for being unstable.'

Tom nodded. 'I'm considering anything and everything, at the moment. And so should all of you. The one certainty is that an extremely volatile object was lodged inside that huge cone, and it was placed there deliberately.'

Max emerged from his office at that point, and entered the discussion. 'Although I didn't witness the explosion I saw the damage it caused, and there's no doubt in my mind that the foreign object was highly unstable. I've been discussing it with Captain Knott of Logistics, who's sending his explosives team along to the Sports Ground to study the evidence George and his lads have already found. They'll join in the search of the entire area and study the findings. Captain Knott is certain his men will be able to identify the cause of the explosion from them.' He frowned at them all. 'Once we have that we'll have something to work on. But that'll be just a start. Finding the perpetrator promises to be a bloody sight more complex. It's unfortunate that we have just absorbed the Scots – another several thousand personnel. As they only marched in during yesterday afternoon it's highly unlikely that they could be involved, but *unlikely* is not *impossible*. One of them could have wandered in to mingle with the crowd, and inserted something while all attention was on the fireworks. As Mr Black says, we must consider everything. Right, get to it!'

Taking up mobile phones and car keys, they all left the building discussing who each of them would take as interviewees. Max headed for the shelf bearing an electric kettle and a cluster of mugs.

'I didn't have time for breakfast, and you look as if you need some immediate caffeine, Tom. What time did you eventually turn in?'

He wandered across to join the boss who was also a friend. 'Too late. A case like this is very unsettling. We have no idea what we have on our hands. If it was the work of a local employee we'll have to hand it over to the *Polizei* and have them swarming all over the base. If it was an act of terrorism we'll have the Anti-Terrorist Squad doing the same. In those instances we'll be piggy-in-the-middle, which is the worst place to be in.'

Max opened the snack tin and took out two walnut and sultana muffins, offering one to Tom before spooning instant coffee into the mugs. 'I've to see Major Crawford, Deputy GC at ten. He's come home from the hospital to change and eat breakfast, but he means to return there this afternoon. His wife's staying with their son who was badly burned. Imagine if it had been one of your girls, Tom.'

He nodded gloomily, thinking of their hostility this morning. What if something happened to them before the issue of a new baby was resolved?

As Max poured water in the mugs the telephone in his office rang. 'Do the coffee while I take that,' he said, plonking the kettle down and heading to the small partitioned area he used as his own domain.

Tom was still brooding over Maggie and Gina's attitude towards their parents' continuing sexual habits, when Max returned looking rather grim.

'Mrs McTavish died in the early hours. We're dealing with a case of manslaughter, or a religious or political killing. Take your pick, my friend.'

THREE

Max approached the Deputy Garrison Commander's house with misgivings. Major Crawford was one of what Max thought of as black and white officers. Everything either was, or wasn't; no room for might be. Never bend the rules. Tom's demand for high security implementation had been the correct thing to do following the explosion, but Max could not dismiss Piercey's protest that a bonfire was an offbeat site for a terrorist bomb. Unfortunately, they dare not dismiss the possibility when Miles Crawford asked if the situation still warranted a red alert, as he surely would.

The Major looked hollow-cheeked and red-eyed, and invited Max inside as brusquely as if he were an offender coming before him for a reprimand. Max gritted his teeth as he followed him to a room set up as an office, and told himself the man was under stress because his son was suffering. Although there were two padded chairs as well as a chintz-covered box seat, they remained standing. Max began by enquiring about the progress of young Gavin, and received a bitter reply.

'He'll be scarred for life. A boy of fourteen years faces resembling a monster for the rest of his days. So what have you done about apprehending the maniac who's done that to him?'

Choosing words carefully, Max explained that they had done all that was possible so far. 'My team conducted interviews well into the early hours, sir, and they're continuing to do so this morning. Captain Knott's explosives experts are presently evaluating any evidence scattered around the stadium, and they'll shortly be able to tell us what caused the explosion. Once we have that, progress will speed up.'

'I sincerely hope so,' Crawford said icily. 'I've given orders for every local resident we employ to be intensively questioned by Redcaps before being allowed entry.' He picked up a ruler and began slapping it against the palm of his other hand. 'I've never approved of having civilians on strength. We're a unique Force which knows best how to look after itself on every level. These nine-to-five Fritzes can possibly handle what's needed at a manufacturing company's site, but they're totally wrong on a military base. They simply don't understand us.'

Max wondered where the interview was heading. 'They're doing those jobs the Army is unable to staff in these days of low manning levels. They leave our troops free to concentrate on active service.'

'I know all that, man! The serving women traditionally undertook all the supportive roles – catering, clerking, chauffering, store keeping – and it worked smoothly. Now they want to do everything the men do, including active service, so we have to pay civilians to replace them.' The ruler landed on the desk with a clatter. 'You know where you are with fighting men. The rules are clear. But civilians! They come in here and behave just as they like.'

'Sir, we have no evidence that a local employee was involved in last night's disaster,' said Max, trying to get the conversation back on track.

Major Crawford regarded him with impatience. 'Are you forgetting the fact that we fought two wars against these people?'

'I'll keep an open mind until the explosives boys come up with their professional opinion after studying the debris. Rest assured the blame will be laid appropriately. I'll keep you informed throughout, sir,' Max replied firmly, ending the meeting by moving towards the door.

Driving away Max wondered why he had been summoned by this prejudiced officer. He had to assume Crawford wanted the state of high alert because the man himself was enforcing intensive vetting by Maddox's men at the main gate. Apart from that there had been no instructions, no real interest in what the SIB team planned to do once they had the vital information from Captain Knott's experts. Could Crawford truly believe a local civilian working on the base still regarded his employers as wartime enemies?

On the point of laughing that off, Max remembered Tom's directive to suss out any soldier who might have links with the neo-Nazi groups undeniably active in the area. Would this case have to be handed to Klaus Krenkel, Commander of the local *Polizei* squad? If the perpetrator was German the prosecution would have to be handled by his men even though the victims were British military personnel and their families.

Max was inclined to believe they had on their hands another case of a soldier, or soldiers, making some kind of statement. Possibly one more deadly than they had intended. Mrs McTavish's death now put it in the top league of criminal acts. Expressing condolences was Miles Crawford's responsibility in Colonel Trelawney's absence. Max hoped the Major would not suggest to the bereaved husband that she had been deliberately killed by a Nazi sympathiser.

The sudden reflection that Eva McTavish had been killed only because she had come to stay with friends a week before her husband's regiment was due to march in caused Max to pull up by the Recreation Centre and call Tom's mobile. He took a while to answer against a background of shouts and metallic clattering.

'Problems?'

'Can you recall offhand the name of the family Mrs McTavish was staying with?'

'Uh, Greene, with an e. He's a sergeant in the West Wilts presently in Afghanistan. Are you on to something?'

'Just a stray thought. I have a gut feeling this case is going to lead us in some odd directions, and this is one of them. Where are you?'

'The Armoury, checking if they have anything missing.' He gave a short laugh. 'They're running around like headless chickens.'

'I'll get back to you with anything useful.'

'Ditto.'

Another call, this time to Headquarters where Sergeant Bob Prentiss was on duty, gave Max the Greenes' address, and he made a three-point turn to head towards the sergeants' married quarters. The woman who opened the door to him was tall, slender and very striking. Stylishly cropped black hair and pale skin accentuated chocolate brown eyes that surveyed him frankly as he identified himself and asked if he could speak to her about Eva McTavish.

'Aye, come in.' She led the way through a short corridor to the living room. 'I guessed a body would be wanting words with me, but you're very quick off the mark,' she added in an attractive Scottish brogue.

Max cast a swift encompassing glance at the room sporting bright colours that individualized the standard MoD furniture, then asked quietly, 'Have you been told that your friend has died?'

She nodded. 'Hector called me on the instant, blathering, of course. Crocodile tears! Take a seat. I'll make coffee . . . or would you prefer a dram?'

Taken aback by her calm manner in the face of her friend's sudden death, Max said, 'Coffee would be welcome.'

Crocodile tears? What lay behind that contemptuous phrase, he wondered as he studied the room further in her absence. The colour was provided by throws of complicated design on the chairs and sofa, and by unusual pictures which were actually framed squares of similar fabric. Interesting.

He grew aware of another presence and turned towards the door. At the foot of the stairs stood a girl of around three years, with black curls and big eyes that studied him as frankly as her mother had.

'Hallo,' he said.

'Who are you?' she asked with interest.

'I'm Max. Who are you?'

She gave no reply, simply crossed the room and climbed on his lap with total confidence. Although charmed by this doll-like child Max thought her trust should be curbed before it led to problems. He intended to say as much to her mother, but she then entered with a tray and smiled.

'I see Jenny has adopted you. She misses Billy so much she sees a substitute daddy in any male visitor.' She addressed her daughter. 'Offer your friend a biscuit, darling.'

'He's called Max.' She turned her dark eyes up to him. 'Shall we have biscuits?'

Still charmed, he said, 'Only if they're my favourites.'

'What are they?'

Seeing a couple of custard creams on the plate, he named them. She shook her head. 'No, they're *my* favrits. You must have the others.'

Her mother admonished her. 'Captain Rydal is a guest. He must be given first choice.'

Max felt the purpose of this meeting was being undermined by this enchanting pair. The woman did not seem upset by the death of a friend who had been her house guest for the past week. His attempts to unseat the child met with resistance, so he spoke over her curly hair as she munched a custard cream.

'Mrs Greene, I . . .'

'Jean.' She smiled. 'Jean Greene. Quite a mouthful, I know, but I had a school friend called Joyce who married a Frederick Joyce, which is even worse. I'll put your coffee on this side table where you'll be able to manage quite well.'

He waited until she settled on the sofa with her own mug of coffee. 'This isn't a social call, Jean. I'm here to get from you a few details about Mrs McTavish who was hit by flying debris from the bonfire. SIB is investigating the cause of the explosion so we tend to explore every avenue, however unlikely. I shall be speaking to Pipe Major McTavish in a while, but as he only came on base yesterday few people already here know the couple. I'd like you to put me in the picture. You made a comment just now that suggests they weren't close, and you don't appear to be too deeply upset over her death. Why did you invite her to stay with you to await her husband's arrival from the US with the band?'

Jean leaned back in relaxed manner and nibbled a biscuit. 'She invited herself, Max. With Billy away I had no solid reason to refuse. We were schoolfellows keeping in contact at Christmas and birthdays, that's all. Her email came out of the blue and, as I said, it would have made things awkward to deny her. She was going to be living here and I didn't want to start off on the wrong foot. Time for plain speaking when she had settled in.'

She sipped her coffee, then selected another biscuit. 'She's been aware of my business career so I intended to use it as a means of shedding her as soon as she had made other friends.'

'What kind of business?' he asked with interest.

She waved a hand at the room. 'Before I married Billy I ran a village store selling furnishings – blankets, throws, cushions, shawls, wall decorations all designed from fabrics woven by local women in their homes. Cottage industry. I inherited the business from an aunt, and soon developed a mail order outlet. It took off almost immediately with growing sales to the US.'

She smiled again. It was a very beguiling smile. 'I was set to marry the local doctor and settle in the village, then I met Billy and knew at once that he was the one. Another of my school friends is managing the shop for me and I go home every three months to discuss new products and to meet important customers. I've recruited several here in town. You'll find our goods in *Gunters* and in *Petit Bijou*.'

Once again Max felt his command of the meeting was being undermined, and he wondered about Billy Greene who had made such an instant impact on this woman.

'While Eva McTavish was with you did she discuss the state of her marriage at all?'

'Aye, non-stop. She made the mistake of taking on the boy from next door without playing the field first. Very unwise. I suppose it worked well enough at the start. He wore big boots and she was a handy doormat.'

Sitting with a pretty child snuggled against his shoulder while listening to a vivacious woman who had a way with words, Max was momentarily saddened by memories of his wife Susan and their unborn son they had already named Alexander, who had died in a road accident. There could have been a boy on his knee, and the woman *he* had known at once was the one sitting with him.

'Is something wrong?'

The words reached him and he again focussed on the stranger on the sofa. 'Was he ever violent with her?'

'With words, not actions. Hector can blaspheme for Scotland. Even as a boy. I suppose his real love is music; the pipes. Eva was just there to get his meals, keep his togs clean and satisfy him in bed.'

'And did she, so far as you know?'

'Aye, surely. He's a man whose needs are basic; no frills. It would never occur to him to wonder if *she* was satisfied.' Her eyebrows rose expressively. 'Climb into bed, get a quick fix, turn over and fall asleep dreaming of treble clefs.'

Max had to smile. 'You put it very succinctly. It probably explains why Eva was watching fireworks instead of spending the evening with her newly arrived husband. You and Jenny had a lucky escape last night.'

She shook her head. 'We weren't there. Jenny hates fireworks. The bangs frighten her, and so do sudden explosions of colour in the sky. Eva went on her own.'

'I see. Was she intending to join her husband afterwards?'

'No. She told me their accommodation hadn't yet been allocated. I don't know how true that was but I intended to be rid of her today.' She frowned, and looked disturbed for the first time. 'Oh dear, poor Eva! Such a stupid termination of a life so shallowly lived. It's said we're all born to play a part on the world's stage, but that sad girl stayed in the wings.'

Caught up in her terminology, Max said, 'Perhaps she was the prompter that ensured Hector played *his* part faultlessly.'

'Perhaps, and maybe they weren't crocodile tears he was shedding and his world really has come tumbling down. Oh, dear God, Eva's luggage is upstairs in the spare room. What shall I do about it?'

'I'll arrange for someone to collect it and give it to McTavish when he's ready for it.' It was the moment for him to leave, but Max realized Jenny had fallen asleep so he struggled to rise from the chair, still holding her.

Jean chuckled. 'Don't worry about waking her. She cat naps all the time.'

He succeeded in arranging the still sleeping girl on the seat he had just vacated, however, and departed with guilty reluctance which he managed to dispel by reminding himself he had not been there to interview an actual suspect. And he had gained some interesting facts about Hector McTavish.

Deciding to have an early lunch in the Officers' Mess of which he was a member, his curiosity about the absent Billy Greene was interrupted by the ring of his mobile. He reached out to connect and heard Tom say, 'Nothing missing from the Armoury.'

'Bit quick off the mark to offer that guarantee, aren't they?'

'They had a very recent stocktake, and everything they checked out since then is safely back. I'm off to interview someone at Max-ee-million, the fireworks manufacturer. Anything on McTavish?'

'Zilch.'

'How did it go with Major Crawford?'

'As bloody-minded as usual and understandably angry about the damage to his son. Any news from the explosives team yet?'

'They'll let us know as soon as.'

'Hmm, we're walking through treacle until we get something from them.'

Parking at the Mess, Max called George Maddox and arranged for a Redcap to collect Eva McTavish's things and hold them in store, then he went to the cloakroom to spruce himself up before walking through to the dining room. Spotting Clare in a far corner he collected a plate of braised beef, poured himself a large glass of water, then crossed to sit with her.

'Hi! Your car wasn't there when I went home around three a.m., nor when I left this morning.'

'Ha, checking up on me, Mr Detective? I had a few hours' sleep on the camp bed at the surgery. We had five children in overnight, two women with badly burned hands and a lance corporal with injuries to his eyes. Luckily, his sight won't be permanently affected.'

'Any chance of David Culdrow getting back to work yet, to reduce your hours?' Max asked, sitting beside her and starting on his meal. 'You look completely washed out.'

'Just what a woman wants to hear, Max.'

'I was speaking to a *doctor*,' he said firmly. 'Is there?'

'Not yet. Mumps affects adults badly. But, by lucky chance, the in-comers have their own Medical Officer. Major Duncan MacPherson. Seems he's known to the Jocks as MacFearsome, and I saw why. He's a very fine figure of a man. He's going to replace David on a temporary basis, which means I can resume a normal routine. After I've eaten I'm going home for a leisurely bath and several hours on my bed. Heaven!'

Glancing with irritation at a group of rowdy subalterns who had come through from the ante-room, Max said, 'Did you read the notice on the board announcing a compulsory dinner night on Friday to welcome the new Scottish members?'

She nodded, her mouth full of roast potato. 'Mmm. Nuisance.' Several moments later she was able to add, 'Emergencies never interrupt on those occasions, you notice. You can bet we'll have to sit throughout the entire boring ritual without a single call for our help. Sod's Law! How's the investigation progressing?'

'Slowly. The Scottish woman's death rachets it up a rung, of course. People haven't had time to fully react. Wait a day or two and the trouble will start.'

'Unless you've already got the guy who caused it.'

'Fat chance.'

Tom left Max-ee-million little wiser than when he had arrived. A fat-bellied Estonian with an obvious personality problem and a heavy accent had marched Tom between rows and rows of cardboard boxes explaining, with much arm-waving, that 'every gives a small "pouff", much colours and safe to the hand. Mister has mistake. Max-ee-million never sell with bombings.'

During a tour of the factory Tom saw only what he would expect to see at a legitimate dealership. He had almost to fight off a gift of several cartons of fireworks which the Estonian tried to thrust into his arms on leaving, and he sought refuge in his 4x4 with the man's curious English protests still ringing in his ears. Driving to his rented house in the hope of some lunch, he felt frustrated yet glad that he had not found evidence that would have placed the case in the hands of the *Polizei*.

When he walked through to the kitchen Tom saw that Nora had been crying, and he regretted leaving so peremptorily after breakfast. Even so, he was unsure whether to raise the subject or to keep things light. He had to get back to the base, so it was probably the wrong moment to wade in at the deep end.

It soon became obvious that Nora was already there when she took one look at him and broke down.

Deeply disturbed, Tom went to her and drew her close, thinking yet again how this pregnancy had changed their lives so drastically. All their plans for the future, the pleasure derived from their maturing daughters and, without doubt, their own expectation of having more time free from parenting duties, had suddenly been put back for at least twelve years. He thought they had come to terms with all that, but it looked as if Nora had not. Unless . . . He recalled the scare they had had before Gina was born. He tightened his embrace.

'There's nothing wrong, is there, love?'

Fighting free, Nora stared at him with tear-filled eyes. 'Of *course* there's something bloody wrong,' she practically shouted. 'We didn't want it, we're unwilling to go public on it, and now our children think it's *disgusting*. It's easy for you and the girls. You can walk away from it. I can't. It's part of me and I'll soon feel it move inside me.' She beat his chest with her fists. 'We have to love it, Tom. *Someone* has to love the poor little sod.'

Tom had never been good at handling pregnancy. Living and working in a predominantly masculine environment he knew and understood men in all their moods, but he was always bewildered by Nora's out of character behaviour and the spells of acute emotion in a woman who was normally assured and well-balanced.

Aware of the cowardly wish that he had returned directly to base, he made matters worse by saying, 'You shouldn't have told them. They were heading for school full of excitement about last night's drama. It was the wrong time to spring that on them. Talk to them again when they'll absorb the fact properly.'

'That's right,' she raged. 'It always has to be me to sort them out. I hope to God this one's a boy, because I'll hand him to you on day one.'

'That'll be fine by me,' he replied, forcing a smile. 'It'll be good to have another male around the house to support my stand against all you women.' She glared at him, so he took the only escape route he could think of. 'Suppose I heat some soup and make spicy sandwich rolls with those cold sausages left over from last night?'

Taking her silence as a truce, he set to work providing the light lunch he wished he had instead eaten elsewhere. When it was ready he set two bowls of aromatic soup on the breakfast bar along with a large plate containing the food. The silence continued while Nora drank her soup, but left Tom to eat most of the sausage sandwiches.

He wondered how soon he could leave. He needed to check on the accelerant used on the bonfire, and in what quantity. He also intended to stop at the Sports Ground to see what progress had been made by the explosives experts. Surely they were getting some ideas by now. The fact that nothing was missing from the Armoury was not conclusive on that score. It was easy enough to obtain weapons from all manner of sources, even the Internet. Once it was identified it would be easier to attempt to trace its origins. Now the McTavish woman had died from her injuries it was even more imperative to find who had indirectly caused her demise.

Growing aware that Nora was up and rummaging in the freezer Tom felt fresh guilt over allowing the case to absorb him to the extent of forgetting where he was. It ebbed away when he saw that she had in her hands a large tub of chocolate ice cream, something she invariably devoured in huge quantities when she was pregnant.

'At it again?' he teased softly.

She came over with a full spoon and fed him with his least favourite treat. 'You don't deserve it, Thomas Black.'

He breathed a sigh of relief that the storm had blown over. 'I don't deserve *you*, sweetheart, but they say the Devil looks after his own.' Getting to his feet, he kissed the top of her head. 'Beth was thrilled, and so will the other two be when they absorb the truth that there'll soon be a baby for them to play with and mother. Don't worry. He'll be swamped with love by the Blackies.'

Second Lieutenant Stuart Freeman was a lanky young man with mousey hair and very intelligent eyes. He looked warily at the tall, dark-haired man dressed in a charcoal suit – an apparent civilian with a decided air of authority – who had walked unannounced in to the office where he was very volubly swearing at his computer for wiping the report he had taken such pains to compose before lunch.

Max smiled with sympathy. 'I know the feeling.' He offered his hand. 'Captain Max Rydal, SIB.'

Freeman scrambled to his feet and completed the handshake. 'I'm sorry. I didn't recognize you, sir.'

'No reason why you should have. We've never crossed paths before.'

Max's identity suddenly registered with the subaltern. 'SIB? Is there some problem?' he asked, even more warily.

'That's what I'm here to find out by interviewing four members of your platoon.'

This proof that the focus was not on him did little to reassure, and Max guessed he was fresh from Sandhurst and was trying too hard to be the perfect leader of men. He would soon discover that was a very rare breed. Was his ultra diligence the cause of the 'hard time' given to the four who had fashioned a straw dummy to burn on the bonfire?

'What have they done?' The cadet training came to the fore as Freeman stood ready to support his men. 'I'm not aware of . . .'

Max interrupted by telling him exactly what his men had done, adding, while Freeman's face flooded with colour, that he was investigating the cause of an explosion which had resulted in a fatality and numerous injuries.

'Privates Mooney, Rule, Casey and Blair are under suspicion. I need to know what they might have hidden within that corn dolly. They all sound irresponsible enough to stuff something volatile inside it as a joke, and thick enough not to recognize the danger of such an action.' Max softened his tone. 'It's the kind of thing squaddies do with abysmal frequency, you'll find, when they believe they're being hard done by. If it isn't the Platoon Commander, it's a sergeant or a corporal – anyone who keeps them on their toes.'

He changed his approach. 'On the other hand, this quartet might actually have planned what happened as some kind of subversive statement. Get someone to round them up, and I'll interview them initially in your presence. If I judge there was evil intent I'll have them hauled off to my headquarters for further questioning.'

By now looking really apprehensive, Freeman said, 'I think it would be better for you to see them in the adjacent office. Captain Crooke's on leave so you won't be disturbed. The men will talk more freely if I'm not present.'

Knowing he would say that, Max nodded. 'Fair enough. I'll give you the gist of the info I squeeze out of them.'

'Yes. Yes. Good.' The younger man picked up his telephone. 'I'll organize someone to bring them in for you.' When he had done that he offered Max coffee. 'Or tea, if you'd prefer it.'

'Coffee's fine. Have them put it in the next office for me. I imagine you're anxious to sort out your computer blip.'

Still pink in the face, Freeman said, 'Oh God, yes. A report that had taken all morning to compile vanished from the screen the minute I logged on again after lunch. It's presently swimming around somewhere in the ether until I manage to rein it in.'

Max laughed. 'Along with a myriad pieces of vital info which have never been reined in and will remain in space ad infinitum.'

The corporal who brought the men to the company offices was surely efficient enough to meet Freeman's high standards, for they arrived only five minutes after Max had drunk his coffee. It had been accompanied by two chocolate digestive biscuits. Freeman pulling out all the stops?

'Corporal Furness, sir,' anounced the lean NCO with a long face that reminded Max of Collie dogs. He had appeared in the doorway and saluted with a flourish. 'Privates Mooney, Rule, Blair and Casey are without, sir.'

Resisting the urge to ask 'without what?', Max nodded. 'Thank you. Send the first one in and tell the others to follow one at a time. You needn't wait.'

'Sir!' Another tight salute, a smart swivel on his heels, then a parade-ground command for Mooney to 'See the officer.'

One glance at Dennis Mooney told Max all he needed to know. Stuart Freeman had been giving him a hard time because he needed it. A man who had joined the Army because he could not think of anything else to do, Max judged. No real enthusiasm for the job, no realization of a boyhood dream. It had been the easy way out of unemployment. Signing on had given him somewhere to live, ready companionship, three solid meals a day, opportunities for free participation in sports and other leisure activities that required expensive equipment, a guaranteed wage, the chance to learn a trade, and a uniform to be proud of. Except that he was not, that much was evident. Max guessed the other three would be the same. An unlikely crew for subversion. It would require too much effort.

He went straight in with, 'You and your mates made a straw dummy that was meant to represent Second Lieutenant Freeman, and then persuaded Corporal Naish to attach it to the bonfire last night. Why was that?'

Mooney's lips twitched. 'It was a joke, sir.'

'I see. Did you tell Mr Freeman so that he could appreciate the laugh of having a parody of himself burned in public?'

'It was just some straw put together like a scarecrow. I mean, it didn't look nothing like him.'

'Then what was the point?'

'Um . . . it was a joke, sir.'

'So you keep saying. How many people laughed?' Mooney was by now so far out of his depth he gave no reply. 'Just you, Rule, Casey and Blair. Corporal Naish told me last night that he was not altogether happy about doing as you asked. What did you stuff the effigy with?'

'What?'

'Something wrong with your hearing, Mooney? Or your comprehension?'

Mooney shuffled his feet uncomfortably. 'I don't know why we've been called in about this. It was just a . . .'

'Joke. Your sense of humour is around the level of a junior schoolboy. One of limited intelligence. If you haven't already heard I'll tell you that a woman who was injured when the bonfire blew apart died this morning. Also, the Deputy Garrison Commander's son has severe head and facial burns as a result of that explosion. I ask you again, what did you put inside the straw bundle to make it resemble a scarecrow?'

The coarse face with fleshy lips had paled. 'Christ, we didn't have nothing to do with *that*! Who says we did? Corp Naish? He's a bloody liar. You can't hang that on us. We didn't have no explosives.' He wiped a hand across his wet mouth in his agitation. 'When they said SIB wanted us we didn't have no idea why. Christ!' he swore again. 'No, sir, no way can you have us up for that. That's . . . that's murder.'

'Involuntary manslaughter. You still haven't answered my question.'

'What question?' He was so worked up he had lost even the minimal concentration he had had at the start.

'What was inside the dummy?'

'Just rags, sir. Oily rags we use around the trucks we're working on every day.'

Max changed direction. 'When were you and your mates last on exercise?' Mooney looked bewildered. 'Answer the question, man!'

'Last month we was on mock manoeuvres. We didn't make no scarecrow then.'

'When you returned to base how much of your ammo did you hand in?'

Greenish-brown eyes widened in tardy understanding. 'Every bit I signed out, *sir*,' he added as if that made his statement more veritable.

'How about other times when you've been issued with items from the Armoury?'

That really got to Mooney. 'I need to speak to the Platoon Commander.'

'Why?'

'You're charging me with what I haven't done. I know my rights. I'm entitled to have my Platoon Commander here.'

Max leaned back and surveyed him with dislike. There were born soldiers, and mediocre soldiers who nevertheless put all they had into the job. What he had no time for were men who took and gave nothing in return. Uniformed layabouts, in his opinion.

'You want the support of the officer you parodied as a scarecrow and put on a bonfire to burn? As a *joke*.'

Mooney took a deep breath and began a stumbling defence.

'We didn't mean anything by it. Second Lieutenant Freeman came just five weeks ago and he started laying into us like we was useless. Well, we didn't like it. Lieutenant Cummings what was here before never did that. The scarecrow was just our way of making a protest.'

'And "laying into you" is Second Lieutenant Freeman's method of making *his* protest over your lack of effort and dedication, I suspect. He knows *his* rights, one of which is to expect maximum effort from everyone in his platoon.' Max looked down at the open file on the desk. 'On your way out tell Rule he's next.'

'But what about . . . ?'

Max looked back at him with narrowed eyes. 'I see why you're having a rough time of it. You can't even respond to my simple command. In a war situation you'd be a dead loss, with the emphasis on *dead*. Learn to behave like a soldier and you might eventually be of some use to your platoon. *Now, go out there and tell Rule I want him in here next,*' he ordered in tones that brooked no further argument.

The other interviews followed similar lines. There was always someone in every platoon who failed to pull his weight. Freeman was unfortunate enough to have four of them. Max swiftly assessed their lack of culpability regarding the explosion, but he hoped he had frightened them enough to improve their attitude. It was probably a vain hope.

He gave this opinion to the young subaltern, who had managed to retrieve his report along with some self-confidence, but their conversation was cut short by a call on Max's mobile. He left the building to hear what George Maddox had to say.

'We have a result regarding the explosive material, sir. Are you able to come to the Sports Ground?'

'On way,' said Max with enthusiasm. This information would at least break the stalemate they presently had.

When he reached the Sports Ground he walked through to the spot where the bonfire had stood and found a small group studying a collection of tiny fragments spread on a sheet of plastic. Tom was already there in discussion with the experts who had been scouring the area for evidence.

'So, what's the verdict?' he asked, joining them.

'It was an improvised explosive device, sir.'

Max was taken aback. 'So we're looking for someone who's served in Afghanistan and knows a hell of a lot about those things. An explosives expert.'

'Not necessarily,' came the defensive retort from one such expert. 'Anyone can access the Internet and find out how to make a bomb.'

Max gave a grim smile. 'I agree, but we're on a military establishment and the military know a bloody sight more about exploding devices than the Internet.'

FOUR

'No, no and bloody *no*!' raged Captain Knott leaping to his feet and glaring at Max. 'I've known these men for six years, in good times and bad, and not one of them would use his expertise to *kill and maim*. For six months at a time they risk their own lives to save others by *de-activating* explosive devices. That's what they do. *Day after day*. They know there's a chance of being blown to bits, but they're dedicated guys with immense courage.'

His reaction was almost explosive in its heat, but his blue eyes were icy cold. 'I deeply resent your attitude, which springs from ignorance like everyone else who's never in the front line. Do you know how many times my squad has been in Iraq or Afghanistan during the time I've been their commander? Do you?' he repeated aggressively.

'Yes. I checked the records before I came here. With demanding frequency, because what you do is very specialized,' said Max quietly. 'I also know you've lost two men, and three have had limbs blown off.'

'Yes, and young Barry Tyler is still on life-support from our last deployment. Consider *that*, Captain Rydal.'

Max had also learned that Jeremy Knott had been recommended for an award for risking his life to rescue two of his injured men under fire a month before their return to base at the start of October. Ignoring the man's belligerent stance, he sat and took his time in responding to Knott's hostility with some plain speaking of his own.

'We in SIB are often accused of having no understanding of fighting men, because we're simply plods with unpleasant natures. No, we don't normally go into battle shoulder to shoulder with them; our work begins when they crack under the strain and act totally out of character. For instance: He's just back from a war zone where he's been pushed to the limit, seen his mates killed or maimed, and he discovers his wife has been sleeping around, or the bank has foreclosed on their loan and repossessed the classic car he's been lovingly restoring for the past two years. Or he's told his thirteen-year-old daughter is pregnant. Or he learns his son was set upon and kicked half to death by a gang of local yobbos.'

Knott had sobered considerably during this calm speech, and stayed silent while Max continued.

'The man we meet isn't the one you know. He has assaulted, maybe even killed the wife who betrayed him while he was having a tough time. He has run amok in the bank and been arrested for ABH and criminal damage. He has stripped his promiscuous daughter's room of her clothes and prized possessions and burned them in the garden as punishment, or he goes on the rampage in town attacking any group of rowdy youths to avenge what was done to his son.'

Seeing Knott about to speak, Max forestalled him. 'Yes, the majority of soldiers returning from active service who might face such problems cope reasonably well, but every so often one finds he can't cope. That's when *we* meet him.'

'Yes, of course, I appreciate what you're saying, but . . .'

'We had to ask your permission to borrow your men for a search of the stadium because that was an official request to take them away from their normal duty to perform one for us.' Max stood. 'However, when it's a question of interviewing them in connection with an incident which killed a woman and injured a large number of people, our demands override others. I could have called any of your personnel to our headquarters for interrogation. I'm here merely as a courtesy.' Knott just glared as Max handed him a written list. 'Please arrange for these men to report to us before twenty hundred hours. I'll hold you responsible for any who fail to do so.'

Max left Knott's office and walked the long corridor to the front of the building thinking that his smart grey lounge suit might impress the manager of his bank but, when facing an undoubtedly courageous man whose combats were adorned with medal ribbons, his own appearance was hardly impressive. He could not even depart with a semblance of authority. His leather shoes made little sound on the vinyl floor covering, even if he stamped. George Maddox, in impeccable uniform, gun belt and size twelve army boots, could make a meal of a departure.

On reaching his car, Max checked the time. Brenda would be settling Micky in his cot, then tidying the apartment ready for his arrival. Not that it had been a definite arrangement. He had only told her maybe. All the same, he thought he should call her.

'It's Max,' he said when she answered. 'How's the little lad?'

'Good as gold, for once. When I particularly want him to drift into deep sleep he seems to sense it and stays awake.' She gave a soft chuckle. 'Doesn't want to miss anything exciting.'

'Well, that rules out a visit from me. Something's come up which'll keep me fully occupied for the foreseeable future, I'm afraid.'

'Oh.' That one word expressed disappointment. 'Well, duty calls, as Flip used to say when cancelling a date. Not that you . . . I mean, it was just going to be for a coffee in passing,' she added hurriedly. 'You needn't have phoned. As I said, Micky and I are always glad of company. Please don't feel under an obligation to explain when . . .' What was becoming an unwieldy speech tailed off.

'I'll call you once this problem is wound up. Hopefully, not too far ahead.'

Max sat for a few minutes thinking of his last case concerning a fatality. The dead soldier had been married, but he had fathered Micky with the intention of getting a divorce and marrying Brenda, the true love of his life. Max had had to tell her why that would never happen.

A former army nurse, Brenda was a capable woman. Max had admired the way in which she had accepted the destruction of her planned future just days after the birth of their son, and he had offered to help, if he could. He had meant official help from military sources, but she had simply said his company would be very welcome at any time. Flip was the nickname of her lover, and she had talked freely about him on the two occasions when he had been in the area and taken a chance on finding her at home.

Today was different. He had planned to take the day off to

participate in a motorbike scramble – his new enthusiasm. One route back from the club passed near her flat, so he had let her know he might call in. He guessed she had taken *might* for *would.*

Blonde, with violet-blue eyes, Brenda Keane was an attractive woman. No more so than others he had met – Clare Goodey, for example – yet he owned that he enjoyed his time in an apartment which reflected her quiet personality. Somewhat different from the home he had visited earlier in the day. Jean Greene's artistic flamboyance was the reverse of Brenda's classic elegance, despite the presence of a baby.

Micky was just four weeks old. Max had been in many homes where a baby appeared to occupy the entire house. Packets of nappies, tiny clothes, lotions and creams, soft toys or half-eaten rusks littered the rooms, and chairs had to be cleared before attempting to sit in them. Max had only been in Brenda's large lounge, so maybe she bundled all the baby paraphernalia into another room when he visited. Whatever, he nevertheless admired her efforts to live in reasonable order.

That might change as Micky grew, and she returned to nursing. Max knew that must be inevitable, and he wondered how she presently managed to pay the rent on such a comfortable apartment. Philip Keane had still been married when he died, so any savings or funds due from military sources would go to his family. His illegitimate son did not fall into that category. Neither did his lover. So, unless Brenda married again, they would remain just another one parent family – like his own had been. Was that why he was following the unusual practice of keeping in touch with someone who had briefly been a murder suspect?

Once a case ended he and his team had no further contact with the main players, unless normal military routine demanded it. Max shut his eyes to the fact that if his own plans for the future had not been almost as cruelly ended, Brenda Keane and her fatherless son would never have seen him again.

Eighteen hundred. The usual time for a check on the latest evidence obtained during a major case. Most of the team had assembled, some still busy at their computers getting data. Tom had spent most of the afternoon at the Sports Ground with the uniformed boys, two of Jeremy Knott's squad and the Fire Chief, all of them attempting to assess where the explosive device had been situated within the bonfire pile.

They had reached no firm conclusion when Tom left them to return to his office to find which personnel presently on base would have served in Afghanistan at some stage of their careers. He found that Max's frequent comment about a cast of thousands applied in this case.

Leaving his desk, Tom called for attention and began garnering information. Firstly, he asked Connie Bush about the second interview with Corporal Lines, who had been in charge of the fireworks.

'Did you get anything from him now he's over the concern about his wife's injury.'

Connie shook her head. 'He's genuinely upset over what happened, apart from the personal problem. He loves doing the shows, has a deep interest in it. He studies the content of every display he can get to, watches TV showings of those massive ones from all over the world on New Year's Eve, and he has a pile of mags about pyrotechnics.'

'He's not so besotted he forgets how dangerous they can be, is he?'

'He struck me as very responsible. A careful type of man.'

'Mm, not careful enough to check the contents of those boxes from Max-ee-million,' Tom pointed out.

'He freely admitted that he compared the lists on the labels with what he had ordered, but didn't open the boxes to confirm the contents. He told me he'd ordered stuff from Max-ee-million loads of times and they always sent the right things.'

'So who opened the boxes?' asked Piercey. 'It's my bet they didn't check contents with labels, either.'

Heather Johnson frowned as she joined the discussion. 'But the explosive device was in the bonfire, not set off with the fireworks. Why are we so concerned with those boxes?'

'Because we have to consider the possibility of an outside accomplice before we can rule that out,' Tom pointed out. 'I don't believe the Estonian proprietor is implicated. He's just an alien bent on building up a business here. He wouldn't check outgoing boxes. Like Corporal Lines, he'd compare the labels with the order forms and send them on their way. He'd have overseers to ensure the right stuff went to the right place. In view of what we now know about the nature of the explosive component it seems unlikely to have been sent on to the base by a civilian. We have to keep that possibility on file, however.'

He glanced around the grouped men and women. 'Did any of you trace a link between someone involved in last night's display and a local political organisation?'

There was common dissention. 'OK, so have we any info that poses a question mark over someone who was in any way concerned with the two-day preparations for the Guy Fawkes' party?'

Derek Beeny, Piercey's friend and fellow sergeant, said in his usual unexcitable way, 'In the Boss's report of his interview with Corporal Naish, who constructed the bonfire, there's mention of a Rifleman Carter who had to leave because he'd cut his hand on nails left in a plank, and needed to get it stitched. My attempts to track him down proved negative. Captain Boyce told me his platoon is on a cross-country exercise for three days. He tried to contact Lieutenant Fleet – *Meg* Fleet, sir – but the link was ruptured. He said he'd try again and give us their exact location. He hasn't been in touch.'

'Typical!' grunted Tom, with the usual sergeant major's opinion of officers' efficiency. 'I'll call him up and spoil his dinner.'

'I'll do that,' offered Max, who had entered in time to catch Beeny's report.

'One other thing,' said that sergeant. 'I checked with orderlies at the Medical Centre. Carter didn't go there to have his hand seen to.'

'So we need to speak to that bastard asap.' Tom felt the slight frisson that accompanied the prospect of a lead. 'Why did he leave before the event got underway, and where did he go? Good work, Beeny. Get over to your desk and download all you can get about our lad Carter.'

Heather Johnson had obtained details from all the Quartermaster Stores of what they had sent to build the bonfire, and her report was subsequently downbeat.

'What they had listed was innocuous enough, but they all said they weren't responsible for what the lads might have put in the bins en route.' She sighed. 'An easy let-out, but true enough. I've made a list of everyone who filled the bins and drove them to the venue. Connie and I had planned to question them tonight, but the explosives guys are now on schedule. We'll do it in the morning.'

'Fair enough,' judged Tom, glancing at the clock. 'A couple of you had better get over to the NAAFI and collect some sandwiches, sausage rolls and pork pies. We're in for a long night here.' Seeing Piercey and Roy Jakes get eagerly to their feet, he added, 'Nothing that'll stink the place out like the last lot you brought in.'

They left grinning widely. They were soon back with nothing in their hands.

'Trouble brewing, sir,' said Piercey, addressing Tom because Max had gone to his office to telephone Captain Boyce about the whereabouts of Carter.

'What kind of trouble?'

'Big trouble! The Jocks are marching on the NAAFI. They're a tough-looking lot, and they're clearly out for a fight. Better contact George Maddox pronto.'

By morning, the cells at Maddox's RMP Post along with those at 26 Section Headquarters were full. Civilian workers were sweeping up glass and attempting to mend broken tables in the NAAFI, four overnight casualties at the Medical Centre were discharged with instructions to attend for the next three days to have dressings changed, and Major Crawford was having an uneasy meeting with Major Carnegie of the Drumdorran Fusiliers.

The newly arrived contingent of Scottish warriors had expressed their anger over the tragic death of Mrs Eva McTavish, wife of their highly respected Pipe Major, in their traditional manner. The long-term garrison troops had responded in *their* traditional manner, with no holds barred. Battle had commenced and, in the absence of Colonel Trelawney, the Garrison Commander, Miles Crawford had to negotiate a peace before all-out war was declared. Inevitably, Max was summoned to detail what had so far been done to apprehend whoever had caused the appalling outcome of the annual November 5th celebration.

Telling himself, with smug satisfaction, that he had known all along that the arrival of the Scots would mean trouble, Tom drove out to where Rifleman Carter was taking part in an exercise. Two companies of the Royal Cumberland Rifles were polishing their skills in the vast area used by the Army for every aspect of battle technique. On it were mock villages, open plains, areas of undulating ground for tracked vehicles to tackle, high ground and gulleys, and a stretch of the river which ran through that region of Germany.

As he drove, Tom recalled the first case 26 Section had tackled following Max's emergency appointment to replace the officer whose two sons had been killed in a school bus crash in the UK. They had come to this same training area through thick snow to apprehend an officer who had regarded shooting another officer as justified retribution, not murder.

For two years now they had worked well together. Max had flights of fancy – what the team called his wild geese – but Tom had learned not to dismiss them out of hand because once or twice the investigation had been advanced by pursuing them. Tom kept his feet firmly on the ground, so they complemented each other.

It had been a successful pairing, and he did not envy Max trying to satisfy two aggressive majors that SIB was well on the way to arresting someone for Tuesday night's exploding bonfire. Tom smiled as he approached the training area. How satisfying it would be to discover Carter was the perpetrator and return with him.

The interviews with Captain Knott's squad had proved fruitless. Unless one of them was a very accomplished liar, they all had alibis that could be supported by numerous witnesses. So it was even more to be hoped that Carter, who *had* lied, succumbed under questioning and confessed. The case could be wrapped up and Tom could tackle the problem over the coming baby.

The girls had been in bed by the time he had arrived home last night, and Nora had steadfastly watched a late night film until he dozed off on the sofa beside her. When he had roused she was in bed feigning sleep. He had deliberately made an early start to the day, leaving the house during the usual two-way traffic from bedrooms to bathroom, with a double bacon sandwich to eat in a handy lay-by. He would welcome a large coffee before interviewing Carter. He needed it.

Max had disturbed Captain Boyce's dinner with the biting tone of command he could adopt when angry or frustrated, and the man had called back within ten minutes with the requested information. Another no-nonsense call to Lieutenant Meg Fleet arranged for Rifleman Carter to be available for interview at 09:00 today.

Beeny had provided full details of Charles Carter late last night. The only son of six children he had probably joined the Royal Cumberland Rifles to escape the female majority, thought Tom with a modicum of understanding, and on paper appeared to be an eager soldier. Reports from the RCR Depot on his basic training said he was a promising recruit with a good sense of team spirit. An assessment by his Platoon Commander, Meg Fleet, noted that Carter had been steady and controlled under fire during their recent deployment in Afghanistan, but that he had shown signs of boredom since their return two months ago.

Tom thought that was an unusual comment. It did not reflect on his efficiency or his dedication to duty, which were the two phrases mostly used by commanders. Or did it? Was that a woman's way of expressing a sudden change of attitude towards the job? It did, however, tell Tom quite a lot. Carter had been a good soldier in the making until six months in a war zone had ended. It was a fairly common situation, particularly with young, unattached men. The stress, the danger, the extreme demands, the *excitement* of warfare made normal non-active routine seem flat and . . . yes, *boring*. Tom reversed his opinion of Meg Fleet. Maybe she had it right.

Bored young soldiers tended to get up to mischief. They did things to liven up the sudden predictability of their lives. Like planting an explosive device in a bonfire then making sure they were nowhere around when it went off? Oh yes, Carter could very well be responsible for that.

Gaining admittance to the enclosed military area, Tom then had to drive a kilometre to reach the whitewashed building from which all training exercises were controlled, and park beside a group of Land Rovers and heavy trucks. The flat ground stretching out towards a rise topped by trees was empty of movement and looked bleak on this day of low cloud and biting wind. The Cumberland Rifles must be operating in the far reaches today.

Inside the Operations Command Post a few men and women were gathered around a vast table on which was spread a mock-up of a desert village complete with market stalls, shops and community buildings; the objective of this particular day's operation. Around the walls were screens depicting the reality of what was being shown in miniature on the table. Messages were being passed back and forth; the uninitiated could well believe it was real warfare.

As Tom hesitated, to watch with interest, he was approached by a man he knew. Captain Ben Steele had put himself in danger last year by 'doing a Miss Marple' as Tom had put it. He had also been vaguely involved in SIB's last case, but not by attempting to solve it. He had learned his lesson.

As they shook hands with some warmth, Ben said, 'Nasty business. Is it true the woman has died from her injuries?'

Tom nodded. 'Which puts the case one notch higher. Were you there on Tuesday evening? It was pretty grim.'

'No, but I saw the outcome of a suicide bomb a couple of months ago, over there. Much worse, and we don't want anything like that starting up on the base.' He led the way to a side room containing a desk and several chairs, where it was possible to make hot drinks. 'Coffee?' At Tom's nod he spooned grains into two large mugs, saying, 'Have you managed to assess what caused the bonfire to explode so violently?'

'Yes. It's worrying and adds urgency to our investigation.'

Ben's dark eyes questioned that comment. 'Not a lark gone wrong?'

'That's what we have to discover. So far it points to something more serious.'

Handing Tom the mug of much-needed coffee, Ben said, 'Carter's in my company, so I'll be very concerned if he was in any way involved. And surprised. He's not a beer and bovver squaddie. His platoon commander admits he's been unsettled for the past few weeks and she faced him with his lack of concentration, but he offered no defence. Corporal Landis also tackled him. Carter apologized, but has continued to show little interest in the job. I had a quick word with him last night after Max contacted us. Carter denies any connection with what happened, but you obviously have some info which makes it necessary for you to question him.'

Glad of the coffee and a couple of chocolate digestives, Tom asked how Carter had behaved in Afghanistan. 'You said he became unsettled a few weeks ago. PTSD would you say? Was he caught up in a particularly violent action? Did he witness the outcome of that suicide bomb and react badly?'

Ben leaned back thoughtfully in his chair. 'I only observe him professionally, of course. So does Lieutenant Fleet. We both see a solid, unflappable guy who works well with the rest of the platoon, even under pressure. Post Traumatic Stress Disorder is far too serious a condition to account for the change in Carter. I've seen the victims of what used to be known as Shell Shock. Our man seems simply to have lost interest in soldiering.'

Putting his empty mug on the desk, Tom said, 'Lieutenant Fleet's assessment is that Carter is bored.'

'Ah, that's nearer the mark,' agreed Ben. 'And I can't think boredom would drive a man to do something as dramatic as the incident you're investigating, to relieve it.' He got to his feet. 'Carter's waiting in the equipment room. I'll send him along to you.' He paused in the doorway. 'I'd be glad of some kind of report on your findings before you leave. Hopefully, without Carter in handcuffs.'

The man who entered a few minutes later was sturdily built, with bright red hair and a face covered in freckles. Tom told him to sit on the other side of the desk facing him. 'We're interviewing everyone who was concerned with the Guy Fawkes celebration. In the course of our enquiries we have learned that you left the Sports Ground before the bonfire was fully constructed because you had gashed a hand on nails left in a plank and needed to have it stitched. Is that correct?'

'Yes, sir.'

'Were the nails rusty?'

Carter look wary. 'Rusty, sir?'

'So that you'd also need antibiotics to prevent poison in the open wound.'

'Oh. Yes, well that stuff we were given had been lying around in the stores for months. We even had to ditch some of it.'

'Who dealt with your injury, Carter?'

'One of the orderlies, sir.'

'Which one?'

'Don't know his name,' he replied glibly.

'None of the orderlies know yours, either,' Tom told him. 'In fact, they deny treating anyone with a gashed hand or of giving out antibiotics until the casualties came in late in the evening. How do you explain that?'

Carter's tawny eyes rolled from side to side as he worked out a response, but all he came up with was, 'They must've forgotten.'

'You're still saying you went to the Medical Centre on Tuesday afternoon and received emergency treatment?'

'It was bleeding really bad.'

Having looked at Carter's hands as he entered and seen no sign of heavy dressings or plasters and, aware that the man had kept them under the desk during the questioning, Tom said, 'Why didn't Lieutenant Fleet sign you off this exercise? You can't responsibly handle a rifle with a badly damaged hand.'

'It's a lot better. Almost healed.'

'Overnight?' As Carter stared miserably at Tom, he added, 'You claim to have had stitches in a bad injury on Tuesday afternoon, but by six the following morning it had healed enough to enable you to come with your platoon to participate in a mock battle. That *is* what you're saying, isn't it?'

'It had almost healed,' he mumbled again.

'Did you volunteer to help construct the bonfire, or were you detailed to do it?'

Taken by surprise by this change of direction, Carter said swiftly, 'No way was I going to volunteer, and Corporal Landis knew why.'

'Yet he detailed you for the job.'

As if aware that he had said too much, Carter gave no response.

'Why were you so set against volunteering? Most of your mates would have seen it as a good skive from normal duties.'

'I'm not like them.'

'You take your duties seriously?'

'Yes, sir.'

'Show me your injured hand,' Tom demanded. Then more sharply, 'Show me your hand, Carter.'

It was held up with the palm facing away from Tom. Then, when he could stand the long, cold stare and unnerving silence no longer, Carter set his hand palm upward on the desk. On the fleshy area at the base of the thumb was a narrow plaster of the kind used to cover a minor scratch or small blemish. Tom maintained his silence and continued to gaze right into the eyes of the other man until Carter was forced to speak.

'I couldn't stop it bleeding,' he insisted. 'Handling all that guff that'd been stacked in a filthy yard for yonks, Corp Naish said I could've got poison in my bloodstream. Said it was too risky to carry on.'

'He actually said that to you?'

'Yes, sir.'

'The staff at the Medical Centre deny seeing you for treatment.'

'All those people with burns, they forgot who came earlier.'

Tom leaned back and took his time before saying, 'If you return to base with me now, you'll be able to show me the person who put that very small strip of plaster on your hand, will you?'

Carter gazed miserably at the hand still lying on the desk, and kept silent. At that moment, Tom's mobile rang. A swift glance at the screen told him Derek Beeny had significant information, so he got to his feet and moved out to the corridor.

'This had better be worth interrupting my interview,' he told his sergeant.

'It's very relevant, sir.'

'Go on.'

'Your Red Alert was put into operation on Tuesday at twenty-one hundred. From then on everyone passing through the main gate was thoroughly vetted. Private C Carter is recorded as *entering* the base at twenty-two thirty. The guard does happen to have seen him drive *out* some time around sixteen thirty, which means he was well clear of the base when the bonfire was ignited.'

'Good work! He can't talk himself out of *that*.'

Returning to the room, Tom sat for a full minute silently studying the young soldier. Carter grew visibly more and more anxious, until Tom confronted him with this new evidence.

'Where did you go on Tuesday afternoon when the guard at the main gate checked you out?'

'He's lying,' countered Carter swiftly. 'There's no check going out.'

'He says he saw you.'

'Couldn't have. He was inside the booth looking . . .' Carter's defence tailed off as he realized his mistake.

'There's documentary evidence of your return after twenty-two thirty when a Red Alert was in force, so where were you prior to that?'

Tom recognized Carter's silence as a battle between telling the truth or fabricating a story which could be easily disproved by SIB. He waited without prompting him. Eventually, a hesitant, embarrassed explanation was put forward. The first sentences heralded a familiar tale.

'I met a German girl at a disco. She's not one of those tarts who go there every night to pick up a soldier and help him spend his money. She's a really nice girl. Classy. We hit it off right away, sir. I mean, it's serious.'

Tom said nothing, letting him tell the whole story uninterrupted. Carter's tanned cheeks darkened slightly as he confessed they had not yet slept together.

'She took me to meet her family and we got on very well, except her father's a bit protective. They all speak good English. She's a really nice girl. Classy,' he repeated emphatically. Then he studied his hands and fidgeted until he realized he had to continue.

'Tuesday was her birthday. Eighteenth. Her people had laid on a party. Not a rave-up; a family do with aunts and uncles. Corporal Landis knew I wanted to go, but he added my name to the bonfire detail. I put up an objection, so he said I hadn't been pulling my weight since we got back from the Stahn, and it was time I did.'

All Tom said then was, 'And?'

'Well, I cut my hand on some nails. It did bleed a lot at first and Tommo Jenks said it should be stitched. Corporal Naish was busy with some guys who'd brought a straw scarecrow, but he said I should go along to the Medical Centre.'

'And did you?'

Carter shook his head. 'I went back to my billet, held my hand under the tap for a bit and slapped on a plaster.'

'So you lied to me just now?'

'The bonfire was almost finished, and everyone was knocking off early because of the fireworks and that.'

'So?'

'So I went to Greta's party.'

'We'll need corroboration of that.'

'Why?' he cried in mild panic. 'What happened that night has nothing to do with her family.'

'We need proof of your whereabouts when that explosion took place. The girl's full name and address,' invited Tom firmly.

Carter was deeply upset. 'Her father's not too happy about me going on active service; says Greta will be left abandoned and unhappy if I get killed. He wants me to leave the Army.' He studied his hands again. 'I don't know what to do about that yet.' He glanced up earnestly. 'Greta and me want to . . . well, we want to get married soon as possible, but if I leave the Army what else can I do? The RCR is all I know. It's all I've ever wanted to do . . . but her father . . .'

Deciding that this mixed-up young squaddie was not the person who had sabotaged the bonfire, Tom was about to tell the lad to talk things over with Ben Steele when he had cause to reverse his thinking.

'Greta will confirm I was with her that evening,' Carter said urgently, 'but can you talk to her at work? If SIB turns up on her father's doorstep asking about me that'll be the end of it.'

'So where does she work?' asked Tom.

'Max-ee-million, where we got the fireworks.'

FIVE

Max went to the meeting with the Officer Commanding the Drumdorrans prepared to face a proud, unyielding man. He had compiled a carefully worded account of the efforts being made to trace whoever had been responsible for the death of Eva McTavish.

However, Major Dougal Carnegie was a battle-hardened soldier with a great deal of common sense, who handled the discussion with more understanding than did Miles Crawford. Max tried to make allowances for the DGC's tetchiness, but he knew the man was difficult to deal with even when not stressed over his son's injuries. Against Carnegie's professional approach, Max found Crawford's attitude highly irritating, if not verging on the disparaging – to the Scot as well as to himself.

Seated in Carnegie's office they eventually broached the subject of the brawl in the NAAFI.

'Very regrettable that my men should have begun their deployment here with a violent expression of their anger over the loss to one of our most respected musicians. Hector McTavish's knowledge of Scottish airs is second to none. It's always he who pipes in the haggis, leads brides and grooms from the kirk and plays the lament at the graveside.'

With a frown, Carnegie continued. 'That's no excuse for what occurred last night, of course, and I shall be addressing the battalion at sixteen hundred to express my displeasure. I promise you there will be a marked improvement in relations with the resident units from then on.' He turned his attention to Max. 'It'll make my task easier if the ugly business you're investigating is swiftly cleared up, allowing tempers to cool on both sides.'

He raised a hand in a silencing gesture, although Max did not believe he had expected a response to that. 'I appreciate the difficulty of the task facing you, believe me.' He turned back to Crawford. 'I also appreciate that concern for your son, and the absence of Colonel Trelawney at this difficult time, makes life burdensome for you, but it would be helpful if you could tell all regimental commanders on this base to read the riot act to their personnel, too. It's been an unfortunate start and we must all make every effort to nip aggression in the bud, don't you agree?'

Receiving a vague nod from Crawford, he continued with his next point. 'The funeral of Mrs McTavish will, of course, be a traditional Scottish service. To this end I've asked our regimental chaplain to officiate and Angus Salmond will play the lament. Assuming the body will be released either today or tomorrow, we've provisionally arranged for the interment to take place on Saturday.'

He then stood, signifying the end of the meeting. 'Thank you, gentlemen. I think we're all of the same opinion that, after an unfortunate start, we can work alongside each other amicably if the willingness is there.'

Once in the car park, Miles Crawford turned on Max. 'Willingness has nothing to do with it. They're looking for blood, and until you pull out all the stops to get who was responsible for my boy's injuries and that woman's death, those tartan bastards will be on the rampage at every opportunity.' He slid behind the wheel of his car. 'Sort it, and bloody fast!'

Max stood watching the car disappear around the corner by the Garrison Church wishing Colonel Trelawney was in command right now. He would handle the present problems with far more tact and finesse, which would have ensured Major Carnegie had not acted as if he and not Crawford, was the Deputy Garrison Commander. All the same, Max had warmed to the Scot's assured manner and professionalism and, unlike Crawford, he did believe willingness could go a long way towards stabilizing the aggressive situation. Staging the funeral without delay was probably wise.

He got in his own car and sat for a while staring into space. Resolving the case would also go far towards calming tempers, but he could not work miracles and there really was a cast of thousands to pick from. The only hint of a lead so far was

Rifleman Carter, who had gone to have his hand stitched but never turned up at the Medical Centre. Tom had pounced on that with enthusiasm as if it were a major breakthrough, but Max guessed it was nothing but a red herring. Experience, and his well-known sixth sense, told him there was something more devious than a soldier telling lies about a cut hand behind the disaster of the exploding bonfire.

He had cause to rethink when Tom rang his mobile to report on the interview with Carter, ending with the information that he was en route to see Greta Gans.

'I contacted Krenkel. He's sending two of his guys to Max-ee-million and I've called up Heather to meet us all there. It's a real link. She's an overseer at the factory. Checks the contents of boxes before they're sent out. Perfect opportunity to slip something extra in one, mark the label so that Carter would identify it and liberate the stuff when no one's looking.'

'Mmm, sounds reasonable . . . but what's Carter's motive?'

Max could picture Tom's expression as he said with slight irritation, 'We'll find out when we have enough evidence to pull him in for a recorded interview. I've left him with his platoon until I check out Fräulein Gans.'

'Good luck with that, but if she's involved it'll be taken out of our hands by Krenkel.'

'Yes, well . . . How did your meeting go?'

'Like a lead balloon, although Carnegie's a reasonable man. Once the GC's back everything will run much more smoothly. Call in if you find anything significant.'

Max disconnected and was about to drive off when the mobile rang again. Thinking Tom had recalled something he should have mentioned, Max was surprised to hear Clare's voice.

'Where are you, Max?' When he told her, she added, 'Something of interest to you. Call in.'

That was Clare, he reflected. Brief and to the point. Glancing at the clock he saw it was nearing lunchtime. If she was free, he would suggest they repaired to the Mess for a light meal. That idea was dashed when he saw the number of people waiting. Burns and cuts suffered on Tuesday night had to be treated, and dressings changed. The four orderlies were dealing with that while a couple of pregnant women, and three soldiers with black eyes and bandaged heads sat waiting to see a doctor. From the way two soldiers sat as far as possible from the single one suggested that last night's aggression had not yet eased.

The door normally bearing David Culdrow's name now had an insert announcing that Major D MacPherson was occupying that consulting room. The door then opened and a woman with a boy whose leg was in plaster came out, followed by a man who remained in the doorway surveying the waiting patients. His attention was caught by the tall, dark-haired man in a smart grey suit, who looked too fit and healthy to be there.

'Are ye by any chance Captain Rydal?' he asked in an assured and very easy-on-the-ear brogue.

Max decided there and then that a majority of female patients would switch allegiance from Clare to this imposing Scot, whose physique made even a man as well built as himself seem puny by comparison. Max walked to him, offering his hand.

'Come you inside for a wee moment,' MacPherson invited. 'We'll no keep you long.' After closing the door behind them, he added, 'Clare told me she'd asked you to come in in passing. I'll tell her you're here.'

While he tapped, then opened the door connecting the two consulting rooms, Max wondered if he was about to participate in another discussion on last night's set-to in the NAAFI. From a medical angle, this time. Why else would this handsome giant with curling dark red hair be muscling in on Clare's request for a word with him?

MacPherson appeared to have made David Culdrow's domain his own within twenty-four hours. Max reflected that David might have problems wresting it back when he had fully recovered from the mumps. Being a civilian doctor would weigh against him, apart from the question of what this Scot would do if he returned. No, Max had a strong feeling MacPherson was here to stay for as long as his countrymen remained on the base.

When Clare came through she was holding several sheets

of paper, which she waved at Max and said in a totally professional manner, 'Medical assessment and death certificate for Eva McTavish which arrived this morning from the hospital. I thought you should know right away that the injury she suffered on Tuesday evening was not the cause of her death. It was serious, but in their opinion she would have recovered from it and lived a normal life.'

Max frowned. 'Corporal Stubble reported back from the hospital that same night that she had been put on the critical list. When we were informed that death had occurred during the early hours, we naturally assumed that she'd died of her injuries.'

Clare shook her head. 'When she was admitted, along with the Crawford boy, all their attention was concentrated on the chest wound. The more serious problem only became apparent shortly afterwards, when her failing responses caused them to grow suspicious. There was nothing they could do at that late stage.

'I know you're regarding her death as involuntary manslaughter, but it wasn't.' After a swift exchange of glances with MacPherson, she continued. 'Prior to attending the Guy Fawkes celebration Eva McTavish had swallowed enough diazepam washed down with vodka to kill herself!'

Tom arrived outside Max-ee-million to find Heather and two local policemen already inside the office talking to a tubby Estonian. From the speed of their intercourse, Tom guessed the man's German was better than his English. Heather was fairly fluent in the language of their host country because she had attended the advanced German course last year. Never hesitant when interviewing, she was making SIB interest very marked. Although most of the *Polizei* personnel seemed to be either bi- or tri-lingual, Tom let Heather continue to liaise in German, most of which he understood. According to Carter, his girlfriend was able to converse in English, so he would take over when she was summoned.

With a great deal of expressive waving of hands, the Estonian disappeared in to the workshop area to fetch Greta Gans, and then Tom discovered that the two fresh-faced policemen spoke reasonable English. One remained in conversation with Heather while the other subjected Tom to intense scrutiny with cool blue eyes.

'We have no trouble here. This is well known for the *Feuerwerk*. For the New Year party and the summer concert, all are using Max-ee-million. You have evidence for this girl's guilty?'

Having no intention of being 'interrogated' by this man who had left the cradle around ten years after him, Tom replied in officialese.

'We have reason to believe Frâulein Gans could be implicated in a case of involuntary manslaughter by abusing the trust of her employer, and using the privilege of her senior position to aid and abet the possible perpetrator of this serious crime.'

Clearly baffled by Tom's deliberate attempt to deflate him, the youthful German nodded, muttered, 'Ah, *so*,' before showing great interest in whatever his companion was saying to Heather which was making her eyes sparkle. Tom would also have liked to know, and to remind her that she was not here on a blind date.

When Greta Gans arrived with her boss, Tom saw at once why Carter was so taken with her. And why the girl's father would be so protective. Even with wide, scared eyes, and wearing an ill-fitting dark blue overall, she radiated a discreet sexuality any healthy man would respond to. Yet Tom saw Carter's point that she was in a class above the girls who haunted the discos in town preying on British soldiers who flashed their money around.

The two Germans explained why they were there, and looked set to conduct the entire interview until Tom intervened, speaking in English.

'Miss Gans, I understand that you are friendly with Rifleman Charles Carter, who is stationed at the military base. Is that correct?'

Looking even more scared and worried, she just nodded.

'He told me that you were thinking of getting married.'

Again she nodded.

'So you think highly of him, do you?'

Seeing her puzzled look, Heather asked gently in German if she loved Charles Carter. Greta replied in a flood of words of which Tom understood enough to confirm what Carter had said of her father's condition that he should leave the Army.

Using a well-known tactic Tom changed direction with the questioning, and reverted to English. 'You work here as an overseer. Can you tell me what that entails?'

Encouraged by Heather's smile, she finally spoke to Tom. 'It is that I see the order that has been made, and I look at what is to be sending to this persons.'

Tom nodded. 'You check the contents of boxes being dispatched?'

'Yes,' she half-whispered, still frightened by the presence of two uniformed *Polizei*. More scared of them than of an Englishman in a dark suit and a young woman in a feminine version of the same, who looked nowhere near as threatening.

'So did you check the boxes being sent to the army base last week?'

Greta nodded.

'The fireworks were for a display on Tuesday evening – your birthday.'

Another nod.

'Was there a party?'

'Yes.'

'Tell me about it.'

The girl glanced at Heather seemingly at a loss.

'Was the party at your family home, or at a hotel?' she prompted. 'Who came to wish you a happy birthday?'

Speaking to Heather, Greta finally relaxed a little. 'Mutti has made all very special. It is for *Familie*. All have come with *Geschenken*. Presents, you know. I am very happy.'

Heather continued while she had Greta's attention. 'How about your boyfriend? Was he invited?'

More nods. 'But Charlie is to work. He is angry about this . . . this *Korp*, who is making him stay when he ask that he come to this important party.'

'His work as a soldier is more important,' put in Tom firmly.

She turned to him. 'No, it is this *Feuerwerk*, that is all. That is why he is angry to do such things when he has told why he wish to leave. He say this Korp is meaning to punish him for no reason.'

'So he was very angry?' asked Tom, pursuing the point. At her familiar nod, he went further. 'So angry that he asked you to put something extra in one of the boxes of fireworks that he could use to punish the Corp instead?'

Greta looked totally uncomprehending, so Heather asked quietly, 'Did you add something to one of the boxes that wasn't written on the label – something Charlie could use to show his anger over not being allowed to come to your party?'

'But he *did* come,' the girl said, still unsure of what was being implied. 'His hand it was hurt, so this Korp has say all is right for him to leave.'

By this time Tom knew this particular train had hit the buffers, but he pitched one more question. 'Miss Gans, has Rifleman Carter ever asked you to give him something from this factory without anyone knowing you had taken it?'

Fear returned. 'You say me I have taken money? I *steal*?'

'No, Greta,' soothed Heather. 'We just wish to know if Charlie has ever asked for fireworks for himself to use. Something in addition to what was in the boxes.'

She shook her head vigorously, turning to her boss with a flood of explanatory German. The *Polizei* men now intervened, the more arrogant one saying, 'All is now clear. Fräulein Gans is not the villain. You have mistaken.'

Turning to the Estonian, he spoke rapidly in German and indicated that Greta should return to work. The girl, however, grabbed Heather's hand.

'Tell me that Charlie is not hurt. That Korp is not to punish him because I have say wrong today.'

'Charlie will be fine,' Heather assured her with a smile. 'Call him this evening on his mobile and he'll tell you all is well.'

Back on the pavement, Heather became engrossed in conversation with the young German who appeared to be flirting with her, which left Tom to give the parting shot by advising his partner to investigate the factory before many days passed.

'If that girl is an example of their overseers, I imagine things could be smuggled out with ease – and they have the ingredients to produce items vastly more explosive than *Feuerwerks*, chum. Can't be too careful these days.'

Walking to his car with a depressing conviction that he had been aping Max in chasing a wild goose, Tom saw Heather exchanging cards with the young policeman who, as far as he saw it, had contributed nothing to the investigation apart from a cheeky smile and a body as virile as his own had been at that age.

Driving back to the base Tom mentally struck Carter's name from the list of suspects. What list? he asked himself sourly. They were landed with one hell of a job. He had never worked on a case with so many victims. Just one death, but enough injuries to make it imperative to find the perpetrator swiftly. To add to the urgency, there were ravening Scots at the door, snapping at their heels.

Nearing his house he was momentarily tempted to call in for a snack lunch, but he abandoned the idea after recalling the outcome of calling in yesterday. One problem at a time. He would cheer himself up with a good hot lunch in the Sergeants' Mess.

George Maddox looked harassed, as well he might with complaints against him and his staff piling up over the exploding bonfire, to say nothing of the fight in the NAAFI the following night. Max appreciated the man's workload, but he had as much and of a more serious nature on his own hands.

The senior sergeant got to his feet and left his desk where the computer screen showed a column of close-listed data. 'Morning, sir. Anything interesting?'

'That's debatable. Captain Goodey's just had the hospital report which puts a bloody different slant on the entire case. Eva McTavish died as the result of swallowing a mixture of diazepam and vodka.'

George's eyebrows rose. 'Suicide?'

'Or murder. Whichever, it means I have two cases on the go now. The report states that she would have recovered from the chest wound.' Max gave a sour smile. 'The Jocks'll have to keep their heads down now, and you'll have to set patrols outside their quarters for a few nights. Sure to be a return match.' He waved a hand at the inner door. 'Do you still have the woman's stuff collected from the Greenes' house?'

George reached out to take a key from a board on the wall. 'He's been informed that we have it, but there's been no request for access from him. It's possibly because the Drumdorrans are still allocating quarters, and because McTavish was virtually living at the hospital I guess he wasn't regarded as a priority.' He led the way to the secure area where lost property, vital evidence in ongoing cases, and the effects of the dead were kept. 'The daughter of a close friend took a load of happy pills. Doctors fought for hours to save her, and they did. Problem is, she's so brain damaged she needs twenty-four-hour care. Geoff and Eunice have virtually given up *their* lives to look after her. Makes no sense to me.'

How many times had Max wondered about his own future if Susan had survived the car crash as a semi-zombie? He pushed the thought away and concentrated on real problems.

'I'm hoping to find a suicide note,' he said as the other man unlocked the metal door allowing entry to the chilly, stone-floored store. 'An envelope gathered up by whoever collected the stuff, unaware of its importance because we then believed Eva had died from the chest wound. A suicide note would clarify the situation.'

Walking to the far end of the racks, George indicated two suitcases, a zipped holdall and a sensible black handbag. 'Babs Turvey did the necessary. She's out on patrol right now, but you'll catch her at fourteen hundred if you need to question her.' Preparing to leave Max to it, he asked with a frown, 'You're not seriously considering murder, are you?'

'No, not yet, but the lack of any indication that the woman meant to kill herself will force me to. Face the facts, George. The Drumdorrans marched in that very morning, yet neither Eva nor her man made an effort to meet. Perhaps understandable during that afternoon when the men were settling in, but why did Eva stay another night with Jean – or, at least, plan to? She hadn't seen Hector for three months because he'd been with the band touring the US, yet she was apparently in no hurry to meet him. It's not difficult to guess there were outstanding issues between them, is it?'

'Which could only be settled with Eva's death?'

'That seems to be a possible case, until we delve deeper into their lives and discover an alternative scenario. A suicide note would clarify the situation and maybe tell us why she felt she had no reason to live.'

George hesitated in the doorway. 'Funny way to commit suicide, watching a firework display. Most pill swallowers do it at home; in bed, in the bath, on the fireside rug – even sitting in the car in the garage, the point being that they can be sure of not being found before life's extinct. Doing it in a public arena would surely result in help being summoned too soon.'

'Exactly why I have to keep an open mind. As you say, it's a curious venue to choose. We may find it was just a cry for help on her part. Being injured scuppered her plan to collapse amid a helpful crowd, and that very injury delayed recognition of the fatal symptoms in the one place where resuscitation would have been swift. Sod's Law, George.'

Max first opened the no-nonsense handbag. It contained all the essentials, but none of the clutter many women carry around. The leather purse held fifty euros, a credit card, half a dozen postage stamps and a slip of paper on which was written Jean Greene's address. A pair of spectacles were in a black leather case. There was also an old-fashioned gilt powder compact, a pale pink lipstick, a handkerchief with an embroidered thistle in one corner, and a plastic folder containing a faded photograph of a very young man in the dress uniform of the Drumdorran Fusiliers. Written in red ink on the back was the name Tammy. A nickname? Never having met Hector, Max was unable to tell if this was an image of him on joining the regiment. He could be a brother or a cousin. Or lover.

Max soon dismissed the idea of a lover. This handbag

had clearly been owned by a very unadventurous woman. A doormat, according to Jean Greene. What he found in the suitcases bore out that description. The skirts, jumpers, trousers and blouses were more suited to a sixty-year-old than to a woman in her late thirties. A swift glance at the underwear explained why Hector McTavish had his mind more on music when they went to bed than on exciting his wife.

The first things Max saw on unzipping the holdall were two brown bottles crammed with pills. They told him nothing. The labels had been mutilated. Someone had tried to soak them off, then scratched at them with a sharp point so even the name of the dispensing pharmacy was effectively removed. An analysis of the contents would soon identify the medication. Two full bottles? Had Eva been a recreational pill-popper, or had she suffered from a condition that had to be controlled daily? Clare had made no mention of it on the hospital report, and she surely would have done.

Apart from a polished box which held Eva's passport, birth and marriage certificates, a folder stuffed with bills, invoices and bank statements, and two bunches of keys, all the bag contained was a thick plastic sleeve protecting a cream brocade dress, matching shoes and a folded plaid on which was pinned a Celtic brooch. Eva's Burns' Night finery. All-in-all two things were surely missing. A mobile phone. And a suicide note.

As he placed everything back on the shelf Max wondered how best to progress this unwelcome complication. McTavish would have been told of the true cause of his wife's death by the hospital doctors. Had the news come as a further blow, or had it been no surprise? Was it possible that Eva had met him that evening, and had he made her ingest the fatal mixture? Easy enough to overpower a woman, tie her down, then cram pills in her mouth and force her to swallow them with large quantities of vodka. Messy though. And where would McTavish have done the deed?

There was a small copse with picnic tables and stone barbecues used by families during the summer, and all year round for dog walking. That would be ideal. The only snag with that was that McTavish had not been on base long enough to know of it.

Brushing that aside, Max continued to pursue the theory by imagining McTavish then bundling his semi-comatose wife into his car, driving the short distance to the Sports Ground where he deposited her on a seat in the stand, before hot-footing it to join colleagues who would doubtless swear he had been with them the entire evening during the settling-in activity. He nodded thoughtfully. It *was* possible. The priority must be to search for a suicide note.

Returning to his car, Max headed for the married sergeants' quarters. Jean Greene was fairly certain to be at home giving her dolly-like daughter her lunch. She was, and greeted him like an old friend.

'Max! I didn't expect to see you again,' she said with the attractive smile he remembered from yesterday. 'You've come at the right time to have a sandwich and a glass of wine with me. Come you in. Come you in,' she repeated warmly, leading the way to the room brightened by her colourful throws.

For a woman who had seen Billy Greene and known at once that he was the one, Jean was very welcoming to little-known male visitors in his absence, Max reflected as he followed her to where Jenny was sitting in a child's chair before the coffee table to tackle a meal of fish fingers and mashed potatoes. Also there was a plate of sandwiches and a large glass half-filled with Chardonnay from the bottle beside it.

Waving a negative as Jean raised the bottle invitingly, Max said, 'This isn't a social call. I need to talk to you about Eva.'

'Surely we can do that in a civilized fashion over a glass of wine,' she coaxed, still smiling. 'And a small ham sandwich. Even policemen have to eat.'

Irritated by this woman's extraneous bonhomie, he repeated that it was not a social occasion. 'The situation has become more complicated and there's a need for further details of Mrs McTavish's time with you. Perhaps we could talk in another room while Jenny eats her lunch.'

'I don't want it,' Jenny said immediately, making signs of leaving her chair. 'I want to go with Max.'

'No, darling, we're staying here,' Jean hastened to tell her. 'You must eat it before it grows cold. You can watch Paddington Bear while I talk to Max over here. The *new* Paddington Daddy left for you when he went away,' she added persuasively, going to the TV and taking up a DVD to insert in the player.

Watching this activity, and Jenny's complete change of focus, Max realized just how much a child can monopolize parents' lives. Would he ever experience that first hand? The TV screen came alive with images of a teddy bear wearing a mackintosh and wellington boots, which took all Jenny's attention. Jean then crossed to the far corner where Max had taken up position beside the door leading to the hallway, a direct sign that a cosy chat over wine and sandwiches was not on the cards. The lack of a smile suggested Jean had got the message.

'I told you all I know about Eva yesterday. If it's about the funeral on Saturday you're out of luck. The Drumdorrans will take that on. Because she's just a wife it'll no be a regimental ceremony, thank God. I'll attend the service but have no desire to participate in the rigmarole afterwards.' She rolled her eyes. 'I'm a Scottish lass, but I have no time for Celtic grieving. I live in the twenty-first century, not in some legendary mists of time.'

'The funeral is likely to be postponed,' he said quietly.

'Why?' Then, as if recollecting his earlier words, she asked, 'How has the situation become more complicated?'

Max avoided that for the moment. 'Do you know if Eva needed medication for an ongoing condition, or for a short term infection? Were you aware of her taking pills during the week that she was with you?'

'Och, she was forever swallowing this and that. For her nerves, she said, but she spent too much time fancying that she had everything under the sun. A sneeze, and she had the flu. A crick in the neck, and she had dislocated her spine. A tiny blemish, and she had terminal skin cancer. Over the years, of course,' Jean inserted with a faint grin. 'Not just during last week. She's been like it from way, way back. She had a miscarriage six months after they wed, and reckoned the gynaecologist told her another pregnancy would kill her. It continued from then, I guess. She felt she was doomed to die.'

'Did her husband bear that statement out?'

She tutted. 'That's no something he'd discuss with any *woman*! Hector's as full of pride as any Drumdorran.'

'So Eva was prone to take some kind of medication fairly often?' At Jean's nod, Max then asked, 'How about alcohol? Was she fond of a glass or two?'

She stared at him. 'What's this all about? Eva was killed by something piercing her chest, wasn't she? Are you suggesting it was because she was an alcoholic?'

'She set out for the Sports Ground from this house, didn't she?' he riposted. 'Did she seem perfectly sober to you?'

'Yes, of course,' she said indignantly. 'A glass of wine taken at lunchtime doesn't mean it flows freely all day in this house.'

'I'm not suggesting it does. You misread my question.'

Jean continued to glare at him while jolly music emanated from the TV where Paddington was walking jauntily along a country lane. Max waited until Jean had calmed down; waited until she gave a response to his question. She then confessed that she had not actually seen Eva leave.

'The truth is we'd had a spat in the morning when she said she'd have to stay with me for a few more days, until Hector had sorted their accommodation. She didn't ask if she could, just told me very firmly that that was how it would have to be. I was highly annoyed. I had expected to be rid of her that day. We had words but, apart from pushing her out the door with her baggage, I had to accept it. I did try to contact Hector, but you know how it is when a regiment is settling in a new base. Total organized chaos.'

'She actually mentioned staying here for *a few more days?*' Max asked, reading significance in such a statement from a woman who might have been planning to commit suicide within the next few hours.

'Her exact words were "a wee while longer", which certainly indicated to me not the next day or the one after that. I suspected she was in no hurry to leave. This was a safe haven, wasn't it?'

'Safe from her husband?'

She waved her hands expressively. 'Och, I don't know. Hector had no reason to hurt her; she did everything he wanted without argument. Safe from acting the doormat, mebbe.'

Over Jean's shoulder Max's attention was half taken by flickering colours on the TV screen as Paddington appeared to be choosing a tablecloth at a village stall, and a narrator spoke above another jolly tune. Only then did he grow aware that Jenny was no longer watching. In fact, she was lying face down across the coffee table.

Max moved forward, saying urgently, '*Jenny*!'

Jean actually chuckled as she crossed the room beside him. 'She's just fallen asleep. It's the TV. It somehow mesmerizes her.'

'But her face is in the food,' he protested. 'She can't breathe.'

Raising the little girl, Jean began wiping mashed potato from her nose and chin. Down her left cheek was a streak of red, but it was only ketchup, Max realized, as Paddington expressed his delight with his new tablecloth and the titles came up on the screen. At that point, Jenny woke up and began to cry, holding up her arms to Max for a comforting cuddle.

'No, no, darling, Max is just leaving,' said Jean, picking her up. 'We'll sit together and eat some sandwiches while we watch Paddington again.' She cast a glance at Max. 'I told you she does this, which is why we couldn't go elsewhere to talk.' She nodded towards the hall door. 'Please let yourself out.'

Strangely shaken by the sight of the child comatose over the table, Max voiced his thanks and headed to the front door. Then he returned to the doorway of the sitting room. Jean was re-starting the DVD with Jenny still in her arms. The child's eyes looked extra large and unfocussed as she stared in his direction over her mother's shoulder.

'Just one more question,' he said. 'When Corporal Turvey came for Eva's luggage and personal items, did she take everything? There's nothing still here?'

The jolly music was starting again as Jean glanced across, wine glass in hand. 'I had nothing to do with it. She told me to leave everything to her. I was glad. When Hector called me yesterday morning I went up to her room to see if there was anything I should put away for safety, and seeing her things scattered there upset me so much I left everything just as it was. Except a letter addressed to Hector. Thinking it mebbe was something important, I sent it across to him.'

SIX

Drum Major Andrew Lennox proved to be a hurdle to leap before gaining access to Hector McTavish. The band of the Drumdorran Fusiliers had moved into the headquarters vacated by the band of the Royal Cumberland Rifles, which had returned to the UK. This consisted of a large rehearsal hall, a series of small individual practice rooms, and living quarters for the musicians.

The Bandmaster, Captain Rory Staines, was away from his office discussing with Major Carnegie the final details of Eva McTavish's funeral so Max, who had recruited Connie to accompany him on this sensitive mission, was confronted by Andrew Lennox on entering the large complex. Coming from an office which already bore his name on the door, the barrel-chested, sandy-haired man stood four-square demanding the business of the man and woman wearing dark business suits.

Max had not seen the band march in with this man at its head, dextrously twirling the mace as he moved with a proud swagger in his impressive dress uniform. What he presently saw was a khaki-clad sergeant major of the old school, ready to make intruders about turn and exit with all speed. He swiftly identified himself and Connie.

'Glad to have you with us after what I've heard was a most successful tour of the US,' Max began. 'A great pity your arrival coincided with the tragic death of Mrs McTavish. Not the best omen for easy integration with the regiments already in residence, but I'm sure time will soften attitudes.' He adopted a tone of greater authority then. 'We need a private word with Pipe Major McTavish.'

Lennox stood his ground. 'And why would SIB need to speak to a man just two days bereaved?'

Thinking, as he so often did, of how mufti robbed him of the respect a uniform with three pips on his shoulder would command, Max said cripsly, 'That concerns only SIB and

Mr McTavish. Will you fetch him, or shall we look in every room until we find him?'

The other man's hesitation lasted just long enough to convey the message that he did not jump to Redcaps' orders, but not so long as to be regarded as insubordination.

'I'll call him to meet you in practice room three.' He waved an arm at the corridor leading off to the right. 'End door facing this way. He may be a wee while coming if he's at his prayers, sir.'

'I'm sure the Lord will excuse him in order to talk to us. He'll know we have to find whoever caused injuries to some of His flock, before further harm is done.'

Reaching room three, Max held open the door for Connie to enter then left it open behind him. Connie glanced up and mimed wiping sweat from her brow.

'Not a man to meet in a dark alley at night. I confess he was a splendid sight on Tuesday all togged up in kilt and white gaiters, but in combats he looks a real force to be reckoned with.'

Max grinned. 'He was on the point of pushing his luck out there when he thought better of it. He's worth keeping an eye on, however. He very obviously has no love for the English, so he'll play no part in defusing the aggro stirred up last night. Might even fan the flames.'

Connie perched on the edge of the table in this room furnished with two chairs, two music stands, recording equipment and an upright piano. 'I suppose to the Scots, Guy Fawkes was a hero for trying to do what they would have applauded.'

'Quite likely,' Max agreed with amusement. 'They're not a very forgiving race. Tend to relish old battles and resentments. Even amongst themselves. If it's not religious, it's clannish feuding.'

'Mmm, more deep-seated and, perhaps, more understandable than we English, who fight each other over football match results. How pointless is that?'

The sound of heavy footsteps on vinyl prevented an answer to that frequently asked question, and Hector McTavish entered the room. Max was surprised to see a man of very striking appearance pull up and stand waiting for whatever came next.

McTavish was about forty, with a body that suggested regular workouts. Nothing unusual for army men who had to be very fit, but his black hair and black eyes were almost startling in their compulsive effect. Max's first reaction was to wonder why he had remained married for so long to a frumpish hypochondriac. Indeed, Connie was visually responding to this man dressed in dark cord trousers and a long-sleeved polo shirt.

Max identified himself and Connie, then expressed their sympathy for the loss of his wife. Hector thanked them solemnly and stood waiting once more to hear the reason for their visit.

'We're now in receipt of the hospital report on the true cause of your wife's death,' Max said quietly. 'You were told the facts by the doctors, I assume.'

'Yes.'

'Did it come as a shock?'

McTavish blinked several times while he thought that through. 'Yes and no.'

'Would you explain that?' said Connie. 'We have to submit a report in cases of suicide.'

His dark gaze bored into her. 'She was nae in the armed forces. Just a wife.'

Max thought those three words said a lot. *Just* was dismissive, *a* instead of *my*, and *wife* was spoken as if suggesting an accessory.

'As Sergeant Bush said, we have to send in a report on all deaths that occur on this base, suicides included, so please elaborate on "yes and no".'

'Yes, their conclusion came as a shock. No, because Eva was very careless with her medication and it's obvious that she took an overdose without knowing. I was forever telling her it was dangerous and that she should get one of those gadgets that register the times and dosage to prevent such an accident.'

'You didn't buy one for her?' probed Connie.

Hector frowned as if puzzled by her question. 'She was the one taking the pills. Her responsibility.'

'So you believe Eva took an overdose in error?'

'It was bound to happen sooner or later.'

'How about the excessive amount of vodka your wife had drunk during that evening?' asked Max.

Hector shrugged. 'What do they mean by excessive? She was nae planning to drive anywhere. Or work with machinery,' he added, as if recollecting the warnings written on some medication.

'She liked vodka, did she?'

'How should I know? I'm away a great deal with the band. She never gave me a rundown of everything she'd done when I got back.'

'You didn't ask, show interest in how she'd filled the time during your absence?' asked Connie with deliberate surprise in her voice. When McTavish ignored that, she pushed him further. 'So, as far as you are aware, your wife wasn't unhappy, depressed, worried, ill; had any kind of problem that would drive her to take her own life?'

'But she didn't. Yes, she forgot she had already taken her pills and swallowed another dose. Yes, she had a dram or two of something to warm her while she watched the fireworks. But a bloody English dickhead put some effing explosive in the bonfire and puir Eva was struck down by a flaming wooden shard which kilt her. Put *that* in your sodding report, Sergeant Boosh,' he concluded in explosive manner that highlighted his accent through lack of control.

Max allowed a long silence to develop after that proof of Jean's description of this man's temper. He held eye contact until McTavish looked away and the angry colour faded from his face and neck. According to Jean Greene he was violent with words not actions, but suppose he had been pushed beyond bearing by Eva on Tuesday evening, and snapped.

'Now you have regained your control we'll continue,' Max said coldly. 'Mrs Greene told me she found a letter in the room your wife had occupied in her house, with your name on the envelope, and sent it across to you yesterday morning. What was in that letter?'

The black eyes narrowed. 'What has that to do with SIB?'

'Just answer my question.'

'It was a press cutting about our tour of the US. I promised my mother I'd send it on when Eva had read it.'

'Do you still have it?'

'No, I sent it off first thing this morning.'

Until now Max knew McTavish had been inventing answers, but he was lying, coolly and calmly about this. Without doubt, he had destroyed the contents of that envelope and they might never know the truth. Pointless to pursue that line of questioning.

'Mr McTavish, did you meet your wife on the evening of Tuesday last, or at any time during that day?'

'We marched in through the morning, and even you will know the demands of settling in and allocating quarters. We're hardly organized yet today.'

'That doesn't answer my question. Did you meet with Eva anywhere on this base two days ago?'

'I did not, sir.'

Max made signs to Connie that he was going to leave, then said, 'The funeral might have to be delayed, I'm afraid.'

'*Why?*' The red colour flooded McTavish's neck once more.

'In my opinion there is some doubt over the way your wife died. There are further questions to be asked. It shouldn't take more than a few days, depending on how soon people start giving us truthful answers.'

As he was passing through the doorway Max turned back to ask, 'Who is Tammy?'

'Who told . . . how did you . . . ? He shook his head as if to clear his confusion, and Max saw real distress now in those deeply dark eyes. 'He was my young brother. He died early this year.'

Max was assuaging his mid-afternoon hunger with several cereal bars, an apple and a large mug of coffee while he and Tom exchanged reports on their morning activities, when a staff car drew up outside. Seconds later, Major Carnegie and Duncan MacPherson entered. The two detectives got to their feet, Max cursing the evidence of his much delayed lunch scattered over his desk. With the whole team out on the job it looked as if 26 Section was a ramshackle unit, with its OC lounging and snacking.

Major Carnegie showed no actual signs of disparagement

as he got straight to the point of this surprise visit. 'I understand you told Hector McTavish his wife's funeral will have to be delayed, due to your doubts over the cause of her death.' He indicated the Medical Officer at his side. 'Duncan assures me that you've seen the hospital report which gives a full medical assessment. Is that correct?'

'Yes, sir,' agreed Max, realizing this man was behaving as if he was the Garrison Commander, as he had earlier that day. Max resented it more this time.

'Then what doubts can you possibly have?'

'When a person ingests large quantities of pills washed down with equally large quantities of alcohol in order to expire, it's a slow, deliberate act leaving time to write a note of farewell and explanation. Mrs Greene, with whom Eva McTavish lodged for the last week of her life, found an envelope addressed to Hector amongst the dead woman's things, and sent it across to him.'

'And?'

'He told me it contained a press cutting about the band's US tour which he had promised to send to his mother. He couldn't produce it because he claimed he had posted it first thing this morning. He prevaricated throughout the interview, but *that* was surely highly questionable. The wife he had been parted from for three months apparently swallows enough noxious substances to kill herself, apart from being seriously injured in the chest, yet he hastily sends a mere press cutting to his mother barely a day after the tragic death of his wife. Don't you find that curious?'

Carnegie's eyes narrowed. 'Sudden, shocking bereavement causes people to behave in ways that might seem inexplicable to others. Perhaps you've no experience of that to guide you.'

Flashbacks to a day of thunder and torrential rain when a duo of uniformed men had arrived to tell him Susan had been killed outright in a road accident ran through Max's inner vision, but he said nothing. Those memories were crowding in more often since the humiliating end to his hopes of a new future with his father's ADC. No way would he allow them to interfere with his job now.

Duncan MacPherson asked, 'You thought the envelope contained a suicide note from Eva?'

Max nodded. 'A natural enough assumption.'

'And you suspect Hector of destroying it?'

'He lied about it. I have enough experience of *that* to guide me,' he returned grittily.

'Why would he lie?' demanded Carnegie, causing Max to feel he was being interrogated the way 26 Section treated a proven perpetrator of a crime. His anger rose.

'That's what I attempted to find out. If he had answered truthfully I'd now have the answer. If Eva took her own life she chose a bizarre method. I need to know when and where she took all those pills and drank about three-quarters of a bottle of vodka. I certainly regard the fact that she left in Mrs Greene's house an envelope addressed to her husband as very significant . . . and the fact that he lied to me about it even more significant.'

Tom suddenly entered the lists. 'Sir, we were told only this morning that Mrs McTavish didn't, as we all believed, die from the chest wound. Our entire team is out gathering evidence to enable us to find whoever caused the explosion on Tuesday evening. In addition, we have to submit a report on the death of Mrs McTavish to the Garrison Commander. As Captain Rydal said, it's a most unusual suicide pattern. One we've not come across before in all our combined years of investigation, and when the victim's next of kin shows little sign of grief and palpably avoids the truth, we're obliged to dig deeper into the background of this sudden death. We have never taken the easy way out, particularly in a case of loss of life. In short, Major Carnegie, we think it's possible someone forced Eva McTavish to swallow that lethal mixture.'

The Drumdorrans' OC was looking thunderstruck now. 'What evidence do you have to support that wild theory?'

'So far, none, sir,' Tom returned swiftly. 'The truth about her death was only relayed to us three hours ago. We need time to resolve the case to our satisfaction.'

'And this is why you propose to delay the funeral?' asked Duncan MacPherson. At Max's nod, the red-haired doctor said, 'That's quite unnecessary. Whether or not Eva took that fatal mixture willingly or under duress, there's no dispute over what killed her. Her corpse will tell you nothing more if you keep it from the grave than it can tell you now. I'm referring to medical evidence, Max. Since we spoke this morning I've examined the body, and I can tell you now that the report from the hospital is comprehensively correct. There was nothing to suggest maltreatment or any kind of restraint. There is no legitimate cause to postpone Saturday's funeral. I give you my professional word on it.'

Carnegie looked set to depart, and his next words supported this. 'You have from now until ten thirty on Saturday morning to check Duncan's assurances. The cortege will leave for the church at precisely eleven o'clock.' His final comment was made over his shoulder. 'The sooner this affair is concluded the sooner we can work on establishing good relations on the base, even if it's no more than unarmed neutrality. Good day to you.'

During the heavy silence following the Scots' departure. Max assimilated the impression they must have received of the Section he commanded. Empty desks, silent computers, an office littered with confectionery wrappers, apple cores, biscuit crumbs and coffee mugs, and the two senior members sitting amongst this debris minus their jackets and with shirt sleeves casually pushed up.

He grimaced at Tom. 'Do you have the feeling we were the losers in that Anglo-Scottish scuffle?'

'We had 'em rattled, though.' He began collecting the snack debris. 'That MO's a giant. Can imagine him tossing the caber with ease. He needs watching where women are concerned, especially your doctor friend who'll be working closely with him.'

'Mmm, it's a pity David Culdrow's still not recovered from the mumps. I've a suspicion MacPherson's here to stay.'

Throwing the rubbish into a metal waste bin, Tom muttered, 'I knew they'd be trouble, and they've not been here a week yet.'

If the first half of the day had been trying, the second half offered no relief. Having had enough of Scottish guile, Max and Tom switched their attention to the case of the exploding bonfire and discussed at some length how to proceed before the team returned for the evening briefing.

Piercey and Beeny had tracked down everyone who had been involved with the fireworks. They had a few things to report, but nothing to get excited about.

'Corporal Lines is something of an anorak where pyrotechnics are concerned,' offered Piercey. 'Soon loses it if there's a hitch. Seems there was a box missing from the original order, and he went beserk; threw an artistic tantrum according to two of his helpers.' He glanced at his notebook. 'Privates Stone and Bartholemew.'

'And?' asked Tom tetchily.

'The Corp called Max-ee-million on his mobile and let rip. According to Stone and Bartholemew the stuff in the missing box was meant to form the basis of the fixed display, so nothing could be done until that was all in place.'

'What was the outcome?'

'Max-ee-million sent a van out here pronto with the box, and a smaller one packed with some extra fireworks for free. Bartholemew said these were a dozen massive rockets.' He grinned. 'The kind you want to push up someone's arse when they don't move quickly enough.'

Tom was in no mood for levity. Why had that late delivery not been mentioned at the fireworks factory a few hours ago? Nor had Lines spoken of that hitch and the gift of giant rockets to Connie or to himself when questioned. How easy for someone to filch one, split it open and use the contents to make an IED!

'Did Corporal Lines include those freebies in the display?' he asked, deep in thought.

Piercey nodded. 'Right at the end.'

'Did you speak to whoever set them off?'

The Cornish sergeant looked again at his notebook. 'Rifleman James. Because Corporal Lines was in an artistic tizzy over the set piece which only he was allowed to control, he had to delegate. James told me he boobed; was late sending up the rockets so that the last two spoiled the effect of the start of the set piece which was producing great showers of gold and silver. Lines was giving him an earful when the bonfire exploded.'

'Did James say anything about there not being a full dozen of those rockets when he came to deal with them?'

'I asked him about that.' Piercey again referred to his notebook and read from it. *I didn't count them, Sarge. I was late setting them off and knew I'd be for it. That's all I was thinking of.*'

'Right,' said Tom. 'First thing tomorrow we question all those involved in the firework display again. Find out if anyone counted those rockets as they went up. I also want to know who opened the box they were in, what time that van delivered it, and where it was from that moment until the rockets were removed in readiness for the display.'

'Might prove negative, sir,' put in Beeny. 'I got the impression it was a hell of a shambles all day Tuesday. The lads I questioned said Lines, and Corporal Naish who constructed the bonfire, were like a pair of headless chickens. Normally highly motivated, they behaved as if they were creating a global masterpiece. Checked everything ten times over and treated them all as if they were idiots. Several said if no one had been hurt, they'd have been delighted the bonfire blew apart so dramatically.'

'But people *were* hurt, so go back tomorrow and put on the pressure. Someone must know where the box of rockets sat during the preparations, shambolic or not,' ruled Tom.

Heather Johnson glanced up from her notebook. 'There was no mention of a late delivery and freebies when we were at Max-ee-million, was there?'

'No, and Greta Gans had every opportunity to tell us,' Tom agreed. 'There's more to that girl than meets the eye. And that leads us back to Carter and his bogus cut hand that gave him an excuse to be well away from the Sports Ground that evening.'

'Greta's not the only overseer, sir. There are three. They work shifts so that there are always two on the premises.'

'Who told you that?' asked Tom sharply.

'Bruno Borg.'

'That walking advert for active healthy living you were giggling with when I left?'

Both Heather and Connie had learned long ago not to rise to provocation from their male colleagues, even their 2IC, so she simply nodded. 'Yes, him.'

'Why didn't you see fit to pass that info on to me?'

'We were investigating the connection between Rifleman Carter and the girlfriend who could have passed him something. I didn't think it was relevant to an enquiry which seemed to be proving negative,' Heather said in her best detectivespeak. 'Now we know about the late delivery and highly explosive freebies it puts a new slant on that relationship.'

'So pull out the note your *Polizei* friend gave you, call him and arrange another visit to Max-ee-million first thing in the morning. Bring back a couple of those giant rockets for Captain Knott's lads to examine. And this time concentrate on the business in hand,' Tom added, unfairly because he knew Heather had been fully on the ball that morning.

Max then gave the facts regarding Eva McTavish's death, although Connie had probably already passed the news to her colleagues.

'In the absence of unarguable evidence that the woman took her own life, we'll have to prove it the hard way. Jean Greene admits Eva kept to her own room after a quarrel in the morning over her proposed extended stay in the house. This means Jean was not witness to Eva's state on leaving it on Tuesday evening. The absence of empty vodka bottles in her room suggests she drank it elsewhere, although she could have taken one with her and dumped it. George's team are searching all possible sites for it, but it seems most likely, to me, that she drank that excessive intake at the Greenes' house, then swallowed the pills at the Sports Ground. Gaining Dutch courage to take the killer dose during the fireworks, when all eyes would be on them.

'One theory I have is that she never intended to die; that it was a cry for help that went wrong because of that very fact. Who would notice a comatose woman when there was so much glittery excitement to watch? The other theory is that she was forced to swallow that lethal mixture. There's no physical evidence that force had been used on her; the Drumdorrans' own MO has examined the body and given me his professional assurance on that score.'

'A third theory is that she was suffering from depression and needed to make a melodramatic statement,' said Piercey, leaning back with a self-satisfied smile hovering on his mouth.

'And a fourth is that her marriage was on the rocks, so she was facing humiliation and a lonely future. Already humbled by her husband's failure to contact her on his arrival after three months apart, plus the quarrel with Mrs Greene who had made it obvious she didn't want her there any longer, drove her to act on desperate impulse,' offered Connie, always the most compassionate member of the team.

'While the balance of her mind was disturbed?' Max nodded. 'The most likely explanation, but I'd like proof of that before I report a suicide to Colonel Trelawney. To that end I want you all to get as much info as possible about Eva's movements at the Sports Ground. Who remembers seeing her there, did she talk to anyone or did she stand aloof, was she drinking alcohol, was she swallowing pills from pharmacy bottles? Find out if she was there before the fireworks, looking at the stalls selling gifts, soup, burgers and hot chestnuts, or if she only arrived on the scene as the display began. Did she look drunk or ill? Question the paramedics who took her to the hospital to discover exactly where she was lying when they approached her.'

He frowned in concentration. 'I'm no medical expert but I imagine she would have only just taken the last of the pills or vodka when she was hit by the small missile and collapsed, because she didn't breathe her last until the early hours. Both the paramedics and the hospital staff concentrated on the wound and missed the other problem until it was too late to revive her. Captain Goodey says they tried all they could to keep her alive, to no avail.'

Connie shook her head sadly. 'If she wanted to die she would have resisted their efforts.'

'The expression is *gave up the ghost*,' murmured Piercey.

'Before we all grow soft and weepy, I have further instructions,' put in Tom firmly. 'Get me all you can on Pipe Major McTavish. His colleagues' mouths will be sealed by superglue, but contact the SIB section covering the area where the Drumdorrans served prior to coming over here. And if any of you have friends in the regiments based there still, get what you can from them concerning the band.'

'One more avenue,' interrupted Max before the team members could go off for a decent meal. 'Get a copy of the band's engagements on their US tour, then contact the local rags in all the places they performed and ask them to email copies of their reviews of those performances.'

Beneath the general noise of chairs being pushed back into knee-holes, car keys rattling on desks, and bantering remarks based on the hotch-potch of ideas that had been expressed, Tom murmured to Max, 'Digging into the dregs there, aren't you?'

'Did no one ever read the tea leaves in your cup and tell you something promising? I'd like to know what could have been so sensational our friend McTavish was driven to send it to his mother mere hours after his wife had died in shocking circumstances.' Max gave a weary smile. 'Let's have an early night. We deserve it.'

He was halfway to his office when George Maddox entered the building and stood dripping water onto the standard MOD carpet.

'Is it raining?' asked Max in surprise.

'That fine stuff those who live north of the border call Scotch mist. Mist, my eye! You can get bloody drenched.'

'Are we to guess you've arrived at an hour when all sensible people are tucking into a hearty dinner, because you have news?' At George's nod, Max added, 'Good or bad?'

'Depends how you look at it, sir.'

'Ah, the invariable answer.'

'Well, spit it out,' urged Tom, still tetchy over not having been told about the freebie rockets. He had visited that fat Estonian twice and got nowhere. That was why he had told Heather to go with the German she fancied for a third trip to Max-ee-million.

'Captain Knott has ruled that we can lift the top security state. Seems his squad has found evidence that aerosol cannisters and some Chinese New Year firecrackers had been inserted in the bonfire, which created such a major explosion. They say the IED alone wouldn't have sent stuff flying into the crowd.'

Max frowned. 'He's giving his professional opinion that it wasn't a terrorist attack?'

George pulled a long face. 'I was told we reacted too wildly to their statement that there was evidence of an IED, and imagined the Taliban had breached our security. A smartarse guy told me an IED is *any* improvised explosive device; even the old alarm clock and stick of dynamite in a suitcase favourite of old black and white thrillers. These what they call "stick and string" bombs could be used for a bank robbery or for demolishing a garden wall. Anyone can access the Internet and get instructions on how to make one. He had the gall to say we were all up a gum tree imagining the base had been infiltrated by Islamic Fundamentalists.'

Max was furious and said Jeremy Knott should have had the courtesy to contact him with the information, not allow one of his squad to pass the news with such superiority to George. He headed for his office telephone.

'I'll call Knott and ruin his dinner.'

'He's not on base, sir.'

Max halted. 'He never is when we want him. Where is he this time?'

'He's giving evidence at the NATO conference; be returning with Colonel Trelawney on Sunday.'

Tom was equally angry, but his wrath was directed against those who had put additional explosive material in the bonfire, and lied to him.

The three men left the building together, too depressed to speak apart from bidding each other goodnight as they reached their cars. As Tom drove away he understood why this fine rain was called Scotch mist. It hung in the air shrouding everything and blurring outlines. On this November evening the familiar buildings around the base loomed from the darkness like ghostly fortresses as he travelled the perimeter road. Lights shimmered in the windows of accommodation blocks, and hooded figures moved through the semi-opaqueness as if on sinister business. Tom imagined this damp pall cloaking mountains and glens where unpopulated wildness could hide an advancing horde. One bloodthirsty clan rising up against another!

Telling himself the advent of the Drumdorran Fusiliers had made him ridiculously fanciful, Tom turned his thoughts back to the death of Eva McTavish. There was certainly a veil of Scotch mist over that; the truth was hidden behind an impenetrable curtain of Celtic pride and loyalty. He scowled. Max and his US newspaper reports on the band's tour! He was clutching at straws. It was surely obvious that Hector McTavish had destroyed his wife's suicide note because it reflected badly on himself. He would play the exploding bonfire theme to the full so that he could put the blame elsewhere for her decision to attend the fireworks display rather than get together with him after their three month parting.

When he drove through the main gate the usual lift of gladness was missing. He must resolve the situation regarding the new baby tonight. He had no intention of letting Maggie and Gina create a division in a united family. They were old enough to be knowledgeable about conception, so they were mature enough to receive a straight talk on the subject. Tom knew of families who allowed themselves to be ruled by their teenage children. Not so he and Nora. So far their determination on that score had prevailed. He was going to ensure things stayed that way.

His mood grew heavier. He had had little sleep since the bonfire tragedy, and Nora was suffering the usual early pregnancy blues which made her unpredictable and weepy. This fourth time she had additional reason to be temperamental. Peering through the thickening gloom at the cluster of red lights ahead, which indicated a queue of traffic tailing back at least a kilometre or more from the crossroads, Tom sighed for the days when he had arrived home to find his family happily engaged while waiting for him to join them for the hot, tasty meal. Then there would be games before bedtime followed by relaxation with Nora before lying together in bed and making love. And there lay the cause of this present situation. Was it only yesterday that he had assured her the new child would be greatly loved? He hoped to God he would be able to live up to that assurance when it was put to the test.

He was inching along in the traffic queue when his mobile rang. Cursing, he checked caller ID and found it was a member of Maddox's team. No need to pull over to take the call. The long line of cars had come to a halt, and the klaxon of *Polizei* vehicles told him they were likely to stay that way for a considerable time.

'What's the problem, Jim?' he asked, making no secret of his annoyance.

'Just a few minutes after you checked out the main gate a German guy turned up there demanding to see you. The guard says he's creating merry hell. Refuses to move his car, so incomers have to use the outgoing lane. I've sent Meacher down there to persuade him to put his car in the visitors' layby until you get here, sir.'

'Who the hell is he? Can't someone else deal with him?'

'It's got to be you, I'm afraid. Says you insulted his daughter. Accused her of stealing and being in league with terrorists. Name of Otto Gans.'

SEVEN

When he left Headquarters Max drove towards the Officers' Mess, thinking it would be sensible to dine there; it would take him around thirty-five minutes to reach his flat. More, with visibility limited in the thickening haze. In any case, he was not in the mood for a basic microwaveable meal eaten alone in a room redolent of the humiliating split with Livya a month ago.

Reaching the Mess he realized he did not want the noisy cameraderie usually to be found there, either, so he continued around the perimeter road to the Medical Centre. Parking outside the building, he punched Clare's number on his mobile to discover whether she was still there or had left for home. No reply, so he tried her mobile.

Her greeting came against a background murmuring that suggested that she was in some public place. 'Hi, Max! Are you still working?'

'Just locked up. I wondered if you'd like to go to Herr Blomfeld's to carry on where we left off on Tuesday.'

She laughed. 'I'm here now, drinking a glass of our favourite Riesling.'

Max was on the point of saying he would be there as soon as possible when her next words silenced him.

'I've introduced Duncan to Herr Blomfeld. You know his funny English; he beamed and said, "So now we have the double doctors", adding that the wine was with the greetings of the house. We assume that means we don't have to pay for it.' A short pause while she murmured something and MacPherson's base gave a reply. 'Come and join us, Max. You two can get to know each other socially and you can drive me home to save Duncan a lengthy detour.'

'No thanks,' he replied curtly. 'I'm not in the mood to play gooseberry . . . or run a taxi service. Have a nice evening.'

For long minutes he sat at the wheel, staring into the murk

while painful memories paraded before him. The shattering break with the second woman he had really loved had revived his grief over losing Susan and their embryo son. For a few short months Livya had driven it to the recesses of his mind, made him feel whole again. Now he was once more aware of isolation, even when among his colleagues. The yearning to have something to go home to was still strong in him. A wife, a real home, children. Why were those normal things so difficult for him to find and hold on to?

Cutting through his jumbled thoughts came the sudden certainty that Eva McTavish *had* taken her own life. Doormats, like worms, finally turned. Years of petty humiliations at the hands of an uncaring man had culminated in the final act of public contempt on returning after an absence of three months. A hundred imagined or stress-related ailments had failed to draw his sympathy. *She was the one taking the pills. Her responsibility.*

Too browbeaten to walk away and start a fresh life, Eva could not face the long procession of lonely years ahead, so decided to go out with a shower of gold and silver stars, cascades of red and green and blue, swirling, glittering wheels and a thunder of explosions to make her departure more impressive than her existence had been. What was it Jean Greene had said? *We're all born to play our part on the world's stage, but that sad girl stayed in the wings.* Maybe, but Eva gave a bravura farewell performance.

Still staring into the shadowy distance, Max took up his mobile again and punched in the number of a woman facing the prospect of her lonely years with great fortitude.

'It's Max,' he said when Brenda Keane answered. 'I'll be passing your way shortly. Will it be convenient to call in?'

'Oh, yes!' came the enthusiastic response, 'It's such a gloomy old evening, Micky and I will welcome company. If you haven't already dined you can help me eat a chicken casserole I've made.'

'On way,' said Max, his spirits lifting immediately.

As he drove through streets where lamps silvered the fine rain that was not visible in the darkness, he was glad he could avoid the main highway into town which was sure to be gridlocked at this hour. Coming up to the turning which would take him to his flat he had the momentary thought of going there and telephoning Brenda with an excuse, but he still shied from the prospect of some pre-packed concoction with only himself for company, and drove on.

When Brenda opened the door and smiled a welcome he was glad of that decision. Short blonde hair shining with health, cheeks rosy from the warmth inside her flat, and violet-blue eyes showing her pleasure at his arrival; at the end of a day like he had just spent this woman in black jeans and sky-blue jumper was a lovely sight.

'Come in out of the rain,' she urged, and led the way to her L-shaped living room softly lit by two attractive Tiffany lamps. 'I'm glad you decided to come. I've made a ridiculously large casserole. It's so difficult to cook for one. There's always too much and I get sick of eating it up day after day.'

She turned in the centre of the room and gave a soft chuckle as she indicated the wooden rocking-cradle of old Germanic design. 'Can't wait for him to be old enough to share meals with me.'

'How is he?' asked Max, crossing to the cradle.

'Bathed and fed, but wide awake. I told him you were coming, so he stayed up for you.' She joined Max, smiling at the baby who was kicking his feet and waving tiny fists with excitement. 'Say hallo to Max, Micky.'

The baby gurgled and blew bubbles, which made her laugh. 'I'm sure he said your name, Max, aren't you?'

He was lost in marvelling at how small this love child was, how vigorous and aware. Were they all like that? Would Alexander Rydal have looked and behaved so energetically if he had lived? A faint frown creased his forehead. A fatherless child gazing up at a childless father. Imagine if he was looking down at his own son and preparing to eat dinner with Susan. How different everything would be.

'Drink this while I put vegetables on to boil,' said a voice, and a glass of wine was put in his hand. 'Do take off that jacket and relax,' Brenda added. 'You look so smart I feel slightly scruffy in comparison.'

Returning to the present, Max said, 'You're a sight for sore eyes after a sea of men in disruptive pattern combats, believe me. Can I do anything to help? I'm sorry I didn't have a chance to buy a bottle along the way. Everything was shuttered and barred on a night like this.'

She smiled. 'I've just opened the one you brought last time. These days I only drink in company. Parenthood puts the brakes on things like that. Or it should. As a midwife I saw a few women who ought never to have become mothers.' She raised her glass. '*Prosit*!'

He repeated the toast and drank, then stood the glass on a small table and removed his jacket to lay it across a chair. Brenda had disappeared into the kitchen, and he was about to take up his glass when Micky began to whimper. It increased in volume until it became a full-blooded scream. What had seemed to Max to be playful kicking and punching the air was now a violent protest against lying in that cradle. The little face was beetroot red and screwed up as if in pain.

Max picked up the distressed child and began to rock him as he walked back and forth. Amazingly, the screams soon subsided into shuddering snivels as blue eyes gazed up in curiosity into dark ones, and the dark ones saw what they wanted to see.

'Ah, you must have a magic touch.' Brenda was emerging from the kitchen to see to her baby.

'Shhh,' Max said swiftly, because the blue eyes had closed and all was quiet again.

'Give it a few minutes, then put him back in the cradle,' she advised in a half-whisper. 'By then the meal will be ready.'

They sat at the table, Micky sleeping contentedly, and Max asked if all babies fell asleep so instantly.

Brenda nodded. 'It can be very deceptive, though. Just as you're slipping back into bed they can wake just as instantly and start screaming again.'

'I interviewed a woman this week whose daughter fell asleep over a plate of fish fingers and got smeared with ketchup. It astonished me, but her mother says she does it all the time.'

Brenda frowned. 'How old is the child?'

'I'm no good at guessing a youngster's age,' Max said, concentrating on his food. 'Three? Three and a half?'

'She needs to see a doctor. It sounds like a form of narcolepsy. It could be dangerous, Max. Surely the mother can't believe it's natural behaviour.'

Max returned his laden fork to the plate. 'It didn't appear to be of concern to her. She actually thought it rather amusing.'

'Amusing? What if the child's in the bath and the mother goes to answer the phone? She could fall asleep, slip beneath the water and drown. *Amusing*? What kind of mother is that woman?'

Seeing how serious his medically qualified companion was, Max said, 'I'll pass on your concern to our MO and suggest she has a look at the girl.'

'With some haste.'

'If you say so,' he agreed, and continued eating while recalling Jenny Greene asleep with her face in a plate of food while Paddington Bear bought a new tablecloth.

Conversation became general for a while, until Brenda said, 'I've had another letter from my parents urging me to go back to the UK. Neither of them is in good health.'

'Oh? How do you feel about that?' He really wanted to know.

'I haven't told them about Micky, or that I got a job out here in order to meet up with Flip again. Chasing a married man is how they'd see it. They believed it was simply a career move.' She rose and gathered up their plates. 'I'll make coffee.'

That was no answer, and while Brenda was in the kitchen Max gazed at the picture of a desert sunset that hung on the wall. Philip Keane had bought it for her after their tour of Iraq because he knew the desert had fascinated her. Max had been there briefly and could never live with a picture like that one. Endless sand turned red by a huge dying sun; unforgiving terrain with few signs of life. Oh, no, it looked to him disturbingly desolate.

He was still in the grip of that impression when she returned with a tray bearing coffee and two slices of *Sachertorte.*

'Another reason why I'm glad you called in,' she said, indicating the chocolate cake with a smile. 'My great weakness, and I'd have eaten it all myself. Are you all right?' she then asked in concern.

'Fine.' To take attention from himself, he asked, 'Shouldn't your people know they have a grandson?'

As if to underline his right to exist, Micky began to cry, setting the cradle rocking and breaking the tentative intimacy that had arisen on this first extended visit. It had been no more than coffee and biscuits on the previous two occasions.

The baby's demands had to be met, so Max tactfully took his leave after downing some coffee. The cake remained uneaten.

Outside, he found the drizzle had been replaced by fog which grew ever thicker as he drove to his flat. It soon became hazardous, visibility such that other vehicles' red rear lights only penetrated the pall when he was almost upon them. And so it must be for those behind him. Risky to progress, even more so to stop.

Much as he disliked using sat nav Max now found it invaluable. Without it he would most likely never have found the short drive leading to his rented home. Turning into it he almost collided with a Range Rover parked in his designated space. Duncan MacPherson's, he supposed. Well, the large Scot would not be returning to base tonight. If he was fool enough to try he would be out of luck, because Max blocked his vehicle in and wearily climbed the outside steps to his front door.

After tossing and turning for several hours, Max gave up the attempt to sleep and went to his kitchen to make tea. While it brewed he surrendered to sudden impulse and opened the door to the shared lounge between his and Clare's apartments. In the dimness he could just make out the blur of pillows and a blanket on one of the long settees. He then closed the door as quietly as he had opened it, and drank his tea. That did the trick. He fell asleep as soon as he returned to bed.

When Tom awoke in a basic room in the Sergeants' Mess he recalled why he had spent the night there and grew depressed. 'A bloody fine mood in which to start the day,' he muttered, running his hands through his tousled hair as he stomped to the shower. It refreshed him, made him feel less like a bear with a sore head. He had collected his spare shirt, underpants, suit and tie from Headquarters before checking in for the night, and now shaved before dressing in the fresh clothes to go for some breakfast.

As he ran the electric razor over his dark stubble he vowed to have a straight word with Klaus Krenkel the minute he reached his office. One of those *Polizei* youngsters who had been with him and Heather at Max-ee-million had provided Otto Gans with the name of the British soldier policeman who had 'browbeaten Greta and falsely accused her of being a terrorist'.

Brushing his teeth with angry vigour Tom could see the pompous expression on Gans's podgy face. A jumped-up local businessman who was also some kind of town official. The sort who invariably made protests, offered unasked-for advice, criticized fellow committee members and insisted on every word being included in the minutes, Tom was certain.

To clear the incoming lane at the gate Tom had been obliged to lead the man back to Headquarters. It had been out of the question to conduct a conversation with him in the fine misty rain, but the sight of the battery of computers, telephones, maps, security lights and CCTV cameras had simply increased Gans's belief that SIB was the British equivalent of the KGB.

The man would not listen to Tom's explanation. He ranted about his friends in high places who could make things very awkward at a word from him, mentioned his certainty of winning the upcoming election for *Burgermeister*, and warned Tom that he had no notion of what he had stirred up by insulting and threatening his daughter.

On his demanding to speak to the 'chief officer' Tom was able truthfully to say the Garrison Commander was at a NATO conference. This had appeared to strengthen Gans's belief in Soviet-style secret plans, and he had only departed because Tom had been obliged to reveal Miles Crawford's name as Deputy Garrison Commander. The one consolation had been Tom's confidence that Gans would get short shrift from a man deeply worried about his son's burns, who still regarded the 'nine to five Fritzes' as the enemy in two bitter wars.

He had no illusions about who would emerge victor from that meeting. Nevertheless it riled him, because there was little chance of Crawford then brushing the whole incident under the carpet. He was sure to summon Tom to explain, and read him a lecture on keeping good relations with their hosts. He was that kind of officer. With regard to a further visit to Max-ee-million to get the facts on the free gift of giant rockets, Tom realized he must relieve Heather of the duty and go himself.

By the time Otto Gans had departed, fog had descended and looked like remaining. A phone call to the RMP Post resulted in the Duty Sergeant telling Tom there was a reported serious accident near the crossroads, which had closed the route to his house. A call to Nora revealed that Maggie and Gina had arranged sleepovers with friends, but that Beth and she were having a heart-to-heart about the new baby which was going well. That news of the older girls' plans – a deliberate tactic to avoid facing their parents, Tom was certain – strengthened his decision to spend the night and enjoy a good hot meal in the Mess.

He ate breakfast in the communal silence of men who were never chatty in the morning. The women, who were, always gathered as far as possible from their grouchy male counterparts, and talked quietly. Tom just nodded to Connie, Heather, Piercey and Beeny who were grouped as an isolated quartet, SIB not being particularly popular with regimental members. For almost a year their promised accommodation attached to Headquarters had been a distant prospect. Now, with fresh MOD cuts in expenditure, they despaired of ever seeing it built and resigned themselves to their present situation.

When Tom arrived at Headquarters he found Olly Simpson on duty to field calls and take appropriate action, and a fair-haired man in a navy suit and a rugby club tie, who was checking a pile of files on his desk.

'Hallo, Staff,' said Tom with pleased surprise. 'When did you get back?'

Staff Sergeant Pete Melly got to his feet with a rueful smile. 'Not until four this morning. I was making good time from the ferry port, but the bloody fog descended so I joined a group of truckers in an eaterie along the autobahn, then had a few hours' kip until it cleared enough to make driving easier.'

Melly had taken leave in an attempt to mend his marriage

before the divorce became final. The fact that he had returned early suggested that he had been unsuccessful, so Tom refrained from mentioning the subject.

'An *eaterie*? I thought you'd been in the UK not the US.'

Melly grinned. 'It's all the Country and Western I'm into. Gets you talking American.'

'Huh, so long as you don't start on *hoots mon*! We've had a bellyful of that these past few days.'

'So I heard. Olly says everyone's out on the events of Tuesday night, so I've started on clearing up the Gibbons case. We can get a report on the Garrison Commander's desk ready for his return.'

'Good. There's also that charge of sexual harassment that's a non-starter. Get that wound up as well. Then we'll have a clear period to get to the bottom of these other cases that are tenuously linked.'

'Until something else comes in,' said Olly Simpson, eating a Mars bar beside the silent telephone.

'That'll rot your teeth,' Tom muttered. 'Didn't you have breakfast?'

'Three hours ago. A man has to top up on energy foods.'

Tom wondered why Simpson was not overweight. He was forever eating chocolate bars, yet had a physique often referred to as wiry. He was the really deep thinker in the team; enjoyed enigmatic situations as much as Max, and frequently came up with aspects of a case nobody else had considered. His consuming interest was the rise and fall of past conquerers – Romans, Greeks, Normans, Celts, for instance. Unlike Tom, he welcomed the arrival of the Drumdorran Fusiliers and would surely soon have a friend or two in their ranks.

He caught Tom's eyes as he walked past to reach his office, and said in a low voice, 'Hetty's coming over at the weekend to spend a few days to see if she can stand being an army wife any better than she did before. He came back early to fix up somewhere they can live together while she decides. It looks promising.'

At that point Max walked in looking somewhat red-eyed. Tom guessed he had had another bad night, and cursed the Cordwell woman who had let his friend down so badly.

'Morning, sir,' the three men chorussed, one speaking through a mouthful of Mars bar.

Max returned their greeting, then perched on the edge of a desk. 'Everyone's out getting evidence that'll allow us to get this case moving towards a conclusion . . . hopefully! Oh, hallo, Staff. Good to see you back. How did it work out? Any chance of a reconciliation?'

Tom exchanged glances with Simpson that spoke volumes, but Melly smiled and said he had high hopes.

'Great! Good man! Any probs let me know and we'll sort them out. I'll précis what we have so far to put you in the picture.' Max then gave a concise account of the case concerning Eva McTavish, and began to outline the more complex problem. 'Last thing yesterday, George Maddox was told by the explosives guys that the bonfire had also contained a selection of aerosol containers – we've had that problem before, if you recall – and some firecrackers left over from Chinese New Year. These, together with the IED, produced the dangerous big bang. Having been professionally serious on Wednesday about the IED, they last evening accused us of having overreacted, even quoting, somewhat smugly, alarm clocks and sticks of dynamite in suitcases.

'So that's the present state of play, Staff. The annual dickheads decided to put the wind up everybody, and I've a good idea who they were, but we have to work out the who and why regarding the additional item that caused the real damage.'

'Have the explosives guys found remnants of a cheap suitcase?' asked Melly, straightfaced.

Max scowled. 'Men who risk their lives on a daily basis in a warzone tend to regard us as buffoons when it comes to *real* soldiering. My initial belief that someone was bent on causing danger to lives no longer stands up. Without the aerosols and crackers, the IED – we'll continue to call it that – was probably designed just to cause the bonfire to collapse with a loud bang. So we're back to my familiar line that someone was making a statement. Yes, I know,' he added. 'On my hobby horse again. But it's the most obvious explanation, and we have on this base a legion of men, and women, who are well primed on the behaviour of combustible material *and* who are never short of things to complain about.

'The absolute urgency to trace the perpetrator has been reduced, but we still have to find whoever was driven to express a grudge by that method.' He straightened from his perch on the desk. 'We also need firm evidence that Eva McTavish willingly and deliberately took her own life before I can file a suicide report. Although I believe it to be true, there is still a small area of doubt that should be investigated. Don't you agree?' he asked, turning to Tom.

Tom nodded, but he wondered what had made Max so certain the woman had taken her own life.

'When the team comes in at the end of the day, they should bring in enough evidence to clarify what's presently opaque. In the meantime, I suggest we tie up the Gibbons case and that dreamed-up claim of sexual harassment.'

'Yes, sir,' said Melly, giving no sign that he had already agreed that with Tom.

Tom was irked by this issue of orders without consulting him first, but in his present mood he would find most things irritating. At some time today he would receive a summons from Miles Crawford, and he would have to go to Max-ee-million to meet the blond German Heather had arranged to rendezvous with at noon. She had been vocally disappointed when Tom had called to say he would take her place.

'I'm not setting up in competition. I don't fancy him,' he had finished brusquely.

When Max went to his office, Tom followed him. 'Better put you in the picture,' he began. 'Our dearly beloved DGC may be on the blower any minute with another bleat.'

'Before you tell me why, get young Oliver out there to make us some coffee. He's only sitting on his backside beside a phone that's thankfully quiet. If there's a bleat in store I need an injection of caffeine.'

'Good idea.' Leaning from the doorway he gave Olly the request, adding, 'If you've left any choc bars in the tin add a couple of those.'

While they waited, Tom asked if Max had managed to reach his flat before the fog and the road accident had closed the main route through town. Max countered with 'Did you?' which suggested to Tom an unwillingness to reply to that. So where had he spent the night? Was there a new woman hovering in the wings?

'I stayed in the Mess. The cause of the expected bleat delayed me until there was a near grey-out. Too risky.'

'Oh, am I likely to receive a bleat from Nora, too?'

Tom hesitated on the brink of telling him about the expected baby, then thought better of it. He should ask Nora before spreading the news around. Not that Max would say anything to others, but she should agree on when they went public, as it were. Telling their girls had been disaster enough, without a mix of congratulations or gentle sympathy from friends. They, themselves, were still hovering between pleasure and dismay.

Coffee and Twix bars were brought in, then Tom related the substance of his encounter with Otto Gans. When he finished, Max actually grinned.

'Ever see that film about a Colonel Blimp? Gans sounds like an inflated dogmatist.' The grin became a chuckle. 'I'd love to listen in when he encounters Miles Crawford. Who d'you reckon as the winner?'

'The DGC, no doubt, but he'll still give me stick. Possibly you, as well.'

'Won't be able to resist it,' Max agreed. 'Colonel Trelawney's back on Sunday, thank God.' He bit into the second Twix baton. 'Unless the team brings in evidence that must be acted on immediately, I suggest we let things lie until Monday. We have a mess dinner tonight to welcome the Drumdorrans – attendance obligatory – and the funeral's being held tomorrow. Adequate reason to keep relations sweet while emotions run high. I don't know about you, but what appeared to be a mountain is fast turning into a molehill.'

'Those guys and their bloody IEDs!'

'Mm, but even an alarm clock and dynamite in a suitcase is more sinister than aerosols put in for a laugh. We *have* to discover who was behind that.' His telephone rang, and he raised his eyebrows enquiringly. 'Do I say you're not available at present?'

'Yes.' He got swiftly from his chair. 'I'm off to Max-ee-million, but don't tell him that.'

Having deflected the bleat with the truth that Tom was not available, Max pondered what action he should take about Jenny Greene. He had told Brenda he would speak to the Medical Officer about the child's habit of falling asleep at any time of day, but he was curiously unwilling to drive to the Medical Centre. When he left home this morning MacPherson's vehicle had still been on the forecourt. Blocked in by his own, of course, but the Scot could have asked Clare to move hers, then back out through the gap. *If* he had wanted to leave. But he had clearly been in no hurry to do that.

Max decided he would instead talk to Jean Greene himself; suggest she take Jenny to Captain Goodey for advice. He took a chance on finding her at home. If she was not, he could always telephone later. He could telephone now, come to that, but he felt the need for action.

The spur had been removed from both investigations, which left him feeling restless. An alarm clock and a stick of dynamite. How often had that ploy been used in the black and white war films he had collected over the years? The description *improvised explosive device* had been used so often in connection with the war in Afghanistan one's mind immediately read terrorist activity into the letters IED. Particularly in a military setting.

What he had now to ensure was that whoever inserted one into the bonfire with the intention of making a point, drawing attention to his anger over some personal sense of injustice, was given appropriate punishment. As for Eva McTavish, the team would surely come up with evidence to show she had been pill-popping at the Sports Ground, or knocking back the vodka. A suicide note would clinch the matter, but Hector had almost certainly destroyed it. If challenged, his mother would doubtless have no hesitation in backing up his claim of a newscutting having been sent to her. It was a lie Hector knew they would recognize, but be unable to prove. Frustration in every direction, and a boring dinner tonight to make much of the new Scottish members of the Mess. Small wonder he felt distinctly unsettled.

Arriving at the familiar house, it looked as if Max had caught Jean Greene on the point of going out. Jenny was being lifted into her car seat, and several stout carrier bags stood on the pavement by the open boot. Max drew up and got out. Jenny spotted him and yelled his name while resisting her mother's attempt to put her legs through the restraining straps. Laughing, Max joined Jean who had realized she was facing the impossible and was lifting the wriggling child out of the car again.

'I'm not used to such flattering female attention,' he said, still laughing as he took Jenny from her. 'Hallo. Not watching Paddington buy a new tablecloth today?'

Jenny shook her head. 'Mummy has to get rid of the bloody bottles.'

Trying hard to wipe the smile from his face, Max looked at Jean and was surprised to see a tide of red flooding her face.

'She repeats everything I say,' she offered lamely. 'I didn't know she'd overheard my phone conversation just now.'

Max nodded but he had seen the furtive glance she gave at the bags on the pavement, and guessed there was more behind her unease than her garrulous child's embarrassing repetition of an oath.

'Maybe she was asleep again, and woke while you were still speaking to your caller,' he suggested. 'That's what I've come to talk to you about.'

'I have an appointment, Max,' she said hurriedly. 'Make it this afternoon, then you can have tea with us. Jenny'd love that.'

'I won't keep you,' he assured her. 'I happened to tell a friend yesterday about how Jenny falls asleep so easily at any time of the day, and she said you should talk to a doctor about it. She's a nursing sister, so she knows what she's talking about. I told her I'd pass her advice to you.'

'Oh, yes. Thank you. I'll do that.' She took the small girl back from him. 'Jenny, we have to go to see Stephanie. She's waiting to show you her new kitten.'

The kitten proved to be a greater attraction than Max, so Jenny was soon strapped into the seat and urging her mother to hurry.

'Thanks, Max. I'll do that,' Jean repeated, and when he made no move to go, added, 'It's good of you to take so much trouble. I appreciate it.' Then, when he held his ground, smiled a goodbye. 'I really should be on my way.'

'Of course. I'll help you to put the bloody bottles in the boot,' he murmured, returning her smile. 'Taking them for recycling?'

'Yes. I can manage them, thanks.'

Ignoring that, he walked to where the bags stood and lifted the first. When Jean tried to take it from him, insisting that she was quite able to deal with them, Max's guess became a certainty. Setting the bag inside the boot he pulled a vodka bottle from it – then several more – strangers in a collection bearing wine or lemonade labels. Jean was now looking as guilty as he expected.

'I'll take these to check for finger prints,' he informed her crisply. 'Eva McTavish's prints, which I've no doubt will be on each one of these vodka bottles.'

EIGHT

The flush slowly faded as Jean Greene offered an agitated explanation for the fact that she had been intending to rid herself of the bottles now in the boot of her car.

'I discovered them under the bed right up against the wall when I cleared her room first thing this morning.'

'So why didn't you call me? You knew I was interested in knowing if Eva was sober when she left your house. *Didn't you*?'

Jean licked her lips nervously. 'She'd been with me for a whole week. She probably liked a tipple in private now and again.'

'And maybe she drank a lot on Tuesday afternoon as the overture to her plan to end her life,' he said coldly. 'Destroying evidence of a suicide is a crime, Mrs Greene. I must ask you to come with me to Headquarters to make an official statement.'

She looked aghast. 'That's ridiculous! The medical report is indisputable proof that she meant to kill herself. Where she actually drank the vodka is surely immaterial.'

'The medical report is indisputable proof of what caused her death. It's not proof of suicide.'

She stared at him wide-eyed. 'But of course it is! You're surely not suggesting . . .' Cries of urgency from Jenny took her attention for a moment or two, then she resumed her protest. 'She's to be buried tomorrow. For the good Lord's sake let her rest in peace.'

Max returned her look unwaveringly. 'I suggest we drive to your friend's house and leave Jenny there while you come with me to Headquarters,' he said in a tone that left no room for argument.

'You're not serious?' she asked in disbelief.

'Very,' he assured her. 'And I'll take those bottles.'

He waited in his car while Jean took the little girl in to the friend whose daughter had a new kitten. He had no idea what excuse was offered for leaving her there, but she came through the front gate looking stormy and refused to travel with Max.

'Have nae fears I'll no come,' she told him bitingly, lapsing into her native brogue. 'I've a wee girl who needs me, remember, so don't continue with this nonsense aye longer than needs be.'

Max drove to Headquarters at a sedate pace, Jean following, which allowed him time to ponder this development. Could her behaviour be regarded as suspicious rather than unthinking? Admittedly, the medical report gave no mention of violence being used on Eva to make her swallow the mixture that robbed her of her life, but he knew there were ways of making victims swallow noxious substances without laying a hand on them.

Vocal threats could be powerful weapons, particularly if the threats were against loved ones. The McTavishes had no children, but what of Eva's parents or siblings? Had she been blackmailed into killing herself? Max realized he must discover a lot more about the Pipe Major's kith and kin, and also about the depth of the relationship between Jean and Hector. Eva had married the boy next door who could blaspheme for Scotland from an early age, she had said. Jean had grown up in the same village, so she must know him well. Just how well, he now wondered.

Using the hands-free facility he called up Connie to report in asap to assist with the interview, then drove on to the forecourt. Jean pulled in to park beside him, and climbed from her car still looking stormy. She marched past without a word as he opened the main door for her, then refused his offer of tea or coffee with an icy 'No'.

Staff Melly glanced up curiously from his work on the Gibbons case but said nothing, so silence reigned until Connie arrived. Max spent those minutes checking out Hector McTavish's details. Both parents still living; father the local sexton, mother a cook. Brother, Fusilier Callan Richard (deceased). The date of his demise tallied with the period Hector had spoken of.

Max then entered Callan's name and was referred to Redundant Personnel. That produced a thought-provoking fact.

Callan Richard McTavish had died from wounds received in action in Afghanistan on January twenty-ninth that year. Max now better understood Drumdorran rage over Eva's death believed to have resulted from the exploding bonfire. Two grievous losses for their much loved and respected Pipe Major within six months. Also, one for the regiment itself, as the death of any member would be, albeit in a different battalion. A regiment was like a very large family. Members frequently quarrelled, but they would let no outsider harm their fellows. One soldier might fight tooth and nail with another, yet stand beside him in defence against any threat to who they were and what they stood for.

When Connie arrived, Max was considering the truth that Jean would also have known Callan McTavish equally well. He should have questioned her more closely on the subject of that family, instead of allowing the woman's easy warmth and the charm of a vivacious child to lull him into wistful thoughts of what might have been. He had accepted Jean's caustic assessment of Hector without question. He now sensed there were depths to be plumbed; depths that should explain why Eva took that fatal step and maybe clarify whether she took it willingly or was driven to do so.

Once Jean was sitting in an interview room facing Max and Connie across a table on which Max had deposited the bag containing the vodka bottles, he made it clear to Jean that she was not under arrest then began the questioning.

'You told me that you found these bottles under the bed in the room occupied by Eva McTavish for seven days, until she left your house to go and watch the fireworks at the Sports Ground on Tuesday evening. Is that correct?'

'Yes. It was the first I knew of their presence. I'm not in the habit of searching my guests' rooms.' It was clipped and angry.

'When I came to your house yesterday morning you told me that you and Eva had quarrelled and avoided each other for most of Tuesday, the day her husband arrived here with his regiment. You gave that as the reason why you couldn't offer an opinion on her sobriety when she left your house.'

'Yes.'

'So it must have been obvious to you that I felt it was important to know the answer to that.'

'But I couldn't give it, could I?' she returned swiftly, watching Connie recording everything in her notebook.

'When you found these bottles this morning, what did you think?'

She was ready for that. 'I supposed she'd taken a dram or two each night to help her sleep.'

Max changed direction. 'Outside your house about half an hour ago you said that the medical report on Eva's death is indisputable proof of her suicide. You could only know that because someone who had read it told you so. Was that person Hector McTavish?'

Her dark eyes challenged him. 'Is that surprising? His wife had been staying with me for a week, until she walked away that evening and never came back. I still had all her things. Who else would he talk to about his loss?'

'The Padre, Major Carnegie, Duncan MacPherson, the Bandmaster, Drum Major Lennox, a particular friend. For the members of a regiment there's always someone to talk to when in trouble. That he chose you suggests that you have a closer relationship than you've revealed so far.'

Her eyes blazed with anger. 'What's that supposed to mean?'

Max ignored that and indicated the bag containing the bottles. 'When you found these this morning why did you feel you must immediately "get rid of the bloody bottles", your words repeated by your daughter in my hearing? Why did you try to prevent me from seeing them?' When she remained silent, Max aired his suspicion. 'That telephone call during which Jenny overheard you say that, was it to Hector McTavish?'

For around half a minute she struggled with the decision on how to answer that, studying her hands that lay on her grey wool trousers that had probably been made by the cottage industry she promoted in her shop, like her red roll-neck jumper. Then she looked at him defiantly.

'You do nae see it, do you? The deed is done. It's over. Eva is to be laid to rest tomorrow. Let her receive God's mercy in peace.'

Whenever witnesses began to bring God into their evidence, Max grew very suspicious. He decided it was time for shock tactics. 'If Eva's prints are on those bottles I could charge you with attempting to destroy vital evidence. That's a serious offence.'

She was visibly rattled. 'Are you totally inhuman?'

'No, I'm simply doing my job. In any case of sudden death I have to establish how and why it happened. People don't end their lives without strong cause for doing so, unless they are insane. Eva McTavish was not. I can't report to the Garrison Commander that a soldier's wife committed suicide on this base *for some reason or other*. Hector claims she must have taken an overdose of pills by mistake, but a woman doesn't drink most of a bottle of vodka at the same time by mistake. Something or someone drove her to do what she did, and I believe you can help me to find the answer. By refusing to do that you're hindering a police enquiry, which is also an offence I could charge you with.'

Connie, who had been scribbling her own version of shorthand, suddenly intervened. 'Maybe you'd appreciate a cup of tea while you think that over.' She smiled a message at Max. 'I'll get us all some, shall I?'

He nodded, got to his feet and flexed his shoulders. After his restless night he was feeling tense and achey. Connie had gauged the situation right. She usually did. She was very perceptive. There had been a tragedy in her own life and Connie had supported both her mother and grandmother through their hard times, which was why Max always selected Connie when empathy was needed during an interview.

'You have to understand that Hector's a very proud man.'

Jean's voice broke into Max's thoughts and he swung to face her. 'That was apparent when we met.'

The rigid pose she had maintained had become more relaxed, and there was now sadness rather than defiance in her expression. 'It came as a terrible blow. Can you no possibly understand that?'

Oh yes, he understood the impact of terrible blows, but all he said was, 'Go on.'

'He can only accept what happened as a mistake. I told you

Eva was forever popping pills, so there's every chance that she lost track of how many she had taken. People do.'

'Yes, people do. Old people who forget easily, or who are generally confused. People in their thirties might, in a stressful situation, double dose, but they soon realize what they've done and rush to get medical advice.'

She gazed at him for some while. 'You just refuse to help him, don't you?'

'You think I should write an official report stating that a woman died through accidentally swallowing more drugs and alcohol than she intended?' Max demanded.

'She's gone, so does it matter what you put in your report? It's just a piece of paper that'll be filed and forgotten about.' She leaned forward urgently. 'When relatives ask if their loved ones suffered, aren't they always told death would have been instantaneous? Lies to comfort, Max.'

His suspicion that Jean and Hector were closer friends than he had been told became more of a certainty with every comment she made. With that certainty came a growing dislike of this woman who had seemed refreshingly pleasant on earlier encounters. He resumed the seat facing her.

'Words of comfort for grieving next of kin don't go on the official medical documents, Jean. *They* give every detail of a patient's death throes, the physical traumas, the fight for survival against the odds. Yes, these reports are filed, but not necessarily forgotten. There are numerous cases when suspicions have arisen months, even years, later and the medical facts are used as proof in an investigation.' His voice grew harsher. 'Hector will have received many words of comfort from his fellows, but my job is to record the facts. Don't expect me to go along with the fantasy that his wife was a confused idiot, because that's what he's implying.'

At that point, Connie arrived with a tray bearing cups of tea and a hiatus was created by adding sugar, stirring and sipping, during which Max mentally reviewed the implications of why Jean had given him such a scathing description of Hector on his first visit. Then he continued the interview along a new direction.

'Tell me about Callan McTavish, Jean. You grew up in the

same village as the brothers, must have attended the same school, so you'd know a lot about their background.'

It brought a frown, a new wariness in her expression. 'That has nothing to do with Eva's death.'

'She carried a photograph of him in her handbag. Why was he called Tammy?'

'Foolish woman,' she said in a half-whisper. Then, because both Max and Connie watched in silence for her reply, she was eventually driven to respond.

'The family lived in the house next to Eva's parents. The boys were known in the village as Satan and the Saint. Hector was up to every kind of devilry, while Tammy just dreamed of having heroic adventures. His fondness for Tam o' Shanter earned him that nickname. He was the better-looking brother, but Hector had the village girls in thrall because of his wickedness.'

Thinking of the sexton father, and Drum Major Lennox's reference to the widower being at his prayers, Max asked, 'Real wickedness or just a lively boy's escapades?'

Jean gave a reminiscent half-smile. 'Unruly, daring, defiant was the verdict of the kinder village residents. His father believed he was a disciple of the Devil and enrolled him in the Drumdorrans as soon as he was old enough, believing the discipline would drive the evil from him.' Seeing Max's raised eyebrows, she nodded. 'He's a deeply religious man and lives by those strict tenets even in this enlightened age. And I'm telling you, Max, that his boyhood years have become a source of shame to Hector because his father had it right. But the Drumdorrans have tamed him too much. He's well on the road to righteousness, and this could destroy what remains of the old Hector coming so soon after Tammy's death.'

She addressed the next remarks to Connie. 'His young brother secretly admired Hector's dash and daring, longed to emulate him, so he joined the Drumdorrans, too. Hector had never revealed to his family the part he actually plays in the regiment, so he now blames himself for Tammy's loss in action.'

Connie bore out Max's confidence in her compassionate understanding by saying gently, 'That's why he's desperately holding on to the theory that Eva died through her own carelessness, not through any fault of his own.'

Max had departed early in order to change into uniform to attend the welcome dinner in the Mess, so Tom co-ordinated the reports brought in by the team at the end of the day. His visit to Max-ee-million had not improved his mood, but he had brought away two of the giant rockets they made and given them to the explosives experts with a snide apology for not providing an alarm clock and a small suitcase to put it in.'

The Estonian, whose name was so difficult to pronounce he was known simply as Maxee, had been only too pleased to make him a present of the fireworks; would have given him an entire boxful in order to get rid of him and the blond German, who had made no secret of his disappointment that Heather had not turned up. Both policemen were told that Greta was no longer working at the factory. Herr Gans had 'made of the big complainings' and because he was 'enormous in the town' would 'make the many cancel from old orders'. It was 'disasters and much unfortunates'.

The young German had dismissed Maxee's melodrama, telling Tom Max-ee-million was the premier fireworks supplier in the region, and Otto Gans was no more than a balloon, which Tom took to mean a windbag full of his own importance – a description he could endorse after last night's encounter with the pompous fool.

There was probably little doubt that Charlie Carter's predicament over whether to leave the Army or lose Greta had been solved for him. Just as well, because Carter would not be off the hook for Tuesday's explosion if Captain Knott's boys claimed material from those rockets was used to produce it. How satisfying it would be to deflate Gans with proof of his daughter's involvement.

For Tom, finding the person or people responsible for that was their premier task of the moment, not the suicide of Eva McTavish. Max was making a big thing of something straightforward; seeing depths where there were none. The medical findings proved she had swallowed enough noxious substances to end her life: there was evidence of an unhappy marriage and a selfish, uncaring husband. Surely her death was unquestionably by her own hand.

Max did not, or would not see it. He had set someone the task of contacting US newspapers for copies of their reviews of the Drumdorrans' concerts – a pure waste of time in anyone's book – then he had learned from Jean Greene this morning that Hector had kept his family in total ignorance of his role in the regiment, so he would never have posted to his mother a rave review of the band's performance. Max had imparted that news just before he left for home, along with the fact that Hector had 'found God' after joining the Drumdorrans. That had killed Tom's dwindling interest in the case, and he now bent all his efforts on the bonfire fiasco. No bible-thumping and bagpipes involved!

Aware that he really must settle the baby situation with Maggie and Gina that evening, Tom nevertheless prepared to spend as long as it took to collate the information brought in by the team at the end of a day of monotonous questioning; that boring but essential task in every case. However, the first reports were sparse and added nothing new. No witness could say exactly when the late-delivered box containing the rockets arrived, exactly where it had stood during final preparations of the set piece, or exactly how many rockets had finally been set off.

Beeny said, 'Corporal Lines thought he had probably opened the box himself, because he had been waiting for the items to complete the set piece, but he was adamant that he hadn't counted the freebie rockets.' He grinned. 'He went all arty and told me I wouldn't understand the pressure he had been under. I swear, if he had long hair he'd have tossed it back and sighed theatrically.'

'Yes, most amusing,' grunted Tom. 'Don't spread it around the Army now employs luvvies.'

Piercey revealed that he had again questioned the men who had collected and delivered the stuff designated for the bonfire. 'They all maintained that Corporal Naish had checked each load and rejected anything he considered duff or unsuitable. Under pressure, Naish admitted to agreeing to tie a straw effigy to the cone.

'I know the Boss has already interviewed the wankers who made it and talked Naish into doing as they asked, but now we're aware of the alarm clock and stick of dynamite IED, I thought it was worth talking to them again.'

Tom said irritably, 'Can we now drop the alarm clock and stick of dynamite?'

'Might explode, sir,' murmured Piercey, with a Cheshire cat smile.

'Get on with your report, Sergeant,' he snapped. 'If it's at all useful.'

Still amused, Piercey said, 'I tracked down three of them. They, sir, are not at all useful. Not to the Army. First time in a war zone they'll . . .'

'We're not here to listen to your personal opinions. Do you have any info appertaining to the case you're supposed to be investigating?' Tom demanded in parade ground volume.

Schooling his expression, Piercey said, 'They're mechanics. Officially. But they appear to be little more than greasers. I doubt they'd have the nous to do anything more than stick a few firecrackers inside the effigy.' He glanced swiftly at his notes. 'All three claim they're being victimized. Told me they're going to apply to Second Lieutenant Freeman for advice on what to do about it.'

Tom gave a snort of derision. 'As the straw man they wanted to burn was meant to represent him I can imagine what advice they'll be given.' He scanned the faces before him. 'Come on! We're getting nowhere. Hasn't any one of you something of real import to say?'

Heather had been riffling through the pages of her notebook, and now offered her contribution. 'I spent all day knocking on doors after making a list of families with children, who were the most likely attendees at the Sports Ground.' She pulled a wry face. 'Got a mouthful of complaints from most of them, but several gave me useful info regarding Eva McTavish.'

Oh God, back to her, thought Tom. 'We're presently discussing the events on Tuesday night,' he reminded her shortly.

'This does concern Tuesday night, sir,' she pointed out, still cool after being deprived of another meeting with the blond German at Max-ee-million.

He waited in silence for her to continue, casting an eye on the large MoD clock on the wall behind her and thinking of the difficult evening to come when he reached home.

'Mrs Grace Sparsholt remembered seeing a woman sitting in the stand by herself and swallowing some pills. She imagined the woman was waiting for someone to join her, and perhaps had a headache.' She referred to her notes. 'This was shortly before the fireworks began. Her attention was then taken by them. She didn't see the woman again.'

Heather flipped over the page and continued. 'Mrs Poole said a woman came to the stand and, although there were plenty of places, climbed to the back row and huddled in the corner. She thought it might be because she was making calls on her mobile and the children on the lower levels were making a lot of noise. She told me the woman was not someone she'd seen around the base before, and she wondered why she was there alone. She didn't look very happy.'

She turned over several more pages, saying, 'I've statements from five others which bear all this out. A stranger on her own either swallowing pills or making calls on a mobile. One – a Mrs Lyons – said she thought the woman was crying, and she would have approached her if she hadn't got hers and a neighbour's children to keep an eye on.

'I then spoke to the paramedics who came with the ambulance. They told me Eva was lying on the ground very near the ropes preventing any approach to the bonfire, so she must have left her corner in the stand as soon as it was lit and walked as close to it as possible. I wonder why.'

'We'll never know,' mused Connie, 'but if she was really making a cry for help she would need to be close to those who could answer it. In a dark corner at the back of the stand she wouldn't be seen until it was too late.'

Heather had not finished. 'I was about to call it a day when Mrs Cleeves at my last port of call told me her friend had been standing beside the person who had been injured and taken off in the ambulance. She called her then and there, and handed the phone to me.' She cast a swift glance at her notebook. 'Gwynneth Jones works with the Forces Welfare Service and lives in town. She told me that she grew aware of a woman on her own coming up beside her because she stumbled and almost fell against her. Mrs Jones had the impression that the stranger was unaware of what she was doing; said she looked set to walk straight at the bonfire without realizing that she was risking danger. Looking back, Mrs Jones remembers a vacant look in the woman's eyes which were red from crying. Of course, what happened next put an end to her intention to lead the woman away and question her.'

Heather summed up what she had learned. 'There's no doubt Eva went to the Sports Ground fully intending to swallow the pills there, *where she would be surrounded by people who would help her*. If the explosion hadn't occurred there's every possibility that Gwynneth Jones would have recognized her condition, called the paramedics who'd identify signs of an overdose, and her life would have been saved. Perhaps.'

'Good work,' said Tom briskly. 'We can now close the case and report the death as intentional suicide.'

Olly Simpson, who had been on standby at Headquarters, looked up from his doodling and added a footnote. 'A messenger from the hospital turned up this afternoon having been redirected by Captain Goodey. Eva's mobile had been found behind the locker in which her clothes had been stored, so they sent it to the doctor to pass to the husband. She thought the Boss would want to do that, but he'd already left so I contacted the provider and said we urgently needed info in a case of sudden death. I exaggerated somewhat, but the girl was impressed and emailed the list of calls made on Tuesday.' He pursed his mouth. 'There were seventeen. All to the same number. I checked it out. A mobile registered to Pipe Major H McTavish. I'd say his wife was desperately calling for help, wouldn't you?'

'And Hector chose not to hear it,' said Connie. 'Poor woman.'

NINE

The ante room of the Mess was crowded when Max reluctantly entered. Loud voices, loud laughter, loud uniforms. Instead of the universal khaki the regimental officers were displaying their colours tonight, not simply for protocol's sake but also so that the new Scottish members could tell at a glance with whom each of them served. The Drumdorrans outshone them all in their tartan trews.

Although Miles Crawford was officially a member of a different mess on the base, he was present in his capacity as Deputy Garrison Commander. Max spotted him standing, drink in hand, in a group of senior officers which included Major Carnegie, who appeared to be holding forth with an ease more in keeping with a host than a guest. A very commanding personality who would surely meet his match when Colonel Trelawney returned on Sunday.

Standing close to these 'élite' was Major Duncan MacPherson talking to someone who, when bodies shifted, Max found to be Clare Goodey. Natural enough for doctors to be drawn to each other, he supposed. He had crossed their shared lounge to knock on her door thinking they would return to base in one car, but there had been no response from her.

One glance from his window revealed that her car was missing from its alloted parking space. He had felt unjustifiably nettled. After all, she led her own life, had her own friends. Just because they occasionally ate at Herr Blomfeld's riverside inn together, it was only when they'd both had a long day and were averse to preparing a meal at home. It was sensible to use one car then. And tonight, an inner voice said. Only when he was backing his car prior to heading for the base did Max remember his churlish refusal of her invitation the previous night. He had thought her above taking umbrage over something as trivial as that. In any case, the dashing

Scottish major had stayed the night as her guest. Surely a more attractive outcome.

'By God, I do believe it's ma old buddy Max Rydal.'

Max turned from his reflections to see a face he'd known well when it was above a school blazer. He smiled warmly. 'Jock Madison! I thought your entire family had emigrated to the land of Oz.'

'So we did. I joined their army, then transferred to the Drumdorrans when Mother died and the old man yearned for the banks and braes. My sister Fran married a guy with a smallholding near Adelaide.' His eyes narrowed. 'Didn't you have a thing about her in the Upper Sixth?'

'Among others. She liked to play the field.'

'Still did until she met Griff. He gave her an ultimatum. Him, or half a dozen. Couldn't have both.'

'She settled for that?' asked Max in surprise, recalling Fran Madison's love of tempting and teasing.

'She grew up, Max. It comes to all of us sooner or later. I married a Danish girl last year and there's a babe on the way.' He smiled. 'I don't regret abandoning the pursuit and conquer regime. Fun, but there's something very satisfying in having a home and a family to return to. With active service very much on today's agenda, it's good to know you'll leave something worthwhile if you cop it. Those lads of eighteen, nineteen – hardly have time to know who they are before they're gone.' He glanced around. 'Let's have another bloody drink before we grow too maudlin.'

A steward caught the hand signal and weaved his way towards them, giving Max time to prepare an answer to what he knew he was certain to be asked once Madison had another sherry in his hand. His former schoolfriend, whose real name was Kenneth, would have no notion of how his talk of home and family had affected Max. The pursuit and conquer regime had never been a real part of his life. There had been girls at university who offered sex freely to almost any male student they fancied, and Max had sometimes taken advantage of a short-lived, carefree episode, but he had probably even then been looking for a stable, loving relationship.

His mother had died when Max was six. Andrew Rydal's

military career had made it impossible for him to keep his son with him, so Max had become a prep school boarder. From then on he had never known a home life. If his father was stationed somewhere easily accessible, Max went to him for school holidays; if he was not, Max stayed at the school or accepted invitations from friends' families who took pity on him.

Andrew had not married again despite being a man whom women found irresistible, so those times that father and son did spend together were in hotel rooms or bachelor accommodation. Polite conversation; the correct expressions of enjoyment of visits to zoos, short voyages on yachts, days in the sun watching Andrew play cricket, treks over mountains; earnest declarations of not minding being left alone while Andrew fulfilled his social duties. It had been a relief to them both when school began again.

The youthful military policeman had encountered Susan while investigating a claim that the dispenser at the local chemist had sent the wrong pills to a soldier's wife, causing her to collapse. Proof that the patient's child had emptied the contents of several bottles, then replaced them in mixed quantities had cleared Susan of blame, but Max had found the woman he wanted to spend his life with.

It had taken Susan no more than two years to realize that winters on Salisbury Plain and a husband whose duty took him away a great deal were not what she wanted. A corporal with come-to-bed eyes apparently made her life bearable, but they had died together when his car crashed during a storm. Max could have checked who had sired Susan's baby, but he preferred to believe Alexander had been his son.

When Livya Cordwell had entered Max's world he had been as sure as with Susan that he wanted to spend his life with her. Two months ago two shocks had penetrated his determined courtship. Firstly, he had received an invitation to his father's marriage to a French Cultural Envoy ten years his junior – a relationship Max had been completely unaware of. Two nights after the wedding the second, most wounding, shock had come when he discovered that Livya was hopelessly in love with the new bridegroom whom she served as ADC.

Jock Madison, slender, dark haired and self-assured took two glasses from the steward's tray and handed one to Max. 'So, what about you? Whatever prompted you to use your school Officer Corps experience to become a *policeman*? You were one of the brightest among us; could've entered any of the most élite regiments with your natural ability and your father's backing.' He smiled reminiscently. 'A number of us aspired to emulate him. Did you know that? Couldn't do much about the film star good looks, of course, but we worked hard at cricket and rugger and athletics, trying to reach his standard. Envied you having a parent like him.' He cocked his head to study Max shrewdly. 'Didn't inherit his skill, did you.'

'No,' agreed Max, thinking of the rows of silver cups with Andrew Rydal's name engraved upon them. He had taken the easy option and given up team sports on leaving school. He now enjoyed rowing a hired skiff on the river, and cross-country running over nearby heathland – solo activities at which he could not disappoint anyone's expectations that he would be as brilliant a sportsman as Rydal Senior.

Realizing Madison was one of those men who, at social events, asked questions then rattled on without waiting for a reply, Max headed him in a new direction.

'Did the Drumdorrans allow you to retain the rank you had in Oz?'

Madison grimaced. 'Made me drop from captain to lieutenant, but I'm due to pick up the third pip early next year.'

'Pity about the trouble on the regiment's arrival. Aggression at the start takes a long time to cool. We're putting out extra patrols tomorrow night. The funeral's certain to revive resentment in your squaddies, who'll go to the bars and discos bent on relieving their feelings.'

Madison was intent on trying to attract the steward's attention once more and persuade him to cross to where they stood beside a table bearing mess silver dating back several hundred years.

'Aye, I daresay they will,' he agreed, turning with a sigh to concentrate on Max again. 'Having lived in Oz for some years I no longer have the fervour of the born and bred Scot whose life revolves around pride of heritage and clan loyalty. We have a number of them in the regiment. A small number, mind, but they soon rouse up the rank and file who enjoy a good set-to for the pure pleasure of a fight.

'Hector McTavish is a guy who revels in the words and music of the ancient songs and airs that extol Scots as prime specimens of manhood who can outwit and overcome any enemy. It's not surprising that he's regarded with great respect and affection by laddies who like to think themselves supermen. They showed their support for him with their fists.'

'And a lot else,' Max reminded him sharply. 'Did they react like that when his brother died?'

Madison shook his head. 'Killed in action is a different matter. There's an element of pride in that death, if you understand my meaning. The lads drink to the memory of their comrades, but soberly. Their fight is with the enemy and they can't wait to get out there and wreak vengeance. What happened on Tuesday was the result of carelessness, of stupidity by those men already on this base. They saw it as murder of an innocent woman who was the wife of one of their number already mourning the loss of his brother.'

Hearing this Max realized that the truth of how Eva McTavish had died was known by only one or two senior members of the regiment, who seemed set on keeping it that way. Closing ranks, which was understandable enough, but Max's team had the facts and so had Maddox's Redcaps. So had Jean Greene. Sooner or later rumours would begin circulating about police interest in the woman's actions during the firework display, and witnesses would discover that too many of them had seen Eva swallowing pills and making calls on her mobile. Oh yes, to hide the truth on a military base it had to be written on paper and marked Top Secret.

'So long as your lads don't harbour resentment for years to come,' he told Madison. 'We don't want weekly punch-ups over it.'

'Och, no! When she's laid to rest tomorrow the anger will be buried with her.'

Max was not so confident of that. He knew how fast old scores rose to the surface when beer flowed and aggressive young men needed an outlet for it. Their conversation was brought to a halt at that point by the short bugle call that, on formal occasions, announced the moment to move through to the dining room. Immediately after it came the sound of bagpipes, which was greeted with cheers by the incoming members who moved forward eagerly to follow the piper to where the long tables were set for an elaborate meal.

Moving with the flow Max found himself walking beside Clare, who said, 'It's lovely, isn't it. Pity we don't get piped in every time.'

'Tom Black wouldn't think it lovely,' he replied. 'He can't stand the sound.'

She glanced up enquiringly as they shuffled towards the hall. 'How about you?'

'It's my kind of music. Even better in large numbers.'

Still studying him, she said, 'You look something of a stranger dressed in uniform. Quite impressive. Pity you had to discard your red-covered hat that adds a dash of colour.'

He shook his head. 'No competition with tartan trews. Your medical pal puts the rest of us in the shade.'

'Yes, he does. Can't wait to see him in the kilt.'

They were separated while crossing the hall, and Max knew he had been placed on a different table from her. His dining neighbours would be two Royal Cumberland Rifles officers whom he knew on nodding terms from when he had lived in a room here.

Finding his seat, Max then glanced across at Duncan MacPherson. The Scot did look rather magnificent. Although he was a doctor in the same corps as Clare, he had somehow wangled permission to wear the colourful trews with his RAMC tunic. Well, it would be a plucky man who denied the red-haired giant, he supposed.

His attention was then caught by a curious flickering light brightening the window behind MacPherson. It took no more than a moment or two for Max to identify it, and his pulse quickened. Disregarding protocol, he swiftly crossed the room to confirm what he suspected. The hedge surrounding the car park on three sides was alight and burning so fiercely the flames were liable to engulf those cars standing nearest to it.

* * *

They stood in a group surveying the dismal scene as firemen rolled up their hoses that had covered the vehicles on the perimeter of the car park with foam, which a blustery wind was spreading everywhere. The bonus of having fire engines and manpower on the base meant very swift responses to alarm calls. Even so, the hedge was now no more than a three-sided square of bare, burnt twigs. Max's prompt call on his mobile had led to the fire being contained and the threat of exploding cars averted. All personnel in the Mess had been warned to be ready to evacuate the building, if necessary, and worried car owners had watched events from the windows.

'It looks a sorry sight,' commented the Chief Fire Officer. 'Second time in a week. In my experience that doesn't equate with the law of averages. I think we have an arsonist on the base, and if it isn't one of the Jocks it's someone who wants them gone.'

Max continued to gaze at the foam starting to plop in sooty globules on the tarmac, his eyes narrowed in speculation. No, it did not align with the law of averages. Evidence showed that Tuesday's calamity had been the result of a deliberate act; he had little doubt that what had occurred here had not been caused accidentally.

'Don't spread that opinion around, Chip,' he warned. 'Admittedly, both incidents have happened since the Scots marched in, but we've no evidence to show a connection with them. Feelings are running hot enough already without fanning the flames.'

'It's my job to douse them,' Chip Reynolds returned sharply. 'All I'm saying is . . .'

'I know what you're saying, and I'm telling you not to,' Max snapped. 'We presently have the Drumdorrans laying blame without knowing the facts. It'll take very little to set them off again, and we're the people who have to deal with it.'

After a drawn out silence, Max softened his tone. 'I agree that this was a deliberate act, most probably by the same hand as the one that put that IED in the bonfire. How soon can you examine the scene and come up with the cause?'

The reply was brusque. 'Are you booked in for the night?'

'OK, I get the message. We'll leave you to it and get details from the owners whose vehicles were alongside the hedge, dodging the ammo sure to be flying our way from the DGC and Major Carnegie.'

Reynolds moved away to where his men were taking a breather with mugs of tea brought out from the kitchen to slake their thirsts and clear smoke from their throats. Max then concentrated on Tom and George Maddox, both of whom he had called out to the scene.

'He's bloody right. It's too easy to imagine a link with the advent of the Drumdorrans. We have to get to the root cause before anything further develops.'

He shivered in the blasts of cold air sweeping down from the Arctic. Tom was wearing a padded coat over his suit, and George was warmly clad in his greatcoat, but Max was dressed for a social occasion in the smart military uniform he rarely needed to wear.

'I'm going to be stretched this weekend,' George reminded him. 'The funeral's going down at midday, which is sure to revive aggro in the bars and discos later.' He nodded at the foam-covered cars. 'This'll rachet it up a dozen or more notches. Krenkel's been made aware of the situation and he's putting on extra *Polizei* patrols. I'll give him a bell about our increased concern following this.'

Max sighed, his breath clouding in the cold air. 'Until Reynolds gives us a run down on what caused this there's nothing for you to do here, George. This is SIB's pigeon, because it's my guess someone is making a statement that's liable to grow progressively more vicious. This could have been a really serious blaze. Fuelled-up vehicles in close proximity are highly inflammable. If Reynolds' team had been attending another emergency, it could have . . .' He broke off with a frown. 'There's a thought! Chummy could have created a diversion on the far side of the base designed to delay their response to this call from the Mess. That he didn't suggests to me that this wasn't meant to get out of hand and endanger lives.'

Tom rose to that. 'Fire is unpredictable, especially in a strong wind like there is tonight. He couldn't have been certain there'd not be casualties. The bastard who's doing this is careless of lives. The McTavish woman could have died from that chest wound, and any of those kids could have been fatally hurt.'

'But we've already established that the IED in itself wouldn't have created such a dangerous explosion. It was the combination of it with the stuff that had been inserted by brainless squaddies.'

'You think whoever's behind this has brains?' demanded Tom.

'Inasmuch as I'd wager he was here over an hour or so ago checking that all vehicles were empty before setting the fires. I'm no expert but it's pretty obvious he went the whole way around this area starting fires every few yards, because the hedge burned so evenly. He intended the flames to be noticed by people in the Mess before it spread to the cars.'

George made a point as he prepared to leave. 'You're saying you believe it wasn't meant to get out of hand and risk lives. So what was the reasoning behind it?'

'I wish I knew,' Max confessed. 'He's deeply serious about whatever's causing him to do this; prepared to risk damaging cars to make his point. *Does* it connect with the Drumdorrans? He made his first move on the day they arrived, and there is a large number of them in the Mess right now, but he could be deliberately leading us from the truth.'

George Maddox was a calling-a-spade-a-spade type of man who found Max's theorizing too airy-fairy, particularly on a bitterly cold night, so he laid out his plans for the next day and departed.

'Christ, I'm freezing,' declared Max. 'Let's sit in your car while we get things straight before we go in there and take the flak.'

They walked to where Tom had left his 4x4 in the road, and sat in it glad of the comparative warmth and the chance to escape from the smell of smoke and burning.

'Sorry to ruin your evening, Tom, but I thought you'd want to be here. No plans to do something special, I hope.'

'Oh, no.'

It was said in such a curious tone, Max took the subject

further. 'Problems? You've been a bit abstracted for a while. Anything I can help with?'

Tom shook his head, gazing into the distance. 'The weighty business of being a father. You can't give advice on that.'

'No, I can't,' Max agreed hollowly.

As if he had recalled the tragedy that had robbed Max of parenthood, Tom glanced across at him with a rueful smile. 'It's the girls. Playing up. Maggie and Gina are at a tricky age; lead each other on. It gets to you when there's a big case on.'

'Mm, must do. You're lucky to have Nora behind you. If you had a wife like some we come across, *you* might be setting fires to make a statement,' he said in an attempt to lighten the atmosphere.

Tom merely nodded. 'There's one angle we haven't seriously considered. Is Chummy a Drumdorran Fusilier? It's possible for one of them to have put that IED in the bonfire on the day they came in. Difficult, but possible. Tonight's shindig would have been easy.'

Tom had turned on the heater, so Max was beginning to thaw out and relax. 'As you say, Tuesday would have been difficult, but possible. I can't immediately see the motive for that. What happened tonight ought to make sense because something particular was underway in the Mess which concerned the Drumdorrans. The only link with them at the bonfire party was the possibility that Eva McTavish was committing suicide during the fireworks display.'

Tom gave an impatient grunt. 'That case is closed. The team brought in enough witness statements this afternoon to prove the woman was doing just that, while calling her husband's number seventeen times on her mobile.'

Max frowned. 'There was no mobile with her effects.'

'The hospital sent it to Captain Goodey, who passed it to us. Olly Simpson checked on the calls made on Tuesday.'

'*Seventeen*?'

'None of them were answered.'

'The bastard! There's more to this case yet, Tom. That man McTavish is hiding something.'

'So what?' cried Tom irritably. 'Three quarters of the

personnel on this base are, no doubt, but until some crime is committed by them it's not our concern.' He pointed at the car park. 'That mess out there is, and Major Crawford is waiting for us to explain why his flaming dinner has been ruined, giving the Scottish incomers another example of how badly disciplined this base is.'

Annoyed by this outburst, Max said, 'OK, so let's go in and give them the one bit of good news; that out of the cast of thousands they're the only ones not under suspicion for this.'

Tom spent another night in the Sergeants' Mess, seeing little point in driving home in the early hours when he had to make an early start to return to base. There would be no opportunity to tackle the baby issue, anyway, a fact of which he tried not to be glad. Max had driven to his apartment to change from his uniform to a suit and warm topcoat, vowing to have a large early breakfast to compensate for the dinner he had missed out on.

The atmosphere in the Officers' Mess had been generally hostile. Majors Crawford and Carnegie were very angry, the Scot coldly so and the DGC on the verge of igniting with rage. The catering staff were furious over the long delay in serving food they had prepared with such care.

Beneath all this there had been an element of antagonism from the Drumdorrans that deepened to contempt when speaking to Max or Tom. Their opinion on the security and policing on the base was freely aired, and they were not in the least placated by the promise that everything possible was being done to trace whoever was responsible.

The dinner was finally served an hour and twenty minutes late, and the officers ate in silence food that had been kept hot beyond the limit of freshness, having been assured that transport would be laid on to take them to their quarters at the end of the evening. That Miles Crawford and Dougal Carnegie barely exchanged a word during the meal registered with the diners, and it strengthened the antagonism. The piper, who normally played during the dinner, sensibly left the scene.

Having already used his fresh shirt and underwear kept at

Headquarters, Tom had washed both before going to bed where he stayed awake troubled by this case which had wider-reaching involvement than any he had previously dealt with. Early morning saw him ironing his white shirt and pressing the trousers of his dark grey suit ready to set in motion a new programme for his team. He had called them all at six a.m. and told them to report in at eight. The only member excused from so doing was Pete Melly, who was strictly still on leave and was due to meet his estranged wife at the airport mid-morning.

Piercey had tried to get out of it by saying he had a date and there was no way of letting the girl know he was unable to meet her at the fixed rendezvous. As Phil Piercey picked up and dropped girls with swift regularity, Tom merely suggested that she would have a lucky escape and told him to be at Headquarters dead on time.

While eating a substantial breakfast Tom tried to see a way through the veil hiding the truth behind the two attacks, which surely must be attributable to the same person. Or persons, he supposed, which would complicate the case further. With a twinge of irritation he wished Max would divorce the Eva McTavish suicide from what was clearly a separate issue. That was the trouble with Max; he worried at vague oddities trying to inflate their importance to fit the facts they had and only succeeded in clouding them further.

The members of the team drifted in, some looking disgruntled and others only half-awake. Heather Johnson kept smothering yawns, which suggested to Tom that she had been on a late date with the blond German policeman she fancied. He was not happy about that connection. Pillow talk might acquaint the *Polizei* with facts SIB would prefer to keep confidential. Only Connie Bush, in a dark blue suit and white blouse, looked fresh and ready for anything, but she invariably did. Tom had often thought she would make a good career with an advertising agency promoting soap, cosmetics or health foods.

For the benefit of anyone who had not heard about the previous evening's disaster, Tom outlined what was known and what was surmised.

'Needless to say, relations between the Scots and the rest of us have worsened. The uniformed guys will be on overtime to cover the certain trouble in town tonight, and they'll be watching the Garrison Church during the funeral. The cortege is due to arrive from the hospital mortuary around eleven forty-five. Time it gets to the church the clock should be striking twelve.

Connie looked concerned. 'Why're they watching the church? A hearse is sacrosanct. Whoever Chummy is, he surely wouldn't violate Eva's coffin.'

'We're not insuring against that,' Tom snapped. 'There's evidence that the true cause of her death hasn't been made public. The tartan lads still believe she was killed by debris from the bonfire so feelings are still running high. Even more so after last night, and George wants to keep an eye on excessive behaviour at the funeral.'

Piercey, wearing with his grey striped suit a tie of vivid blue, yellow and green diamonds which Tom had warned him not to wear on duty, looked bored.

'Why hasn't the DGC ordered Major Carnegie to give out that it was suicide? He's condoning and encouraging bad feelings. I propose our first task is to spread the fact around the Drumdorran accommodation blocks.'

'And start a war?' asked Heather disparagingly. 'Colonel Trelawney returns tomorrow. He has the rank to sort it.'

'Whereas a sergeant hasn't,' said Max, who had entered in time to hear the last comments. 'Carry on, Mr Black. I have a few phone calls to make.'

Tom waited until Max closed the door, then gave out the tasks that they had both decided on before parting last night.

'Seek out every person who was involved with the display on Tuesday, including the guys who delivered the stuff from the QM Stores, and find out where they all were last evening.' He scowled at Piercey who raised his hands in an 'I don't believe it' gesture. 'Everyone who was involved in that calamity has to be a likely suspect for this second fire, so we find out who had the opportunity to be in the vicinity of the Officers' Mess. They all need a firm alibi before we strike them off the list and move on.'

'Where to, sir?' asked Piercey pugnaciously. 'We pretty well cleared them of making and inserting that IED, and we have no other leads on that. Why are we wasting time questioning that lot again?'

'Because those are my orders, Sergeant.' Tom turned away from him to address the others. 'Until we get a report from the Chief Fire Officer we can't be certain that an identical accelerant was used on the hedge but one was definitely used so concentrate on the dickheads who took it to the Sports Ground along with a straw effigy which could have contained the IED.'

'Not big enough for an alarm clock and dynamite bomb in a case,' murmured Piercey, careless of whether or not Tom heard it.

His friend Beeny spoke up swiftly. 'You're not asking us to question any of the Drumdorrans. Surely there's a possibility that last night's incident could have been a tit-for-tat attack.'

'I'd consider that if it hadn't occurred outside the building in which all the regiment's officers, including its OC, were gathered.'

'As were several hundred others,' Heather added. 'If there's a pyromaniac on the base his urge is to start fires where they'll create the greatest visual display and command the most attention.'

'A nutter, you mean? There's plenty of them on this base,' said Piercey. 'Take your pick.'

Olly Simpson, who had apparently been intent on his scribblings, as usual, looked up at that point. 'One aspect is surely unarguable. If he is a nutter, a pyromaniac, the affliction only began dogging him on the day the Drumdorrans marched in. As for last night, on a normal evening there could be less than fifty officers in the Mess, because most of them are married and live in quarters or in hirings in town. The fact that he selected the night dedicated to welcoming the new regimental members must be significant. If he's making a statement it's surely against the arrival of the Scots.'

Tom wagged his head. 'That's stretching credibility. How would setting fires change the situation?'

'It's just a *statement*, sir,' said Heather, then clearly wished she had remained silent.

'So why not just hang banners reading, Go home, Jocks? Easier and less risky,' Tom pointed out, irritated by this fanciful reasoning. It was the kind of input Max would relish. 'Let's get back to reality and interview those involved in the Guy Fawkes explosion. That bonfire wasn't lit by a pyromaniac, and we know the four guys who brought the straw effigy have access to accelerant. Right, get to it.' He nodded at Piercey. 'I want a word with you.'

The Cornish sergeant appeared at ease as he waited until the rest had departed, which annoyed Tom even more. He had twice suggested to Max that Piercey should be transferred, but his friend would not agree. He felt that the man's maverick personality was an asset in that he had several times followed a line no one else had thought of and come up trumps. Well, Max himself did that, so he found it possible to excuse Piercey's lack of regimental conformity, but Tom was a stickler for it and found the laid back attitude and flippant comments infuriating at times like this.

He walked up to the six footer and gazed coldly into light brown eyes from his extra few inches of height. 'You're treading a very fine line between contempt and insubordination. We're not dealing with two squaddies having an alcohol-fuelled punch-up. It's a highly dangerous situation which could escalate unless we swiftly put a stop to it. I've no space on this team for clowns who think they're above the basic task of information gathering, and who treat a briefing session as if it's a TV quiz game. You're one step away from demotion and a transfer, Sergeant, and this is my final warning. Now, get out there and do the job you're trained and paid to do, and do it with the zeal and dedication your colleagues put into it. Do I make myself clear?'

'Yes, sir.'

'Good. Start behaving like a responsible detective with the difficult task of tracing someone whose next "statement" could result in people being burned to death. It's *that* vital, man.'

'Yes, sir.'

Piercey made to depart, looking serious but not in the least chastened.

'And replace that bloody awful tie. You look like a dodgy car dealer!'

Only after the main door had closed behind Piercey did Tom remember that his father was a car dealer. If he was anything like his son he probably *was* dodgy. Needing a coffee, Tom tapped on the door of Max's office meaning to make a cup to mouth gesture, but Max was just replacing the receiver of his landline telephone with a frown. He gazed at Tom for a few seconds before leaning back in his chair and signalling him to take a seat.

'I've just heard from Chip Reynolds. He says the fire last night was caused by a number of incendiary devices linked together by an electric cable, and ignited simultaneously from a master switch. The devices contained the same accelerant that was used on the bonfire, which is why the blaze was instant and so uniform.

'Tom, we're dealing with a man who's not only intelligent and very skilled, he's also a genius at invention. That narrows the cast of thousands down to a few highly specialist soldiers.'

'Who know how to do more than put an alarm clock and a stick of dynamite in a suitcase,' added Tom significantly.

TEN

Max was furious and he made the fact obvious to Miles Crawford. 'This is *not* the work of a terrorist. I thought I'd made that perfectly clear during the past fifteen minutes.'

The Deputy Garrison Commander had red anger spots on his cheeks showing he was in no mood to be thwarted. 'What you've *failed* to make clear, Rydal, is who you imagine *is* responsible for these attacks. A squaddie up for some mischief? For a lark? For a touch of one-upmanship?' All this said in a biting, derogatory tone. 'This is out of SIB's league, which is why I intend to call in the Anti-Terrorist Squad.'

'Has Colonel Trelawney agreed that?'

The red colour deepened on Crawford's cheeks. 'He's presently involved with high-powered NATO talks, during which I'm deputizing for him with regard to any matter concerning this base.' His eyes narrowed. 'You're under my command until he returns, and I now relieve you of the duty of investigating these enemy attacks.'

Max stood his ground. 'At least wait until tomorrow, when I can give the GC an account of the evidence we've collated and on which we're working flat out. The pattern is not that of a terrorist.'

'So you keep saying. On what experience do you base that statement? A few cases of drug abuse, theft of mess funds, marital infidelity – commonplace military crimes. You're out of your depth here, Rydal. Be man enough to admit it.'

Desperately fighting the loss of his temper completely and giving this senior officer his frank opinion of his fitness to deputize for John Trelawney, Max said stiffly, 'Terrorists aim to *kill*. The IED placed in the bonfire was constructed to do no more than make a big bang and cause the cone to collapse. Only the additional items inserted by squaddies resulted in that forceful explosion. We have been told that by Captain Knott's experts, who aren't out of their depth when it comes to explosives,' he could not help adding, 'Last night's fire in the mess car park was set at a time when all vehicles were empty, and when it would swiftly be seen from inside the building and dealt with. The Chief Fire Officer's report will bear that out.' He took a deep breath. 'At neither incident was there deliberate intent to take lives. I say yet again, the pattern is not that of a terrorist.' Into the taut silence, he added more quietly, 'Your son, sir, suffered injury from the outcome of something not intended to be harmful but which went badly wrong.'

The third man in that office, who had been silent after his initial greeting, now offered his opinion. 'The bonfire incident occurred while I was settling my battalion in its new home with as few problems as possible. I'm not equipped to give a slant on SIB's findings although, of course, a life *was* lost that evening. The lady will be interred at noon today and there is no belief that she died at the hands of a terrorist.

'As for yesterday's fire, I was there in the Mess alongside you, Miles, and witnessed the whole incident. It was alarming, certainly wicked, but I agree with Max that the prime object did not appear to be to endanger life.'

'The building was filled with more than three hundred people,' protested Crawford. 'How can you say there was no threat to lives?'

'Because there was ample time and opportunity to evacuate the Mess,' responded Dougal Carnegie. 'The fact that hedges standing well distant from the building were targeted surely upholds that belief. If, as Max suggests, the two incidents are linked with the possibility of more to come, that's a highly disturbing prospect.'

He turned to Max, grim-faced. 'In your resumé you mentioned the coincidental timing of these incidents with the advent of the Drumdorran Fusiliers. I'm extremely concerned by that theory and, because of that alone, I support your request to leave the status quo until Colonel Trelawney gets back tomorrow.' Ignoring Crawford's gusty breath of protest, he continued. 'You say Captain Knott will be returning with him? Good. His evidence regarding the devices used will be invaluable.'

Max countered that swiftly. 'I haven't requested that we do nothing until the GC gets here, just that the ATS shouldn't be called in at this stage. My team will work throughout the weekend following up info received and analyzing those facts we already have. The coincidental timing with your arrival is only one theory of several, sir. I hope to have an in-depth report ready for Colonel Trelawney tomorrow, but SIB's main task is to prevent another incident by tracing the perpetrator as swiftly as we can.'

The Scot stood indicating an end to this aggressive meeting, once more acting as if he was the driving force on the base rather than Miles Crawford.

'I have a funeral to attend, gentlemen,' he said, making for the door.

Max delayed him. 'Major Carnegie, there seems to have been no effort made to reveal to your men the true cause of Mrs McTavish's death. They still believe she was killed by flying debris from the bonfire.'

He stopped, half-turned towards Max and said in a pseudo-pleasant tone, 'Do they now?'

'It would reduce the aggro in town tonight if the facts were made public. Our uniformed boys have enough to deal with on these serious cases without having to monitor unnecessary violence in the pubs and discos.' Seeing the glint in Carnegie's eyes, he added firmly, 'At our previous meeting on the subject you suggested that we should all make every effort to work together amicably.'

The glint became a laser beam of real anger. 'And there was I under the impression that it's Major Crawford who is deputizing for the Garrison Commander!' With that shot he departed.

'That man's a law unto himself,' Max told George Maddox fiercely when he called in at the RMP post en route to Headquarters. 'Due to him tonight's brawls in town will be unnecessarily violent.'

'I'm ready for that, sir. Extra cruising patrols. We want to be on the spot before the *Polizei* are called; deal with our guys ourselves. Saves a lot of hassle in the law courts.'

Still angered by Carnegie's avoidance of the issue of Eva

McTavish's death, Max grunted agreement. Law-breaking outside the base or in any way affecting German nationals had to be dealt with by the local police. Like all British military personnel, Max preferred to keep everything within their closed ranks. Defend their own, whatever the charge against them. An age-old tradition in any fighting force.

'George, if Chummy is making some kind of protest against our new Scottish residents what are the chances of him targeting the funeral?' He glanced at the standard MOD clock on the wall above George's head. 'An hour from now the cortège will be arriving at the Garrison Church.'

'Minimal, I reckon. What could he do, what would he gain?'

'What did he gain, apart from satisfaction, from his two strikes? Find the answer to that and we'll find him.' He frowned. 'I guess it's too soon after last night's affair to go again . . . and he'd draw the line at attacking a funeral, surely.'

'To be on the safe side I've arranged for Meacher and Babs Turvey to watch from a respectful distance.'

'Good.' Max prepared to leave. 'I've never been up a creek without a paddle, but I've taken a skiff up to the weir when the river was in flood and I didn't enjoy the experience.'

George nodded. 'I know the feeling. Helpless to fight the flow of events.'

Max glanced over his shoulder and summoned a faint smile. 'We *will* do something about this once the in-fighting stops and we get full co-operation.'

'Chummy has an issue with the Drumdorrans. It's obvious.'

'I wonder.' He pulled a face. 'I have an issue with them, but I'm not thinking of an alarm clock and dynamite in a suitcase. Yet!'

The funeral was a low-key affair. Max sat at the back of the church for the service conducted by the Drumdorrans' own Scottish Padre, who had such a strong accent Max understood little of it. He observed the behaviour of Hector McTavish, who looked very impressive in his kilted uniform despite the raw grief etched on his face. Had Jean Greene been wrong in suggesting the marriage had been a one-sided affair? If so, why had Hector refused to reunite with his wife on Tuesday, and ignore her seventeen desperate calls from the sports stadium?

He was still reluctant to pen a report concerning a suicide. He was certain that for some reason the full facts were being suppressed. His gaze passed to the two majors in the front pew with McTavish; Carnegie and MacPherson. Iron men, both, although the medical man's personality appeared on the surface to be more flexible. Enough to pay attention to Clare whenever the chance arose.

That thought led Max to study the women in the pew behind the two officers and Drum Major Andrew Lennox, who were there to support the bereaved husband. In contrast to her dismissive comment concerning Celtic rituals, Jean Greene had positioned herself next to an elegant woman in black who appeared to be Carnegie's wife. Jean also wore black and presented an appearance of deep sadness which made Max's lips curl.

That woman was certainly a creature of many parts and he was unsure which of them she played in respect of McTavish. Although she had tried to destroy the bottles that were partial proof of Eva's bid to end her own life, Max could do nothing. Strictly speaking, the law allowed her to be charged with several counts of hindering a police investigation, but it was too petty to pursue when there was a very serious case to solve. Yet Max was irked by her duplicity which he had failed to recognize at the start. He wondered then if she had taken Jenny to the surgery for advice on her habit of falling asleep so frequently. Brenda Keane had been seriously concerned about it.

The congregation consisted of grouped Drumdorran Fusiliers who Max took to be McTavish's fellow musicians, and a few women who were probably their wives. He, and the regular padre in a forward pew, were the only 'outsiders' present, and Max slipped out when the coffin was about to be lifted by the pall-bearers. He recognized Corporals Meacher and Babs Turvey hovering on the edge of the churchyard, and joined them as the piper began the lament.

The interment was performed with due respect and the mourners then departed, leaving at the graveside just the widower, Carnegie, MacPherson, the Scottish padre, Mrs Carnegie and Jean Greene. Max pursed his lips speculatively. Just what was that woman's relationship with McTavish?

The reports produced at the late afternoon briefing completed Max's day of frustration. Having been informed of the Fire Officer's report the team had switched attention to soldiers with engineering, electrical or weaponry skill. Being Saturday, they had only traced a small number to question about their whereabouts on the previous evening, and on Tuesday. Each person questioned was able to produce enough evidence to prove he was not the man they sought.

Bearing in mind the proposed meeting with Colonel Trelawney on the morrow, Max resignedly told them all to go off duty, but to remain on call in case there should be another incident.

'Make the most of the short break,' he warned. 'There's a heavy time ahead of us, that's for sure.'

Left alone with Tom, he said with exasperation. 'There's a curtain of mist hiding what ought to be obvious about this. If we could just clear it . . .'

'We'll go at it full power on Monday. It'll be possible to question whoever we wish then. I'd say it's unlikely there'll be another incident tomorrow, and the GC'll be back in command.'

Max nodded. 'At present there are too many people who think we're under their command, and treat us as such. I'll acquaint Trelawney with the facts we have, and the direction we're set to pursue, but if there's any suggestion of taking the case out of our hands, I'll contact our Regional Commander.'

Taking up his car keys, he said, 'Crawford had the effrontery to say he relieved me of the case because it was out of SIB's league. I've tried to make allowances for his stress over his son, but that's at an end after today's meeting. As for Carnegie!'

Tom walked with him to the main entrance. 'The GC will sort them both. He's dealt with worse.'

'True. I've no doubt the Scot is an admirable Battalion Commander and a first-class fighting soldier. It's his bloody-mindedness over the McTavish woman's death I find insufferable.'

Emerging once more to haze caused by fine rain, Tom locked the door and set the security alarms before crossing with Max to where their vehicles stood glistening with wetness.

'The truth will out. He must realize that.'

'But what *is* the truth?' asked Max doggedly.

Tom stared at him with impatience. 'You're not still querying the suicide verdict?'

'That note she left would back my report.' He unlocked the door on the passenger side of his car and opened it to drop his briefcase on the seat. 'When Connie and I interviewed McTavish he seemed quite unfazed by his sudden loss; said it was bound to happen sooner or later because Eva was so careless with her medication. He denied any responsibility for ensuring she didn't overdose. *Her* ailments, *her* responsibility. This morning, however, the man looked as grief-stricken as anyone I've seen at a graveside.' He frowned at Tom. 'There's more to that death than appears on the surface.'

'So what if there is?' snapped Tom. 'The woman's now six feet under and we have a number of witnesses who saw her popping pills on Tuesday evening. For God's sake drop it! We've enough to deal with on this other, more serious, case. We've got the weapons, but no motive or witnesses, much less suspects. I can't come up with a reasonable course to pursue. It's like trying to see beyond this curtain of fine rain. The answer's there, but we won't see it until the mist clears. Don't cloud the issue further by attaching unnecessary importance to that woman's demise.'

Max walked around his car, giving Tom a stormy look. 'We both need a break. Two or three hours of dedicated rowing in the morning will revitalize my energy ready for the late afternoon meeting . . . and I suggest you sort out over the weekend the problem that's been affecting your judgement these last few days.'

As he settled behind the wheel Max heard Tom say stiffly, 'Yes, *sir*.'

Tom drove home through the misty veil unable to contain his anger. He had had very little sleep since the drama on Tuesday, and subsequent annoyances and aggravations had piled one on the other to add further stress. He had swiftly instigated a top security alert only to be told later, in derisory terms, that he had over-dramatized the translation of IED. The dynamite in a case ongoing joke failed to amuse him.

He had followed what seemed to be a hot lead by interviewing Greta Gans, then had suffered her father's wild accusations and a stricture from Miles Crawford. The manner of Eva McTavish's death had changed from day to day, and the fire last night further complicated all these issues. Miles Crawford ruled that they were out of their depth, the Scots were playing their own game, Max was making a mountain from the molehill of Eva's suicide and had just now pulled rank by advising him to get his act together. Maggie and Gina were still playing up over the coming baby and he was in the right mood to sort them out.

With all that running through Tom's head he swung his 4x4 onto the drive with a scowl on his face, thankful only to escape the shroud of fine rain. He would tackle the baby issue straight away so that he could then enjoy his meal and home comforts after two nights in the Sergeants' Mess. He opened the front door to the sound of voices raised in argument.

'You did, you *did*. Because I lent *you* my glitter scarf last week.'

'I never wore it. It's too little girly.'

'You *borrowed* it. That's what counts, so I'm going to wear your sweatshirt tonight.'

Maggie and Gina were at the foot of the stairs mounting a tug-of-war with a scarlet jumper.

'Stop that!' ordered Tom crisply.

They turned, startled by his arrival they had been too heated to notice. Then, when his presence registered with them, they started up the stairs abandoning their quarrel.

'No, you don't,' he said. 'Come down here. I want a serious talk with you two.'

'We have homework to do,' said Maggie, putting a foot on the next stair.

'It's Saturday. *If* you have homework you have all day tomorrow to do it in.'

'I've promised to go round to Jilly's to work on our joint project,' Gina said defiantly.

'Nobody's going anywhere tonight. We're going to spend

an evening as a united family. Now, come down and go in to the sitting room. Put that top on the hall table. Whoever owns it can claim it later. Come on!'

They hesitated, then decided he was in no mood for rebellion and literally slunk along the wall and in to the room where Tom could hear Nora and Beth talking to each other. It was a cosy room, a family room, with a comfortable settee and chairs, a bookcase filled with well-thumbed favourite volumes, jigsaw puzzles and popular board games. Nothing fancy, just a place where they could relax and enjoy being together.

Nora looked up with a smile and gave him her usual greeting after a short absence. 'Hallo, whoever you are.'

Beth jumped up and came to hug him. 'We went to town to buy a bed and things for when we fetch Strudel at the end of the month. They're in the kitchen. Come and look.'

'Later. We're going to have a serious talk right now.' He saw Nora's eyebrows rise in interrogation and gave her a firm nod in return. 'Let's all sit down.'

Maggie and Gina remained standing, both looking apprehensive.

'I said sit down,' snapped Tom. 'I don't want any nonsense from you two.'

The pair flopped moodily on the settee and began picking at their fingernails, which incensed Tom further.

'Maggie, how old are you?' he demanded. When she made no reply he repeated the question more forcefully.

'Nearly fourteen,' she mumbled.

'And you, Gina, how old are you?'

Without looking up she said, 'You know.'

'I want to hear you tell me.'

Scratching at her jeans she took her time to say, 'I'll be twelve next month.'

'Right, can either of you tell me why you're behaving like prim old maids?' Silence. 'I know you're taught the fundamentals of sexual behaviour at school, and you're both at the age when the teachers consider that you should be made aware of the risk of experimenting with boys. Is that correct?'

They both nodded with chin against chest, still refusing to look at him.

'That risk is that you could get pregnant. That's the way the human animal procreates and, because our social pattern is the most complex and intelligent of the creatures on this planet, the accepted ideal is that our young are loved and cared for in a close family group. As you are,' he added pointedly.

'Felicity Barber and Joanne Blake – two of your sixth form girls – are about the produce babies conceived during a drunken binge at Easter. The reason for their sexual coupling was certainly not to further the human race, nor was it due to love of those boys. It was heedless, alcohol-fuelled disregard of personal pride and the consequences of something they had considered as simply part of the fun of that evening.'

He frowned, because they still refused to look up at him. 'The lives of poor schoolchildren have been marred by irresponsible behaviour, as have the lives of four sets of parents. But what about those babies? They'll most likely have to be cared for by their grandparents until Felicity and Joanne marry and have children with their husband. Those husbands might not want the first child to live with them, but even if they do can you imagine how the others will treat the fatherless half-brother or sister?'

Gina, more rebellious than Maggie, spoke angrily, still staring at the floor. 'Why're you saying all this to us? *We* haven't done anything stupid.'

Conscious of young Beth sitting in the corner, Tom softened his tone slightly. 'I'm giving you one side of the coin. The flip side is entirely different. A boy and a girl meet and something happens between them. Nobody can explain why, but the feeling they get leads them to be together whenever they can, to hold hands walking along, to kiss each other goodbye. Like you and Hans, Maggie.'

She looked up sharply at that, cheeks flushed. 'That's *all* we do.'

'I'm sure it is. But in a few years' time you'll meet someone and the feeling you'll have for him will make you want to do a lot more. Not because you're drunk, not because it's fun. Adult love is more intense than teen fancies, and infinitely more lasting if the right pair get together. Like Mum and me,' he said meaningfully.

'But you had us years ago,' muttered Gina. 'You're old now.'

'I'll accept that remark as the foolishness of someone who's only eleven. Do you wish you'd never been born, Gina?'

Her head came up. 'Of course not.'

'Do you wish Maggie and Beth hadn't been born?'

Her cheeks reddened. 'I never said that.'

'Maggie, do you wish your sisters hadn't been born?'

'Don't pick on me! It's *her*,' she replied, jerking her elbow into Gina's side.

'So I'll take it that you two are fully aware of how you came into the world, and are comfortable with that fact.' Silence. 'And you're also comfortable with how Beth arrived among us?' Still silence. 'Yet you've decided that someone waiting to become part of this united family has no right to be born and enjoy what you have; loving parents, a nice home, friends and all those things girls of your age like to have. Don't you think that's very selfish?'

'That's unfair. We haven't said anything like that,' cried Gina.

'So you're happy about having a brother or sister?' he shot at her. The girls glanced at each other, then nodded while studying the floor again. 'But you're not comfortable with how it came about? Tough,' he said in teenspeak. 'Get this straight. Mum and I are not old. Even Granny and Grandad aren't *old*. That adult love I mentioned lasts an entire lifetime, as you'll discover, so get used to the idea and return to being acceptable Blackies instead of melodramatic, ill-mannered *strangers*.'

He turned to where Nora sat with a rather pale-faced Beth. 'I'll shower and change before we eat supper. Give me a shout when it's ready.'

He half expected Nora to follow him to the bedroom because she had looked faintly taken aback by his ferocity, but she did not, although the glass of beer on the dresser had not been there before he went for his shower. He rarely had cause to become the heavy father and when he did he suffered slight sadness tinged with a curious suggestion of guilt. He had been involved with several instances of child molestation during his career and, like all policemen, found those cases the most distasteful of all. Girls were so vulnerable. He could more easily have given sons a dressing down. Boys were more . . . He hoped to God Nora was not carrying another girl.

That depressing possibility added weight to his sense of impotence, of being powerless to deal with any aspect of his life at the moment. He drank the beer in one draught, telling himself he was losing his grip.

Going downstairs, he headed for the nook in the hall where his scale models of famous steam engines were set out, and took up the latest edition of the enthusiasts' magazine. Maybe he would drive away his frustrations by immersing himself in his hobby, but he sat gazing at the words on the pages taking none of it in. Then he grew aware of someone beside him and turned to see Beth. She had red-rimmed eyes and was clearly very upset. Her sisters standing behind her had also been crying.

'You didn't come to the kitchen to see what we bought for Strudel, Dad,' Beth said in a wobbly voice. 'There's a lovely basket with a mattress, and there's a pink blanket, and . . . and . . .' She tailed off on a heavy sob. 'Can't we have the puppy now?'

Tom's heart turned over as he reached out to her and drew her close. 'Of course you can. Corporal Casey has told her she's coming to live with us in time for Christmas. That's definite. Nothing will change it.'

'We're sorry, Dad,' Maggie offered in a whisper. Gina simply nodded agreement without meeting his eyes. 'We didn't mean to upset you and Mum.'

Feeling a new man, Tom stood and encircled them all with his outstretched arms to chivvy them gently towards the kitchen door. 'Let's have a look at what every cool puppy should have.'

All sunshine after the storm, Beth told him eagerly, 'There's also a pretend bone, a squeaky mouse and a little ball with a bell in it. D'you think she'll like them?'

'Certain to, sweetheart. She'll become a true Blackie in no time.'

After an evening of fruitless brain searching followed by a restless night, Max rose early and drove to the river for his usual energetic spell in a hired skiff. It relaxed his muscles but did little to relieve his frustration. Blomfeld's bonhomie irritated him as it never had before, and he felt an urgent need to get his thoughts on track in preparation for the meeting with Colonel Trelawney later in the day. He hoped the GC would delay it until the morning. After all, the man had been engaged in heavy talks for the past ten days, so it would be in everyone's interest to allow him time to relax before tackling the problems here.

Returning home to shower and change Max had half-expected to see MacPherson's Range Rover outside the apartments. It had been there last night, but gone when he had set out at dawn. If the Scot had stayed the night he must have departed very early, but there was every chance that he would return to spend time with Clare today. They seemed to have more than professional interest in each other.

She had put a note through his letter box informing him of the nature of the pills crammed into the bottle he had found in Eva's effects; apparently they were merely a homeopathic remedy for the menopause which had either begun early or were held by her in anticipation of the onset. Quite possible for a health-obsessed woman.

At some time during the previous evening Max had decided to take Tom's advice to close the case on Eva McTavish's death, so he had written a report stating that she had taken her own life while the state of her mind was disturbed. He would hand that over at the end of the forthcoming meeting.

Brewing a pot of coffee, Max sat with it beside him on the small desk in the main room of his flat as he made a list of every aspect, firstly of the bonfire incident, then of the car park fire. He then looked for any matching points. There were a few, and he poured more coffee while he reviewed them.

1 The devices which had caused both incidents had been made by someone with good technical knowledge.
2 The attacks had been during the hours of darkness.
3 Neither device had been designed to maim or kill. So a statement?

4 Each had been where a large crowd of people were socializing, so the aggression was not directed against a single person.
5 Both incidents occurred after the arrival of the Drumdorrans.

Max then studied the differences.

1 The IED had been placed in the bonfire while a large number of men were in the vicinity, but the fire had been started in a car park empty of people.
2 On Tuesday evening the Drumdorrans were all on the far side of the base settling into new quarters, but on Friday the Mess was full of them.
3 The crowd at the Guy Fawkes party had consisted of soldiers and families who had lived on the base for some years; in the Officers' Mess were military personnel only, with a good mixture of new arrivals and old hands.

Pouring more coffee and munching biscuits, Max studied these lists for some time before he came up with the facts he would give Trelawney. As he had believed from the start, these incidents had been perpetrated by someone making a statement, a protest. He was not a member of the Drumdorran Fusiliers, but the protest could be against the arrival of another regiment in an already crowded base. The present facilities were barely adequate enough for the long-term residents, and government spending cuts would not allow these to be enlarged. Protests had been voiced in the past, so this could be an escalation into violence.

The next part would be to give the GC details of action already taken and outline his proposed steps to reach a resolution. To do that Max knew he would have to read every report by the team of their interviews. Although the only fact that had jumped out of reams of paper had been Rifleman Carter's lies about his cut hand and subsequent unofficial departure from bonfire duty, that had been a false lead and caused Tom unnecessary problems.

The interviews of families who had provided the evidence of Eva's pill-taking might contain something that would suggest how the IED was put in the bonfire without being noticed. By reading them in the quietness of his office Max might pick up something that was not evident at the time, because the issue had been clouded by the thoughts of terrorism.

Changing into something smart enough to attend the GC's meeting, if it was called later in the day, Max drove to the base and sat in his office with a tall stack of interview reports, prepared to stay there until he had tooth-combed through them all.

With practised expertise he cross-checked them and, after a couple of hours, he had as good a description of the construction of the bonfire as if he had been there. The only opportunity to insert an IED appeared to have been when the straw image meant to represent Second Lieutenant Freeman had been attached to the pile. Max had interviewed the four who had made it and knew they were all too unintelligent to make an explosive device, and Corporal Naish was too dedicated to constructing the perfect cone to then blow it apart.

Putting that pile aside, Max then began to read interview reports of evidence by families who had been present throughout that party evening. The emphasis had been on sightings of Eva McTavish, and Max found his doubts returning on reading the statement by a woman who said Eva had been sitting at the very back of the pavilion, making phone calls and swallowing pills.

I watched her for a while wondering if I should see if she was all right, because she looked very agitated, but I had to keep my eye on the kids with all those fireworks flying about. Then I spotted a Redcap fixing a 'guy' on the bonfire and thought I'd get him to check her. When the fireworks ended and we all moved from the stadium the woman had gone, and I had my hands full trying to keep the little devils in sight and well back. Good thing I did. All those people hurt. And that poor woman killed! I feel awful about it now.

Anger over the Scots' decision to allow the belief that Eva's life had been lost through the carelessness of garrison soldiers began to burn in Max again. These witness statements showed clearly enough the woman's desperate state *before* the bonfire erupted. Where the hell had McTavish been, and why had the bastard ignored seventeen calls from the wife he had not seen for three months?

His mobile rang to interrupt this constant worry. He answered with half his mind elsewhere and briefly acknowledged the news that Colonel Trelawney would not hold the meeting until tomorrow morning. Flexing his shoulders, Max noted the time. Mid-afternoon already. Pale sunshine now filtered through the office window giving him the urge to get out in it.

Filing the reports again he left the base and drove to an area that offered hillside walks with extensive views; one of his favourite 'thinking' places. The fact that there was an excellent old inn just ten kilometres beyond the hills was a bonus. He felt he had reviewed all the information SIB had garnered on both the bonfire incident and the car park fire. He now needed space and silence to mentally mull them over and attempt to lift the veil that obscured the breakthrough that he sought. Switching off his mobile, he left it in the car and strode out.

Darkness fell before he reached the end of his walk, but the paths were well defined and the distant lights of the village kept him heading in the right direction. In any case, no self-respecting detective would be out late on a November afternoon without a torch in his pocket.

Max then discovered that a large number of people had also taken advantage of the sunshine to walk the hills and enjoy a hearty meal in the hostelry boasting an excellent chef. Being a single diner he was able to secure the last table for two, which was in a far corner with the view across the restaurant restricted by a wooden coat stand heavily laden with garments. He added his own topcoat, thinking this would be an ideal romantic rendezvous well hidden from curious eyes. However, he was still wrestling with facts, opinions and sightings, so an obscured nook was just what he needed.

He left the inn having enjoyed a satisfying meal and a carafe of wine, but still seeking that breakthrough that was proving so elusive. The easy run back to his apartment was hampered by the fine rain that had arrived on several evenings recently.

In another month or so it would be snow, and he would have to put chains on the wheels.

Clare's car was not in the usual parking place. She must be making another night of it with Duncan MacPherson. He thought the affair was too hot, too soon. He had pursued both Susan and Livya with that brand of urgency, and lost them. Maybe he should point that out to Clare.

A large whisky while he undressed and showered, then a CD of balalaikas playing Russian folk tunes to calm his mind ready for sleep did not produce the required effect. He lay awake wondering what he could say that would convince John Trelawney that SIB could put a stop to the violent incidents before another was launched.

Some time after the CD ended and before sleep claimed him, Max had a vague conviction that something in the reports he had scanned earlier had struck an odd note. He must sift through them again before the meeting, in the hope that it would shed enough light to strengthen his case for continuing to investigate the two attacks.

Although Max had set his alarm to an hour earlier than usual a loud, continuous ringing woke him long before the hands on his clock reached the desired time. Puzzlement lasted mere seconds before he realized someone was leaning on his doorbell. At five a.m.? Pulling on a robe over the boxer shorts he slept in, he padded to the small hallway to find out who wanted him so urgently.

On the top step of the flight leading up to the apartment stood the Regional Commander, Major Keith Pinkney. Conscious of his own dishevelled appearance, and taken aback at this early morning call, Max took too long to react appropriately.

'We need to talk, and I'm not doing it on your doorstep,' the visitor said waspishly.

'No. Sorry, sir, please come in.'

By the dim light from a bedside lamp the large area that was bedroom and lounge-diner did not look suitable for a professional meeting with his boss, yet when Max switched on the main lights it looked even more unappealing. Rumpled bed, whisky bottle and glass beside it, and discarded clothes over a chair suggested dissipation.

After a swift comprehensive glance at it all, Pinkney said, 'I suggest you stick your head under the tap, then get into some clothes while the kettle boils for the strong coffee we'll both need. This is one hell of a tricky situation and I have to get to the bottom of it.'

Knowing that only something extremely serious would have led this man to call on him at the crack of dawn, Max's spirits sank. Clearly, there had been another incident, with truly dire consequences this time. As he speedily freshened up and donned casual slacks with a woollen shirt, his thoughts raced speculatively and continued to do so as he made a pot of coffee. Carrying a tray through from his kitchen, he suggested that they repair to the shared lounge for their discussion.

'It's more comfortable there.'

'This is fine. Sit down, Max,' said Pinkney with new warmth in his tone. 'We have to sort this out, man, and *fast*.'

Mystified by this chummy change of approach, Max sat at his desk facing his boss, who had settled in one of the easy chairs. What on earth was this all about?

Ignoring the mug of coffee beside him, the senior man embarked on an explanation of his last remark. 'Tom Black called me at midnight to report that a child named Jenny Greene had disappeared from the garden of her home mid-afternoon. George Maddox set up a major search of the base with volunteers, once it became clear she had not simply wandered off but had been snatched.'

Alarmed, Max said, 'Jenny has a serious problem needing medical advice.'

'She was found asleep, wrapped in rugs, in the sports stadium at twenty-three fifteen,' Pinkney continued heavily. 'Unable to contact you, Tom called in the MO. and a woman from the Joint Response Team. Captain Goodey found no evidence of physical or sexual abuse, and Sergeant Kinross asked the bewildered child a few questions before a full session today.'

Pinkney frowned at Max. 'Jenny claims the man she went off with – apparently willingly – was *you*, and Mrs Greene stated that you've shown marked interest in her daughter on several occasions.'

'*What*?'

'You were seen entering the base yesterday morning, but there was no sighting of your car leaving. Your mobile was switched off – still is, I checked – and your home number was set on voicemail. Max, unless you can provide me with proof of your whereabouts between fifteen hundred and midnight, I'm afraid you could be facing a charge of abducting and holding a child captive for eight hours.'

ELEVEN

'CCTV at Headquarters will show the time I left.'

Keith Pinkney nodded. 'Tom guessed you'd been in your office and checked the cameras. You arrived at ten past eleven and departed at fourteen thirty-five. That doesn't prove you left the base and, unfortunately, the timing allows for you to have driven to the Greenes' quarter and taken the girl.'

Still feeling much as he had on being brought down in a rugby tackle, Max said, 'You know how it is on Sundays. The gate guards check anyone entering, but tend just to wave them out. There were four vehicles ahead of mine. Lads going out on the razzle in town, and two more coming up fast behind me. Surely someone witnessed my departure.'

The senior man shook his head gently. 'We need to keep this in the family. Once we start asking for witnesses it becomes an official enquiry, you know that. Now, you can't prove you were walking in the hills, but how about the inn where you dined? You said you'd eaten there on previous occasions.'

'Not often enough to be known by the staff, and you've just said we don't want to make it official.'

'It would be for my own benefit.'

Max stared at him in disbelief. 'You don't think I did take her?'

'Not for a moment, but I'd like something concrete to back my defence if it should grow out of hand.'

'It won't. It can't,' he protested. 'I worked in my office preparing for a possible meeting later in the day, but the GC's adjutant called to say it wouldn't be convened until this morning. That was around fourteen fifteen – you can check with him – so I decided to walk in the hills while I mentally reviewed witness statements I'd studied, hoping for a clue that would suggest a line of enquiry we badly need. I ate at a table practically hidden from other diners by a branched stand bulging with topcoats. I then drove home, arriving here soon after twenty-three hundred.'

As he said that, Max realized why Clare's car had been missing. Not a late-night date with MacPherson. She had been looking for signs of abuse in a child who claimed he had abducted her. Would Clare believe that of him?

'But you can't prove any of that,' prompted Pinkney breaking into his thoughts.

'No.' He frowned. 'You've had my reports on the serious incidents last week. Could this be another attempt to make a statement? You said Jenny had not been harmed, but if he's now targeting children we need to identify him, and fast.'

'I can't see any obvious link with the previous attacks.' Pinkney drank his coffee thoughtfully, then topped up his mug and held up the pot. 'Get some of this inside you. Sharpen your wits.'

The sensation of having had the breath driven out of him remained. Max did as suggested while he tried to come to terms with what was happening. If Jenny continued to insist she had gone off with him he could be in trouble. Crimes against children were viewed with abhorrence by any police force, and Max knew George Maddox was particularly intense on the subject. As was Tom, the father of three girls. Did *he* believe Jenny's claim?

As he drank the strong coffee Max studied his inquisitor, a man he had known for some years but as his immediate boss for only two. Tall, thin, greying at the temples and with a neat brown moustache, Keith Pinkney had spoken of keeping it in the family, by which he meant the Corps. He surely would, to the best of his ability, but without an alibi Max knew his defence was shaky.

'So, let's get to the nitty-gritty,' Pinkney said briskly. 'Why was your mobile switched off yesterday? Isn't that unusual?'

'I wanted to think without any interruptions. Major Crawford was threatening to call in the ATS. He even ordered me to relinquish the case; maintained SIB wasn't equipped to handle it. I need to persuade Colonel Trelawney that we're making headway. Hence why I was reviewing witness statements in my office. I feel it's imperative to retain control of something that is *not* linked with terrorist activity. Tom Black is perfectly capable of dealing with any problem without my advice or intervention. As he did, apparently.'

'Mmm, yes. And I have to tell you your entire team is behind you.'

Max sighed. 'I'd be a poor kind of boss if it wasn't.'

'Agreed. You've been very successful over the past two years. That's why we have to sort this before it goes any further, Now, why did Mrs Greene say you showed marked interest in her daughter?'

Max explained how Jenny had taken a fancy to him when he called to reveal that Eva McTavish had died, and she got very excited on seeing him.

'How have you responded to the little girl's interest?'

For the first time Max was reluctant to answer. He had been charmed by Jenny when she had climbed on his lap and offered him biscuits. He had been alarmed and protective when she fell asleep over her lunch. He had been wistfully delighted when the child had refused to get in the car seat and had yelled his name.

'She's very . . . engaging.' The silence grew awkward as he realized how Pinkney might interpret that. 'I haven't children of my own so I'm unused to the way they behave. Jenny is a very outgoing little girl. Any person would have to be flint-hearted to resist her appeal.'

'I see. Mrs Greene spoke of several occasions. How many times have you been to the house?'

'Initially, on the morning following the bonfire incident. I was curious about a couple who had made no attempt to meet after an absence of three months. I returned with more questions about them when it transpired the woman had committed suicide that night.' He gave a twisted smile. 'I'm still curious about the McTavishes.'

'And that's it?'

'No, I called on Mrs Greene to tell her I'd spoken to a friend with medical training about Jenny's habit of falling asleep all the time, and she advised getting the child to a doctor.'

'So you *have* taken quite an interest in Jenny.'

Max rose to that. 'She fell asleep in my presence with her face in a plate of food. The mother laughed it off, which I considered to be highly irresponsible. Look, sir, I don't have an unhealthy interest in Jenny. My visits to the house were all in the course of an investigation into the death of Eva McTavish, and on that last meeting I discovered Mrs Greene was attempting to destroy evidence pertaining to the suicide. She had also lied to me from the start about the nature of her own relationship with the widower. I pulled her in and questioned her about it, which she strongly resented. If she's fingering me for this . . .'

'No, Max, Jenny gave your name voluntarily. As I said before, this is a tricky situation which needs to be nipped in the bud.' He got to his feet. 'I'll have a word with the Garrison Commander about the proposed meeting. Tom Black reckons it's unnecessary, so I can get it delayed. Preferably indefinitely. I'll also speak to Sergeant Kinross before she questions Jenny again, and tell her you were elsewhere checking witness statements at the vital time. She'll get to the truth eventually. I know her well. She's very good with bewildered kids.'

He headed for the hall, Max following. 'You'll stay here until it's sorted. And switch on your bloody mobile!'

The girls had left to catch the school bus when Tom woke and wandered down to the kitchen. Nora greeted him brightly. 'Morning, Sleeping Beauty.'

'I didn't get to bed until three. Again!' he responded sourly. 'Don't know who you were dreaming of, but you had me in a half nelson before my head hit the pillow.'

'Mm, I think it was Colin Firth last night.'

'Huh, that bloody wet shirt!' He became fully aware of her broad smile. 'Must have been some dream. You're still looking smug.'

She crossed to kiss him. 'I'm feeling fine. It's stopped.'

'What has?' he asked, wondering how large a breakfast he had time for. He really should be on base when Sheila Kinross arrived to question that child again.

'Morning sickness, chump.'

'Ah, good.'

'And the girls are talking freely, with the first hint of real excitement about the new Blackie.'

'Good,' he said again, conscious of just how late it really was. A full English breakfast was right out of the question. 'Can you do me some poached eggs on toast? I need to get in sharpish, love. Max is caught up in something pretty messy.' He headed for the stairs. 'I'll fill you in while I eat.'

'Certainly, oh Master.' Her reply floated to him as he took the stairs two at a time, cursing the fact that he had slept in so long. With plenty of practice at hurried preparations behind him, Tom was ready for work in record time and descended to find a fully prepared grapefruit and eggs ready for poaching, as well as a large cafetière of coffee.

'You're a marvel,' he said warmly. 'Colin Firth has no idea what he's missing.'

Between mouthfuls Tom related what had occurred the previous night, and how he had called in Keith Pinkney as the appropriate person to stand behind Max.

'The Greene woman has it in for him after he grilled her over those vodka bottles, of course, but I don't think she'd go as far as to prompt Jenny to name him out of spite. After all, someone did take the girl and Jean was half-demented until she was found alive and unharmed.'

'As I would be. And you,' Nora said. 'Poor woman. But what was the child doing in the sports stadium?'

'Sleeping. It doesn't make sense to me. What was it all about? The kid was unharmed and wrapped warmly in blankets.' He grimaced. 'Max will doubtless say it was a statement. Once that bee's in his bonnet it's difficult to shift, yet I can't come up with what else could be behind terrifying a little kid for eight hours, can you?'

'We don't know the full story. Once Sheila Kinross gets the details from Jenny it'll make more sense. But *was* she terrified? A three-year-old who apparently went willingly with a man she knew, was not harmed, and then left sleeping peacefully in cosy blankets, hasn't gone through a frightening experience to my mind. Aside from being away from her mother, Jenny sounds to me like a child who'd view it as an adventure. Kids can be very trusting, can't they?'

'Maybe, but my concern is to find who lured the girl away, and why she should say it was Max.'

'Oh, Tom! You have three daughters and haven't learned what liars three-year-olds can be? Jenny had had an adventure; she was tired and well into her deep night-time sleep when she was woken from it to find what seemed to her to be hundreds of people asking questions. Mummy was there to take her home, so what's all the fuss about? Who has she been with? The first name that comes into her head is Max so she says it, drinks her warm milk and goes happily to bed. She has no idea why people are acting so strangely. She's *three*, Tom. She could just as easily have said she'd gone off with Father Christmas or Postman Pat. Surely the most significant aspect is that whoever did take her meant her no harm. A statement? I'd say it was more likely an attempt to hurt the mother. She's the one who had the terrifying experience.'

Tom grinned. 'While we're all reading enormous significance into events, you never fail to offer a down-to-earth explanation that makes perfect sense. Trouble is, that premise opens up a completely new can of worms.'

'Put it aside until you've opened the other cans and found the worms don't provide the right answers.' She lifted the cafetière. 'Got time for another?'

His reply was reduced to a shake of the head as his mobile rang and he stood, ready to say truthfully that he was on his way.

'Where are you?' asked Max.

'At home, about to leave. How did it go with the Regional Commander?'

'Sticky. I can't prove I wasn't on base, but thanks for calling him in on it.'

'Regs demand it, but we're all available to get whatever info is needed to let you off the hook.'

'Even Piercey won't manage to do that. The penalty of deliberately isolating myself. Tom, I've been ordered to stay here pro tem, but I need to go through the witness statements concerning Eva McTavish's behaviour at the Guy Fawkes do. Will you get one of the team to email them to me? I'm sure we overlooked something odd the first time round.'

Some of Tom's goodwill evaporated. Surely he was not still agitating about that suicide when he had this charge hanging over him. 'Do I attend the meeting with the GC?'

'Our boss is going to get it postponed. Concentrate all efforts on questioning the whereabouts on Tuesday and Friday evenings of everyone with mechanical or engineering knowledge. We have to compile a list of likely suspects for the two incidents before that meeting.'

'And before he strikes again.'

'Primarily that. Keep me in the picture, especially on this Jenny Greene affair. We have to discover who took her, Tom. Why she should name me is worrying.'

'She's only three and could just as easily have said she'd gone off with Father Christmas or Postman Pat,' Tom told him smartly, hearing a smothered snort of laughter from Nora. 'I'm liaising with Sheila Kinross to fill her in on the connection you have with the mother to prove it was purely professional.'

He ended the call and shrugged on his topcoat as Nora came to him, saying, 'I expect I'll see you when I see you. If you arrive in the early hours again don't spoil my erotic dream.'

'I'll come to bed in a wet shirt. You won't need to dream.'

After the dreariness of last week's misty rain and fog this one had begun with sunshine that sparkled a heavy frost. As a result colours looked vibrant. Autumn leaves glowed red, gold and amber, newly-washed buses gleamed yellow, net curtains were as snow-white as the grass around apartment blocks, and wares in shop windows looked enticing enough to lure customers inside. The chilly sunshine even brightened people; rosy cheeks, keen eyes and rainbow scarves.

The weather cheered Tom despite the weight of the problems he faced. As he drove he told himself he was being as fanciful as Max in thinking this atmospheric clarity would herald fresh insight. It was certainly energizing. Arriving at Headquarters he found every member of the team primed for positive action on the Jenny Greene abduction. He had to divert their zeal with Max's instructions.

'Have you any idea how many people that directive covers?' moaned Piercey. 'We've been at it for three days and made no more than a dent in the list of possibles. As the bomb boys keep telling us, anyone can access the Internet and read instructions on how to blow something up.'

'You should have learned by now that much of detective work is painstaking elimination that leaves genuine suspects.' Piercey scowled as Tom added, 'The device that ignited the hedge at the car park was the work of someone with advanced specialist knowledge, which allows us to narrow the search.'

He addressed them all. 'It's Monday, start of a week when everyone should be on base. No manoeuvres, no courses at other venues, no block leave for troops returned from war zones and the Christmas exodus is several weeks away. In short, you should be able to find personnel where they should be. Start with the Sappers.'

'We've already quizzed them,' said Heather wearily.

'Do it again. See if they tell the same story. You and Connie search their lockers. Look for magazines, pamphlets, any signs of interest in incendiary gadgets. Piercey, you and Beeny go back to Logistics and the bomb boys who say we overreacted about the IED. Find out if any of them have Scottish links or a grudge against the lads from north of the border. Search their lockers, too. You might fall foul of Captain Knott who returned from the NATO meeting yesterday. If you do, refer him to the Boss, who's eager to have a go at him regarding courtesy of info.'

'He didn't go,' said Connie.

'Who didn't go where?'

'Captain Knott. To the NATO conference. Had gastroenteritis.'

Tom frowned. 'Where'd you get that nugget of info?'

The healthy pink of her cheeks surprisingly deepened. 'Sergeant Carr.'

Tom's eyes narrowed. 'Why didn't you report that earlier?'

'I only heard about it last night.'

It was unwelcome news. He thought she had more sense than to start socializing with a man concerned in an ongoing investigation. Heather was getting dewy-eyed over a blond German policeman which he was not happy about, either. Women! Throwing both of them a scathing look, he directed the remaining members of the team accordingly before heading for the Greenes' quarter in the hope of a word with Sheila Kinross before she questioned Jenny again.

They arrived outside the house at the same time, and he gave her a rundown of Max's movements in a tone of authority that suggested it could be verified.

'Well, she could have been confused last night, but if she continues to name Captain Rydal as the person who lured her away we'll have to question him.'

'But he's the last man to . . .'

'Tom, he clearly features largely in Jenny's life and, if she insists she went off with him, we have to discover why. There might be deep undercurrents here.'

'No. *No*!'

She gave him a significant look which he resented, then asked if he planned to wait in his car or if he'd like her to call his mobile at the end of her first session with the child.

'We have to take things slowly. They frequently change their story as time passes because they grow scared, or because they think it's what we want them to say.'

Impatient with her, yet aware of the sensitivity with which such cases must be handled, Tom said, 'I'll be in my office. Call me there when she decides she went off with Postman Pat.'

In fact, Tom had just remembered Max's request for witness statements to be emailed to him, and returned to Headquarters to do it himself. Until Max had been cleared of this charge Tom knew he could not fully concentrate on anything, but emailing would keep him occupied. Even so, as he began searching the files for the relevant documents he worried about the possibility of Jenny sticking to her story. This could not have happened at a worse time. Max could be suspended while the affair dragged on, his future in the hands of a fanciful three-year-old.

The statements of witnesses who saw Eva McTavish taking pills in the sports stadium had been taken by Connie and Heather, which reminded Tom of Connie's apparent fancy for one of the stick of dynamite and an alarm clock brigade. She was normally level-headed. What had possessed her to get involved with a possible suspect in a serious case like this one?

After making coffee Tom sat at his desk and began to read through each report before scanning it, looking for something odd that had been overlooked. His mood was not lightened by the repetitious descriptions of the woman swallowing pills and making calls on her mobile. He was heartily sick of the McTavish affair Max was still making such a big deal of.

With just two reports left to send, Tom made more coffee and raided the goodie tin for a chocolate bar as a treat for failing to see anything odd that had been overlooked first time around. Max was after a goose even wilder than most he chased. Munching a chocolate-covered biscuit, he speed read the next but last statement and was about to scan it when he realized it was there and had, indeed, been overlooked because they had all been concentrating on the McTavish woman. Bravo, Max, although it raised an unwelcome premise.

Reaching for his landline he punched in the number of the RMP post. The call was answered by Babs Turvey, who told him George Maddox had gone home suffering from the gastro-enteritis that was spreading around the base with the usual speed of such bugs. Could she help?

'Yes, Babs. Look at your duty rosters and tell me who was on patrol at the Sports Ground during the firework display last Tuesday.'

After a few moments she gave him two names, then asked, 'You did mean before the explosion, didn't you? The rest of us were called out to deal with the resultant situation.'

'Yes, that's fine. Thanks.'

He disconnected and sat for a while gazing at the names of two men he knew and thought well of. Then he checked their military careers on screen and discovered Meacher had transferred from REME. Mmm, electrical and mechanical engineers. Very significant. He reached again for the telephone to ask Babs Turvey for Meacher's mobile number, but it rang before he could call her.

'Sergeant Major Black,' he announced with a touch of asperity at being prevented from pursuing this unwelcome lead.

'Sheila Kinross, Tom. Are you free to come here?'

'Developments?'

'Something you should hear. How long will you be?'

'Ten minutes max.'

Shrugging on his padded coat Tom walked out to the sunwashed chill, and drove around the perimeter road to reach the Greenes' house wondering what he was about to be told. Sheila was watching for him and let him in, leading him to the kitchen. From the main room came the sound of jolly music and a soothing voice talking about Paddington Bear. No irate mother, no sobbing child. Just normality. Or *apparent* normality. Someone had taken Jenny from here for eight hours yesterday, which was far from normal.

Confronting Sheila, Tom asked, 'Is she still naming Max?'

The woman gave a wry smile. 'Yes. In her own way. After half an hour of gentle discussion in which Jean and I dropped identifying clues about Captain Rydal, Jenny gave one of those exasperated looks kids do so well when adults get it wrong. She said, 'Not *that* Max. The other one who's sometimes a lady.'

'What?' asked Tom, bemused.

'Sometimes wore a *kilt*.'

'A Drumdorran?'

'Exactly. Someone Jenny has no fear of because he's been to her house and Mummy was friends with him.' Sheila poured herself some coffee from a filter machine, then explained that she would be having another session with Jenny after lunch to get further details of what happened during those eight hours. 'So far, the child's been telling with some delight how he made tunes by blowing into a shopping bag.'

The truth then hit Tom. 'Bagpipes!'

'You've got it! Jean told me that while Eva was living with her last week Jenny called her Auntie *Max*Tavish.'

This time it was a walkover. Drum Major Andrew Lennox was bypassed with ease when two Redcaps arrested Hector McTavish and brought him to 26 Section Headquarters shortly after Max arrived there. On receiving the call from Tom that filled him with relief and also a sense of anticipation that his curiosity about the death of Eva McTavish was about to be satisfied, Max had immediately contacted Keith Pinkney.

The Regional Commander confirmed that the meeting with Colonel Trelawney had been put on hold, and added that this development was strong enough to keep it there ad infinitum. Pinkney undertook to inform Major Carnegie of the arrest of one of his revered pipers. Max knew it would come as a blow, but he felt little sympathy for a commander who had allowed hostility to continue by withholding the truth of Eva's death.

Entering the interview room with Tom, Max saw that the man who, at their previous meeting, had been assured to the point of belligerence was, today, an abject figure with head bowed, hands clasping and unclasping with agitation. Max had seen a suspect full of guilt before, and here was another. Tom started the tape recorder and Max went through the preliminaries, then read out the charge.

He had hardly finished speaking when the Scot mumbled, 'Before God, I meant the lassie no harm. I could'nae help it. The wanting was too strong.'

Exchanging a swift glance with Tom, Max asked, 'You admit to taking Jenny Greene from the garden of her home to some other place where you kept her for eight hours?'

'She was happy to be with me, laughing and dancing to my music. Such a sweet innocent lassie, she is. Laughing and dancing. It did'nae seem wrong.'

'Where did the dancing take place?' demanded Tom.

'Practice room four, where I always go to play the beloved auld airs.' He suddenly looked up, his eyes dark with shock. 'They're all that's left to me now, for the Lord has surely forsaken this sinner.'

Irritated by the religious drama, Max said, 'Didn't it occur to you that Jean Greene, the child's mother, would be frightened and worried over Jenny's disappearance?'

McTavish stared as if unable to understand the question, then whispered, 'She knows I'd not harm her, and the wanting was too strong.'

'Wanting to do what?' demanded the father of three young girls.

The dark gaze swivelled to fix on Tom. 'We were to have

a bairn way back, but Eva went out on the ice against ma wish and fell. She denied me. *Denied me*,' he repeated. 'A McTavish. A man of pride could'nae have the fruits of his seed. Father saw it as reaping as I'd sown. And so it was. I turned to the Lord and repented my ways, seeking peace with my music. But she would'nae have it.'

Letting the man pour out his confession as if to two priests, Max and Tom heard facts that clarified many points concerning Eva's suicide. Some of them echoed what Jean had told Max. Hector's conversion to his parents' religious zeal had driven a wedge between the couple, and the gap had widened as Eva tried to regain his interest with imagined illnesses. Divorce was not an option, so they lived separate lives until the next blow fell.

'Callan joined the Drumdorrans to fight alongside the brother he remembered as being so bold. He mocked me. Said I was no a soldier but a preacher.' The suggestion of shock in his eyes intensified. 'He went to war and died with bad blood between us.'

Max recalled Jean saying this man blamed himself for his brother's death and, as a result, was trying to deny any responsibility for what Eva had done. Although he had not before encountered anyone with extreme religious beliefs, Max knew well enough the lengths to which such people could be driven in their zeal. He sensed Tom's impatience, but gave a slight shake of his head. McTavish was in full flow and best not interrupted.

'The woman grieved for him more than was seemly in public, and the tongues began to wag. I chastised her for always being at the bottle for a dram, as any man would, and forbade her to touch a drop while I was away with the band.'

McTavish fell silent, looking at his questioners as if for vocal support. When their unflinching eye contact became too unnerving he said brokenly, 'She sent letters every week reminding me of him, and how I'd let him go to his death with my curses in his ears. She . . . she even sent photographs of his grave. Every week. Cold earth on the dear brother of my youth.'

He took time to deal with that, and Max had again to signal

Tom to remain silent. The volcano of this burdened man's emotions was slowly erupting.

'I would'nae, *could'nae* face her when we came here last week. You can understand that.'

Getting no response, he appeared to shrink as his head drooped and his shoulders shook. 'She committed the unforgivable sin to dishonour me. A McTavish, to be humbled in the eyes of a regiment of proud warriors. May the Lord forgive her, for I have no will to.'

Max now seized the moment. 'You're saying your wife took her life deliberately? Committed suicide to punish you?'

'Aye.'

'Punish you for what?'

'Taking Callan from her. So she wrote in the letter.'

Max gave Tom a grim smile of satisfaction. 'The letter sent across to you on the morning after your wife's death *was* a suicide note?'

McTavish nodded.

'Please voice your confirmation of that.'

'Aye, it was.'

'Where is that letter now?'

'Burned. It was vile.'

Tom could keep quiet no longer. 'What has all this to do with the abduction of the child Jenny Greene?'

This reversion to the charge he had been arrested for created a hiatus that lasted until McTavish had mastered his distress and got his mind around the new direction it had to follow.

'Jenny Greene,' Tom prompted harshly, to break the silence.

'Aye.' McTavish sighed. 'I went to speak to Jean. I had the need d'ye see? An old friend. For one summer more than friends. Along with others. I was a wild boy. Jean knew how things were and has a kindness for me still.'

'Oh?' said Tom. 'Then why take away her daughter and fill her with anguish?'

Shaking his head, McTavish said, 'That was nae in ma mind. The little lassie saw me and came over with smiles, and I knew she could have been mine if I'd no been denied the right to have the like. The wanting was so strong I took her away to hear my music and to show her the dancing. We were happy.

She laughed and danced to the pipes. We had tea and bannocks and cakes, while I told her stories of the clans and Bonny Prince Charlie. I gave her a plaid to wear, and sang the auld songs from down the ages. She slept awhiles now and then, but wanted more music when she woke.'

He appealed to them with eyes bright with remembrance. 'I knew how it would have been to have a bairn, so I took her to the place where that woman kilt herself. *See how it could have been*, I told her. *See what you denied me*.'

'Why did you leave Jenny there alone?' demanded Tom roughly.

'Och, the lassie was tired from the dancing; fell asleep as I held her. I sat with her awhiles until I heard voices calling her name nearby. I knew then the moment was over and slipped away.'

'And if you hadn't heard the searchers calling her name?'

McTavish appeared unable to answer that, just gazed in puzzlement.

'Was it your intention to return Jenny to her mother and explain why you had taken her?' asked Max to clarify the situation.

All McTavish said was, 'Jean still has a kindness for me.'

Tom snapped off the tape recorder and turned on the Scot to say, 'Which is more than you have for her, you bastard, putting her through eight hours of fear and anguish.'

Max could only imagine a parent's suffering over a missing child so, unlike Tom, he could distance himself from Jean Greene's trauma and consider the depth of emotional torment Eva had dealt out to Hector over the death of his brother in retaliation for the years of neglect she had suffered. If he had answered any one of her seventeen calls, what would have been said between them? No one would ever know if she was asking for his help or wanting to damn him further as her life slipped away.

Over a late lunchtime sandwich Max put forward to Tom his thoughts on that twisted relationship. 'Being a member of a regiment gives a man comradeship, help in need and a sense of communal pride, but it also means that his failures and humiliations are common knowledge. For Hector, who had adopted those narrow beliefs he had rebelled at in his youth, his wife's suicide was the ultimate sin. What's more, in an élite regiment like the Drumdorrans, whose history boasts of clan giants performing Herculean deeds, weakness or failure of any kind isn't tolerated. Hence the fostering of the belief in Eva's accidental death at the Guy Fawkes evening. The Pipe Major's status was being protected, the way Keith Pinkney was preparing to do for me earlier today.

'What I find difficult to equate is that kind of extreme religion with military life. How did he get around the commandment Thou Shalt Not Kill?'

Tom was still looking aggressive. 'Slaughtering the enemy isn't regarded as murder. Anyway, when he joined the Drumdorrans he was still a normal, high-spirited lad. It was his father claiming the death of a foetus was punishment for Hector's wild youth that did the damage.'

'Mmm, if anyone pointed out that that claim had led to years of vindictiveness between a husband and wife, cruel estrangement of brothers, a suicide and public disgrace for his remaining son, the old man would never see the truth of it. Not in a hundred years.'

'You omitted something. It also led to his remaining son becoming a paedo.'

Max shook his head. 'No, he didn't mean any harm to Jenny. The balance of his mind was disturbed. That's what the psycho boys will say when the GC sends him to them.'

'I'd send him to boys who smash men's balls with a sledgehammer,' Tom retorted vigorously. 'Making the kid dance to his pipe music? Taking her to the sports stadium to show her to a woman who had killed herself there last week? If that isn't the behaviour of a pervert, what is it? And he avoided answering when I asked if he had intended taking Jenny home.

'All that bloody bullshit about an élite regiment with a proud history you went on about a moment ago? A regiment is a regiment is a regiment. Each one has its past heroes and glorious victories. They also all have failures and losers. Take those four who put a straw effigy of their platoon commander on . . .' Tom broke off and put down his sandwich. 'Christ, I forgot about Meacher.'

'What about Meacher?' asked Max.

'I found what you said had been overlooked the first time around, and I'm afraid it looks likely that the man we've been searching for is among our own ranks.'

TWELVE

Corporal Douglas Meacher eyed Max and Tom warily across the table in an interview room. 'Yes, I spent five years with REME when I enlisted. The details are on my service record. It was a straightforward transfer, at my request. Nothing dubious about it.'

'And your reason for the transfer?' asked Tom.

'Policing was what I'd always fancied doing.'

'So why not join the Corps from the start?'

Meacher made no attempt to avoid Tom's direct gaze. 'My father said I should learn a useful trade that would come in handy after I'd served my time.' He gave a faint smile. 'Made it sound as if I was about to start a prison sentence rather than an army career.'

'And you did learn a useful trade. One that gave you enough knowledge to show great interest in the evidence the bomb disposal boys found at the sports stadium after the explosion,' Tom pointed out. 'I was impressed by the way you discussed the debris with the experts.'

Meacher's wariness deepened. 'I was eager to learn what had created such havoc. We all were.'

Max had been reluctant to believe ill of a man he had known and trusted for more than two years, but a witness had remembered seeing a Redcap 'fixing' a straw figure to the bonfire minutes before it was set alight. Knowing Corporal Naish had secured the effigy to his meticulously constructed cone when Dennis Mooney and Co had arrived with it earlier in the day, the witness could only have seen the MP *adding* something to the straw bundle.

That statement fully explained how the IED could have been inserted, and it made sense of why every person they had interviewed denied seeing anything suspicious during the two days they had worked on the bonfire and pyrotechnic display. Redcaps had been patrolling the area throughout, so this had been a case of the *usual* not being regarded as *unusual*.

According to the witness this had taken place during the firework display, when she was concerned about a distressed woman making repeated calls on her mobile. Her statement recorded that she had decided to approach the Redcap when the fireworks ended, but when she had looked for him he was nowhere to be seen. Doug Meacher had been on duty during that period, and he knew a lot about all manner of devices.

Before calling him for questioning, Tom had checked out George Maddox's duty roster and discovered that Meacher had been off duty on Friday evening. This meant he would have been free to set the fire outside the Officers' Mess. He now pursued that line.

'There's been a deal of aggro from our Scottish lads over that exploding bonfire. Did you see much of it in town on Friday night?'

Meacher looked slightly happier at the change of direction. 'I was off duty, unfortunately.'

'Unfortunately?' queried Max.

'No chance to give 'em some grief.' He grinned. 'I made up for it on Saturday.'

'So where did you spend Friday evening?' probed Tom.

It took less than thirty seconds for Meacher to realize where the questioning was heading, and he snapped out an aggressive reply. 'Not setting a hedge alight, sir.'

Knowing it was pointless to tiptoe around the subject, Tom asked if Meacher could prove he was elsewhere.

'At twenty fifteen when you, sir, saw flames rising from the hedge around the car park,' he said to Max, quoting the official report he would have been privy to, 'I was working out in the gym with twenty or more others. I'd been there a good hour.'

Knowing then that this really was a wild goose, Max nevertheless followed up with the vital question. 'During the firework display on Tuesday, where were you patrolling, Doug?'

'I wasn't, sir. Some boys had been chasing each other around the vending stalls earlier and I told them to clear off. Shortly after that I heard screaming coming from the area beneath the stand and ran under it, closely followed by a St John Ambulance guy. A kid had crashed into one of the supports and knocked out a tooth. There was blood coming from his mouth and he thought he was dying. Where were the parents? Still in the tent guzzling *Gluhwein*! I'd only just tracked them down when the bonfire blew.'

When Meacher departed, Max gave Tom a pensive look. 'Ralph Styles, who was on duty with Doug on Tuesday, has no technical skills so far as we know, so I'm expecting a negative report on him from Piercey and Beeny shortly. Ralph is also newly married, which surely makes him an unlikely candidate for the attacks.'

'Unless pretty Betty has denied him the fruits of his seed,' responded Tom acidly. 'That apparently allows a man to abduct a three-year-old to make her dance to his bagpipes, then expect no more than sympathetic understanding of his *need*.'

'Leave it, Tom. McTavish is a sad, haunted man. He'll get his just desserts, never fear.'

'From the Almighty?'

Max knew his friend found it hard to be impartial in this instance and moved on to his next point. 'Now our task is to check out the rest of our uniformed colleagues. Including George himself, I'm afraid.'

Tom wagged his head. 'I don't like it. I've known them a long time. Before you joined 26 Section. Why would any of them be driven to do something like this?'

'We'll find out when we get him.'

'The one person I don't know much about is Babs Turvey. She only came out here two months ago.'

'We've ruled out a woman.' Max then shrugged. 'The fire at the Mess? Possibly. But anything putting mothers and children at risk wouldn't be perpetrated by Babs.'

'She'll have to be questioned,' Tom said stubbornly.

'I know.'

At that point Beeny and Piercey came in to report their findings after interviewing Ralph Styles. During the firework display he had been standing alongside the men who were setting them off, checking that correct safety precautions were being observed.

'So that rules out the two known to have been on site, yet who couldn't have been the Redcap seen tampering with the straw figure.' Max glanced at the large wall clock. Late afternoon. 'I want the rest of them questioned *now*. This is the first real lead we've had and we must get to the root of what the witness actually saw. I'll drive out to George's place, where he's apparently taken to his bed, and you two, together with Olly, Heather and Connie, can chase up the rest even if it takes all night. And call in reports to me, no matter how late it is.'

He turned to Tom as they left. 'As back up, have another session with the witness and get a fuller account. The initial report was geared towards the behaviour of Eva McTavish, which was why this snippet of info wasn't picked up first time around. I hope to God this woman won't now deny seeing a Redcap, or become evasive and unsure, because we're going to make ourselves very unpopular with George and his staff who won't forget it in a hurry.'

Tom's eyes narrowed. 'Is that why you're sending me to interview the witness instead?'

The white lie came easily enough. 'She lives near the main gate, so you can head for home once you've got her confirmation. You deserve dinner with your family after spending half the night in defence of a friend you couldn't contact. I do appreciate it, Tom.' He put his hand on the other man's shoulder. 'Speak to the witness then go home to your lovely wife and the fruits of your seed,' he added with a sly grin.

And that was how Tom impulsively revealed that another was due to arrive next year.

Max had an uncomfortable session with George Maddox, who was feeling unwell and took exception to being questioned as a suspect despite being told of the witness statement. Marion Maddox was even more incensed.

'Hasn't George suffered enough from unwarranted backlash

from parents without now being accused of *causing* the explosion?'

'I'm not accusing him, Marion.'

'Well, it sounds remarkably like it to me!'

Max departed reminding himself of his own sense of injustice during that morning's visit from Keith Pinkney, then he sat in his office for the next ninety minutes fielding calls from his team while he began his report on the abduction of Jenny Greene.

Curiously, getting to the truth about the McTavish suicide failed to give him the satisfaction he had expected. Hector's religious convictions prohibited divorce, so two people had lived together in a state of such unhappiness it had finally deprived one of her life, and the other of any hope of personal redemption. How different from the secure, loving marriage of Tom and Nora. Max was unsure how his friend really felt about an unplanned addition to his family, but of one thing he was certain. Tom wanted a son this time.

By mid-evening Tom had called in with the witness's confirmation of seeing a Redcap handling the straw man moments before the bonfire was ignited, and each member of the team had reported failure to find a suspect as a result of their interviews. All their uniformed colleagues had easily-proven alibis, which had been produced with overt hostility. Max guessed there would be a short period of non-cooperation until SIB caught the impersonator, for that was who they undoubtedly had to trace. So it was back to the cast of thousands!

Tired, hungry, and oddly unsettled by Tom's news of another child, Max headed for home in fine rain that once more put a shroud over everything . . . including the prospect of a result by the end of the day.

Clare's car was outside the apartments, along with a Range Rover. Huh! The MacFearsome major was spending another night here. From the rude awakening by Keith Pinkney at five a.m. to the destruction of a promising breakthrough it had been a long, kaleidoscopic day, so Max pushed aside his views on that hot relationship. What he needed was a reviving shower, a satisfying meal, and several large whiskies while watching one of his black and white war videos before falling into bed trying not to think of Livya lying beside him.

After showering, Max dressed in tracksuit pants and a sweatshirt to eat a microwaved casserole which could have been beef or lamb with three of his five-a-day vegetables, according to the packaging. The whisky was more enjoyable, especially when watching *Colditz*. Trouble was, although the film made him appreciate his freedom it seemed to be prodding him into using more ingenuity to solve this difficult case. The answer was there, if only he could see through the haze hiding it.

Towards the end of the film he heard faint sounds of music coming from the large shared lounge. Clare, entertaining her lover with seductive pieces played on her grandmother's piano. Well, she was a professional woman who had survived a recent divorce and knew what was what. She did not need warnings from a neighbour who was a non-runner in the relationship stakes.

He turned his attention back to the film, then must have dozed because the TV screen was blank when he grew aware of voices raised in argument. Clare's strident demands were overridden by an insistent baritone, and Max recognized male persuasiveness that would not take no for an answer.

'Stop that! I'm telling you again to leave. You're drunk.'

'Just enough to make me very imaginative. You like that, don't you. Wild imagination between the sheets. C'mon, you sexy little bitch, let's make the earth move.'

'Let me go! You're hurting me.'

'You women all say that, but you really *love* it.'

After a brief silence Clare cried out, 'No. *No!* Get off me. *Get off me, you bastard*!'

Max was on his feet and across to the connecting door, obeying a different male instinct. He burst into the room to see just the top of Clare's head as she was being pinned down by a man with his shirt flapping loose, who was straddling her and uttering explicit sexual taunts.

Even as he seized and hauled the man to his feet, Max was surprised to see a head of black hair where he had expected dark red. His assault was unexpected, but the man was fighting drunk and attempted to punch Max on the jaw while aiming a kick at his genitals. Both failed to reach the target.

Police training had taught Max how to counter every type of aggression, but personal anger dominated his actions now. Swinging the man around he rushed him forward to slam him against the wall, pressing his knee in the small of his back while jerking his arms behind him in an immobilising hold.

'Christ, that's bloody agony.'

'You all say that,' panted Max, 'but you really love it. Don't you?' To make his point he added further pressure where it hurt most. 'I heard the lady tell you to leave, so you're going to do as you were told. *Aren't you*?'

'Ye–es,' the other moaned, mouth squashed against the wall.

'Where are the keys to your vehicle?'

'Pocket,' came the anguished response. 'You're breaking my arms.'

'So you couldn't drive even if I let you keep the keys,' reasoned Max, as he frog-marched the man across the lounge and through the apartment identical to his own. Opening Clare's front door he thrust his victim out to the square landing at the top of the flight of steps, first removing a set of keys from his trousers.

The fight had gone out of the swaying, dishevelled man, but there was aggressive fury in his dark eyes. 'You'll pay for this, believe me,' he croaked. 'I have friends in high places.'

'So have I,' Max returned. 'Expect a visit from the *Polizei* to investigate the report of an attempted rape.'

Returning to the lounge, still high on adrenalin, Max demanded, 'Who the hell was *he*?' before he grew aware that Clare was trying to button her torn shirt with hands that shook. In fact, she was trembling from head to foot.

Max sank down beside her and took her hands in his. 'Are you all right?' When she nodded, he asked again for the identity of her assailant.

She gave a shuddering sigh and withdrew her hands. 'Thanks for coming to the rescue.'

'From whom?' he persisted.

'Major the Honourable James Francis Matthew Goodey, of the Blues and Royals. My former husband.'

It was so unexpected, Max was lost for words.

'He's over here on a ten-day course and thought it would suit him to lodge with me; an idea I immediately nipped in the bud.' She sighed again to steady herself. 'He appeared to take it on the chin and invited me to dinner at Zillers, for old times' sake. I couldn't see any problem with that, and accepted.'

Seeing Max's expression, she attempted to justify her decision. 'He may be a bastard, at times, but he knows how to behave in places like Zillers. I once told you he's a member of a hugely wealthy family who only eat in top-of-the-range restaurants.'

'And?' he prompted, trying to imagine this woman he knew as carefree, intelligent and professionally dedicated living with a titled oaf.

'And it was a very enjoyable meal – James can turn on the charm – but he drank very liberally. As we went in a taxi and returned in one I wasn't unduly worried about his liquid intake. However, when we got back here he wanted to come in for a nightcap. I refused very firmly, said goodnight and shut the door.'

Her brow furrowed. 'Max, I truly believed he had gone, but he must have been boozing-up out there in the Range Rover. When the doorbell rang forty-five minutes later I was playing the piano and went to open the door totally unprepared for him to come charging in like a rampant bull. You know the rest.' She touched his arm in a brief gesture of apology. 'I'm sorry you had to come in and deal with him.'

He studied her face still pale with shock. 'I told him I'd call the *Polizei*, but you must make the decision on that. I appropriated his keys. In the morning I'll find out where the course is being run and get someone to drive his vehicle over there.' After a moment or two, he added, 'I thought it was MacPherson's.'

She considered that. 'Would you have acted differently with him?'

'No.'

'Duncan's a gentleman.'

A sense of anti-climax hovered. 'So a rescue wouldn't have been necessary.'

Clare shook her head as she once more attempted to button her pale blue silk shirt with fingers still too unsteady for the delicate task.

Max drew her hands down to her lap. 'You'd better let me do that.'

While he slid each pearl disc through a buttonhole, he was conscious of her rapid breathing and guessed she was still shaken by what had happened.

'You're managing that as if you've had a lot of practice,' she murmured.

Eyes on what he was doing, he said, 'I had a wife for two years.' Then he added, 'I'm also pretty nifty at closing out-of-reach zips.'

'And opening them?'

He looked up at her. 'That, too.'

The embrace lasted long enough for him to be aware that she was as reluctant to end it as he, and when they eventually broke apart Clare gazed at him with a tenderness he had never seen in Livya's eyes.

'I've wondered how long it would take you to realize you wanted to do that. I little dreamed a tussle with my ex would work the magic.'

Having drawn a blank questioning men she knew well as her uniformed colleagues, and bearing the brunt of their hostility, Connie Bush drove to meet Sergeant Colin Carr feeling even more guilty than before. Tom Black was likely to put a stop to the relationship, or at least make her put it on hold until the case was finished. Personal closeness to possible suspects was forbidden. She knew the rules, but she had fallen heavily for the blond bomb disposal sergeant on first meeting him.

There had been a previous sergeant who had also taken her by storm, but he had broken their engagement halfway through the wedding plans. No other woman; simply a change of mind. That had put her off men for a long time, but Colin appeared to be as instantly committed as she was. So she was bending the rules and risking a severe reprimand, because now the Redcaps had been cleared of guilt the investigation would again concentrate on those with specialized knowledge of weaponry in every form. She was worried and unhappy over how Colin would surely take the news.

He had told her that Jeremy Knott had been 'ballistic with rage' because SIB had imagined a terrorist attack at mention of an IED. It had been he who had instructed Colin and the others to put forward the idea of an alarm clock and stick of dynamite in a suitcase to 'untwist the plods' knickers'.

Connie had protested, but Colin had laughed. 'You must be used to comments like that, sweetheart. What got him so worked up was your boss calling us all in as terrorist suspects. We don't *make* explosive devices, we take 'em apart.'

'But you could.'

'Could what?'

'Make one.'

He had elbowed her playfully. 'Hey, don't *you* start on that track.'

Unfortunately, it looked very much as if she might have to now. What she did not understand was why the witness was so certain it was a Redcap she had seen. The hypothesis certainly answered the questions of how and when, leaving the who and why. *Why* would remain a mystery until the *who* was found. Easy enough to pose as one of George's team, Connie thought. Add to his uniform a yellow high-visibility vest, a gun and a red beret, and people would see a military policeman on patrol.

Nearing the inn Colin had chosen as a rendezvous, Connie decided to avoid any mention of the case. It would ruin the evening if her new boyfriend learned his colleagues were still on the list of possible suspects. Colin had told her his boss had a very short fuse since returning last month from their deployment in Afghanistan, which had been particularly harrowing.

Connie had heard how Knott had rescued two of his injured men under fire, then had risked his life again to bring in a leg lost by one of them. The other casualty had been so critically injured he was still on a life support machine with little chance of survival. His wife would soon be asked to give permission to switch it off.

Naturally enough, Knott's men practically hero-worshipped the man whose courage was second to none. They would follow him anywhere, do anything he asked of them, Connie had been told. A Messiah and his disciples? Yes, he would explode with wrath over further suspicion of his followers.

As she parked her car at the rear of the inn and spotted Colin watching for her from a window, it occurred to her that Jeremy Knott himself had never been interviewed as a suspect.

THIRTEEN

It was starting to grow light when Max left his apartment to drive to the base. A damp shroud heralded the dawn. Was it Keats who wrote of the season of mists and mellow fruitfulness? He was right on the first count, but the fruitfulness was doubtful. Max had little idea of what to direct his team to do, how to progress the investigation. Until they had been called in yesterday afternoon to question George and his Redcaps, they had been chasing yet again the experts in Logistics and the Sappers. It must have been viewed as a sign of desperation by them because they had proved their innocence the first time around. Pointless to waste more effort on them.

The bonfire had exploded a week ago and all they had by way of a lead was the reported sighting of a Redcap tampering with that damned straw effigy. Even if they tracked the imposter down they could never prove he had lodged some kind of IED within it. Only if he confessed could they close the case on that, but what if he had a solid alibi for the night of the car park fire?

Had they been wrong to believe both incidents were the work of the same person? Must they begin seriously to question the newly arrived Drumdorrans on that score? They had been on the base for three days by then. Long enough to set that up. Hector McTavish had shown there was one bad apple in the barrel. Maybe there was another.

All these problems bombarded Max's brain as he drove through the empty streets, in addition to the question of what exactly had begun between himself and Clare last night. He would have done what he had to any man forcing himself on any woman trying to fight him off but, in retrospect, he recognized that there had been an element of primitive man defending his own in his actions. And in his concern for her afterwards. Yet there had been no dragging her off to his cave to consolidate possession. The kiss had been instinctive and seriously significant, but he had then suggested that she drank a knock-out brandy, took a long shower and went to bed. Clare had nodded, said goodnight and gone to her own apartment, closing the door firmly.

After checking that Goodey was no longer outside the building, Max had lain awake considering the implications of this new aspect of their relationship. How would it affect living in this semi-shared accommodation? He knew they could not resume the relaxed friendship they had enjoyed, so would being neighbours now work? He needed time to get to grips with how to handle the next stage. For him it was a case of twice bitten, once shy.

One ambiguous aspect of his social life had been surprisingly settled. A text from Brenda Keane had come in at some time during the night telling him he had been right to say her parents ought to know they had a grandchild, and she was flying home on Sunday. Micky had no father, so she hoped to give him a grandad, make him part of a real family. The message ended with thanks for his kindness to them both, and best wishes for his own future happiness.

He felt no disappointment at the news. Brenda had only enjoyed his company because of his link to her lost lover, and he had really been more interested in the infant Micky, imagining how it would be if Alexander Rydal had survived to become his own son.

The psycho boys would have some strong words to say to him on that fantasy, no doubt, he mused as he parked outside the RMP post en route to Headquarters. Walking in, he gave a stony-faced Babs Turvey the keys to James Goodey's Range Rover, saying he wanted a vehicle collected from Marienplatz and taken to where he knew the course was being run.

'Leave it in the car park with the keys under the seat. I'll give them a buzz to explain.'

'Yes, sir,' she said, as if her lips were frozen.

Max knew it would be a while before SIB was forgiven for treating them as suspects, so he accepted the icy formality and went on his way. Letting himself in to the deserted building he filled the kettle and plugged it in. His early departure meant he had gone without breakfast, so a large mug of coffee and two walnut muffins would have to compensate. Armed thus, he sat at his desk to review the notes he had made on Sunday outlining the similarities and differences between the incidents, hoping for new inspiration.

Halfway through this task his concentration wandered to remember how difficult it could be to prove where one had been at the time a crime had been committed. How long would he have remained under suspicion if Jenny had not explained which 'Max' she had gone off with? He would have liked to see her, discover if she suffered any reactions to her experience, and to check if Jean had consulted Clare or MacPherson about the child's spasmodic sleeping, but he knew better than to show further interest in the engaging little girl. A man had to be so careful where children and women were concerned in this enlightened age. The slightest word or action could be misconstrued.

When the members of the team drifted in, clearly feeling as frustrated as he, Max set them to trawling through the service records of every soldier on the base, including the Scots, for evidence that anyone had worked in a quarry, a mine or in demolition before enlisting. There would be little enough recorded, but they should follow even the slightest lead.

Tom arrived somewhat later than usual, looking heavy-eyed and depressed. Armed with a mug of coffee, he came to Max's office and revealed that he had had similar ideas about the only way forward left to them.

'It'll take several days to scroll through the service record of every man and woman on the base, and Chummy'll be laughing at us for every minute of them, but what else can we do?'

Max leaned back in his chair and stretched his arms out to ease the ache in his shoulders. 'We've been looking at soldiers trained in specialist skills, but on this base there must be someone who had experience with demolition in civilian life but has chosen a different trade for his army career. Jeremy Knott's boys did tell us that an improvised explosive device means just that – something that could demolish a garden wall, blow a bank safe or, I suppose, could topple one of those defunct factory chimneys.'

Tom gave a wry smile. 'I doubt dynamite in a suitcase could do that.'

There was a light tap on the door, and they both turned to see Connie Bush waiting for permission to enter. Max thought she looked tense and unusually pale.

'Yes, Connie? Something wrong?' he asked just as his landline rang. 'Be with you in five. Don't go, Tom! This might be of relevance.'

The message was brief, needing only an affirmation from him. Max got to his feet giving Tom a significant glance. 'Summons to the Garrison Commander.'

Tom frowned. 'I thought Keith Pinkney had diverted that meeting.'

'According to his adjutant, it's to be a one-to-one, which suggests I'm for it. Maybe Crawford *has* persuaded him to relieve me of this command and call in the ATS.'

'Keith would have given you a warning. He'd have to be told about it before it was put into action.'

'I'd better go and see what it's all about. With luck it'll be no worse than a slap on the wrist for being obstructive with his 2IC.'

Colonel John Trelawney looked every inch the military hero in any one of Max's collection of war films. Tall, with crisp brown hair and alert eyes, his rugged good looks were marred by a scar down his right cheek. There were other scars on the backs of his hands; probably on his body, too. Tokens from the Falklands War as a young subaltern. He greeted Max with an invitation to make himself comfortable in one of the armchairs in his large office. Then he got straight to the point.

'You've a difficult job on your hands, Max. Give me a resumé of how it stands as of now.'

Was this the overture to being relieved of the case? One of Max's strengths was the ability to summarize accurately and pertinently, so Trelawney soon had a good grasp of all that had happened during his absence. He nodded his understanding of the major aspects as Max outlined them.

'So your belief, until proven otherwise, is that one person

set up both incidents purely to make some kind of statement, not to put lives at risk?'

'Yes, sir.'

'In my opinion he certainly *was* risking lives. He had discounted the possibility of blockhead squaddies also adding explosive objects to the bonfire, and setting the hedge fire was potentially very hazardous. There would have been more than a hundred vehicles outside the Mess. It only needed one to ignite to start a chain reaction.'

'But the windows of the dining hall overlook the car park, sir, so the fire was certain to be spotted in its infancy. As it was.'

'What if the fire engines had been dealing with an emergency elsewhere?'

This was definitely turning into a rap over the knuckles, so Max hastened to expound on his reasoning. 'If his object had been to create a real conflagration he would have first sent the fire brigade as far distant as possible on a hoax call. That he didn't, and the fact that he ignited the hedge after the bugle call had sent us all through to the area where flames could immediately be seen, persuaded me that he had been totally in control of what he was doing. It points to an expert in such skills. We've interviewed every likely suspect with no luck. We now have to search for someone with that knowledge who isn't presently using it professionally.'

'Hmm, and what message do you think he's imparting so melodramatically?'

A difficult question. 'The only clue to that is that both incidents took place during the hours of darkness where a large number of people had gathered to socialize. At the Sports Ground there were soldiers and their families. At the Mess was a gathering of military officers and civilian caterers. Whatever the message is, it doesn't appear to be directed at any specific person or group of people. He just wants to convey it to the greatest number.'

Trelawney's expression hardened. 'In other words, you haven't the slightest notion what's behind those two attacks. I can't accept your airy-fairy notion of a message. He's bloody dangerous, man! Concentrate on that, and if you don't get a result before Saturday I'll be faced with a problematic decision.'

Driving back to Headquarters Max was so weighed down by the burden of responsibility he could not appreciate the slightly gratifying aspect of what Trelawney had revealed. Major Carnegie had moved swiftly after the arrest of Hector McTavish. At his informal introductory meeting with the Garrison Commander, he had expressed his desire to compensate for the hostility following the unfortunate death of a Piper's wife, by staging at the Sports Ground an evening of Highland dancing, and music by the regimental band. The Drumdorran Fusiliers would provide refreshments prepared by their own chefs, and there would be shortbread animals for the children to take home.

In other circumstances Max would have been smugly pleased over Carnegie's climbdown, but the GC would withdraw his permission for this olive branch if SIB could not guarantee there would be no danger at this gathering. Max knew they could not, unless the next three days produced the military Scarlet Pimpernel they were seeking here and seeking there.

As he entered Headquarters, Tom followed him through to his office with an urgency that suggested to Max that his colleague was afraid they had been supplanted by the Anti Terrorist Squad. He swiftly quashed that fear, but revealed the challenge that had been issued.

'This proposed evening of Scottish dancing with much marching up and down by kilted pipers is just the kind of event Chummy would relish. The perfect occasion for another expression of his feelings with fire or big bangs. If we haven't got him by tomorrow evening, I'll have to advise that it be a non-runner.' Then he noticed that Tom looked seriously disturbed, and asked sharply, 'What's happened?'

'We've slipped up. *I've* slipped up. Missed the obvious. I should have picked up on it way back, but I got sidelined by Carter's injured hand and Max-ee-million. I've also been distracted by probs at home, as you noticed, or I'd have . . .'

'Cut the guff and *tell* me!' demanded Max, feeling a rush of adrenalin.

'Connie's just pointed out that we've never interviewed Jeremy Knott as a suspect.'

'Because he was off base on both occasions.'

Tom shook his head. 'We assumed he was during the Guy Fawkes evening because I couldn't contact him to ask for his boys to come to the Sports Ground. We had to wait until the next morning.'

'But what about the hedge fire? He was at the NATO conference with the GC at that time.'

'No. Connie mentioned earlier that he had the bug that's going around, and couldn't go.' He sighed. 'I didn't even pick up on it then but, by God, it all fits. Highly skilled, knows his way around IED's and has access to volatile substances.'

Seeing the truth of all Tom said, yet certain there would be a stumbling block somewhere, Max asked, 'How does Connie know so much about the man?'

'She's misguidedly started a hot relationship with Colin Carr. It took some guts for her to come to me with this info. She feels she's betraying Carr by repeating what he told her about his boss. Apparently, Knott is like a fuse waiting to blow since their return from Afghanistan last month. They had a pretty rough time of it. Three casualties. Carr told her Knott always takes losses badly, although he works hard to keep up the morale of his boys. They all love him, but think he's in danger of cracking up.'

Max was reminded of his own words to Jeremy Knott about SIB meeting fighting men when they cracked under the strain and acted completely out of character. Was that what was happening here?

'Let's go, Tom. As you say, it all fits. We'll keep it as low key as possible until we've talked to the man, but the end of this case may be in sight.'

When Max and Tom climbed the steps and trod the long corridor, they found Jeremy Knott's office empty. Tom poked his head around the door of the adjacent room to ask a corporal who was staring in dismay at a blank computer screen if Captain Knott was still off sick.

Glancing up with an ill-disguised lack of interest, he replied,

'Not ill, sir. Some kind of domestic trouble,' then resumed his bafflement over being unable to log on to whatever it was he was seeking.

The Knott family – wife and two children – lived in married quarters, so Tom drove out to the perimeter road and headed for the far side of the sprawling base with no more than a speculative glance at Max, who was sure his friend was still castigating himself for failing to check Knott's whereabouts on Guy Fawkes night.

Max could understand how it had happened. The focus had been on helping the casualties, and making the base secure after what might have been a terrorist attack. He, himself, had had a stormy meeting with Knott the following afternoon over demands to interview his bomb disposal team, and the idea that Knott had been off base at the relevant time had been firmly lodged in his mind.

In addition, Knott's fierce response to any suggestion that men who risked their lives to defuse explosive devices would ever set one to detonate among a crowd of people, ensured that suspicion of their commander never formulated. The suicide of Eva McTavish had then clouded the issue and brought the Drumdorran Fusiliers into the picture.

He looked across the cab at Tom. 'Don't wear a hair shirt, man. We're all to blame. Not one member of the team picked up on an assumption that had inadvertently become a fact. I just hope Connie won't be the loser for putting her duty before her personal affairs.'

The response was just a nod, so Max dropped the subject and concentrated on what they would find on reaching Knott's house. Domestic trouble could be anything from a fractured water tank to a seriously ill child.

When Tom drove up to the house there was no sign of an ambulance, or flooding. In fact, the place had a deserted look about it. No toys scattered about the garden, no sound of raised voices, no childish laughter or petty squabbling. They knocked on the door and got no response. Knocked again. Not a sound.

Max nodded at the narrow passageway between the house and the garage which led to the rear garden. 'He must be out there. This is his vehicle on the driveway.'

They emerged to a deserted garden. No sign that two young children lived there, no washing on the line, no aroma of cooking, although it was lunchtime. Max tried the back door. It opened, and he stepped into the kitchen.

'Hallo. Anyone there?' He called a second time, but there was still no reply. He leaned from the door. 'Tom, I think we'd better take a look around. I don't like this.'

They separated to search each room, then returned to the kitchen unsure what to make of what they had seen. Wardrobes and drawers were empty of all but Knott's clothes. In the bathroom were a razor, aftershave, a man's hairbrush, toothbrushes and paste, and a large-sized dark towelling robe. Nothing else.

'Domestic trouble of the first degree,' said Max thoughtfully. 'His wife and children seem to have gone. For good, I'd say. Nobody takes all their possessions with them on a short break.'

'She must have decamped a day or two ago, and must have been planning it over a period of time. You don't just call a taxi on the spur of the moment and load it with three people and half a household.' He frowned. 'D'you think this is linked with what he did? Your so-called message.'

Max had spotted a small shed at the end of the garden, and he started out through the kitchen door with sudden urgency. 'I hope to God we're not too late to get an answer to that.'

It was with this fear that he eased open the wooden door and peered into what appeared to be a workshop of some sort, with all manner of equipment covering benches and shelves. Jeremy Knott was slumped across a bench. A row of three whisky bottles stood in front of him. One was empty, and inroads had been made to the second, but when he looked up it was apparent the man in uniform was under the influence of more than alcohol. There was a wildness in his eyes, and his voice reached double volume as he identified them.

'Ah, the upholders of righteousness! The wearers of the red hats, who have no bloody idea what it's all about. *She* certainly doesn't. Nobody does.' He gave a bitter guffaw. 'No idea, *any* of you!'

He put the bottle to his mouth and took a long drink, after

which Max said, 'No, we haven't any idea. So why don't you tell us.'

Although Knott appeared to be staring straight at him, Max could tell the man was seeing something quite different. 'You watch him walk forward and your heart stops beating until he stands up and signals that it's all over. Then it happens again twenty minutes later, and your heart stops once more. The next day is the same. And the next, and the next. Then it happens. You see the earth rise up like a fountain, and he's part of it. He doesn't stand and signal that it's over, but you know it is, and there's an empty bed, and an empty chair at the table, and a silence where there used to be laughter, and warmth, and friendly banter. And you can never get him back.' His gaze shifted to the roof, as if it were the heavens, and his voice broke, 'Dear God, when it happens a third time you lose all faith in what you're doing. In everything. What's the point of it all? You need an answer; need to know *why*.'

'I can understand that,' Max told him gently.

'No, you can't. You've no idea. Any of you,' Knott yelled. 'We come home and you're all carrying on the way you always do, as if it hadn't happened. You're playing snooker and football, flirting with the NAAFI girls, charging into town in souped-up cars just as if it hadn't happened. As if it doesn't *matter*.'

'So you needed to demonstrate to us that it does?'

Knott tipped the bottle again, then stared at it as he held it so that light came through the window to shimmer it. 'Bloody Guy Fawkes! Fireworks and a bonfire. For *fun*! You need to know what it's really like. Machine guns sound like fireworks, but you don't get pretty colours in the sky, you get bullets in your guts. A bonfire's like an armoured vehicle burning, except that it makes a bloody great bang when it explodes. It's not *fun*! Why can't any of you see that?

There was a brief silence as Knott seemed to travel again to another place, another time. Then he gave one more brittle laugh. 'Drinks in the Mess, lads. Let's all get totally pissed and stuff ourselves like pigs at the trough. No empty chairs at *that* table, was there?'

'Not until we saw the hedge on fire,' said Tom.

'Put the fear of God in them. For what? Their bloody Range Rovers and Mercs, that's all. They've no *idea*,' he cried with a touch of terrible desperation. 'They can't tell us what it's all about. *Nobody* knows.'

Max had heard all he needed. Bending his head towards Tom's he murmured, 'Call an ambulance and a patrol. He'll need to be restrained to get him to the Medical Centre.'

Tom stepped out into the garden to get a stronger signal and walked towards the house as he made the calls. Max stood at the door of the hut, watching him punch in the numbers, so he failed to see Jeremy Knott stretch out his hand and push a button that turned day into night.

Tom sat in the swaying ambulance as it raced through the afternoon, holding a thick pad over a deep cut just above his right eye. The paramedics were busy tending the two serious cases, fixing plasma drips and monitoring the performance of vital organs. If he had not been in the garden when the shed blew what state would he also be in now?

Gazing at the bloodied mask that was Max's face, and at the gaping wound the green-clad men were dealing with, Tom's shocked senses told him he now certainly knew what it was like, but he could not tell Knott that. The medics had been exchanging looks and shaking their heads over the torn and broken body on the other stretcher. Even if the man was still alive when they reached the hospital, there was no hope of his eventual survival. Jeremy Knott had made his last statement.

It was dark outside when Nora walked down the corridor to sit beside him. She saw the large pressure pad above his eye, but made no comment on it. 'How is he, love?'

'Still in theatre,' he told her dully. 'The staff nurse who patched me up said she'd try to find out, but she's been gone forty minutes, so I guess she's forgotten.'

'If they're operating she can't just walk in and ask,' she reasoned. 'What about Captain Knott?'

'Dead on arrival. I know that because they left him and concentrated on Max.'

She took his hand. 'Have they sent for his wife?'

'She's possibly in the UK. Signs were she'd left and taken the children. Must have been the last straw for him.'

'Poor man, to risk death in action so many times, then go out this way.'

Tom shook his head slowly. 'He *was* killed in action: he was still fighting the war.'

They were still sitting in the corridor three hours and four coffees later when Clare Goodey approached them. Tom thought she looked unusually pale, but she was very composed. Being a doctor allowed her to take these things in her stride, he supposed.

'I only heard an hour ago, or I'd have been here sooner,' she said without greeting them. 'How good of you to wait, Tom.'

He got to his feet. 'A staff nurse promised to give me the situation, but she hasn't. Staff hurry back and forth trying not to let us catch their eyes. It's five hours since we arrived here. What the hell are they doing to him?'

'He's still in theatre, but they'll be transferring him to the ICU shortly. I contacted a doctor I've dealt with here several times and he gave me the most recent update.'

'And?'

'Broken jaw, fractured ulna, two chipped vertebrae. All non life-threatening, of course, but there's a serious chest wound causing some concern. Once that has been successfully closed he'll need at least three months convalescent leave before getting back to work. I know the ideal place for him to relax and regain his strength. I'll take him there when the time comes.'

Tom was still anxious, remembering how Max had looked in the ambulance. 'He'll make a full recovery then?'

Clare nodded. 'There's no way he's going to slip away from us. I'll be checking him for the next few days and will keep you updated.' She turned to Nora. 'Take him home. He looks all in.'

Nora drove them back to the rented house, saying little. Tom sat beside her feeling incredibly weary, with a growing longing to hug his children close, along with this wonderful woman beside him. At times like this having a family made all the difference. Boy or girl, he looked forward to holding the new member of it before long.

He said into the silence, 'I'll have to inform his father. They've never been close, but he is the next of kin and has the right to be told what's happened.' He thought of what Clare had said. 'She may well have an acquaintance at the hospital, but no way will they allow her to interfere with their handling of the case. He's not her patient, and she's not even on the hospital staff. I don't know how she imagines she can influence the situation.'

Without taking her eyes from the road, Nora said, 'By being there when he regains consciousness, of course. That's all it'll take. It would work with you and me, wouldn't it?'

'That's different. They don't have the same kind of relationship.'

Nora just gave a woman's knowing smile, but Tom was gazing from the window and did not see it. He had spotted a woman wearing a three-quarter coat over a pleated tartan skirt. He sighed. Well, SIB had ensured that the Drumdorran Fusiliers could safely hold their Highland fling on Saturday. With bloody bagpipes!